T0000736

MY BEST
PLAN

About the Author

Cris Ascunce is a Miami native, born to Cuban immigrants. She is a voracious LGBTQ rights advocate and hopes to enlighten her readers on the struggles, advancements, and setbacks the community has endured and still faces to reach full equity through her writing. A graphic designer by trade, she has designed advertising campaigns, websites, and other materials aimed at luring visitors to Miami, now she writes about it in her prose. A lover of travel, books, and animals, Cris lives in Miami with her wife of twenty years and their canine and feline daughters.

MY BEST PLAN

Cris Ascunce

BELLA BOOKS
2024

Copyright © 2024 by Cris Ascunce

Bella Books, Inc.
P.O. Box 10543
Tallahassee, FL 32302

All rights reserved. No part of this book may be reproduced or transmitted in any form or by any means, electronic or mechanical, including photocopying, without permission in writing from the publisher.

This is a work of fiction. Names, characters, businesses, places, events and incidents are either the products of the author's imagination or used in a fictitious manner. Any resemblance to actual persons, living or dead, or actual events is purely coincidental. The publisher does not have any control over and does not assume any responsibility for author or third-party websites or their content.

First Edition - 2024

Editor: Heather Flournoy
Cover Designer: Cris Ascunce

ISBN: 978-1-64247-511-1

PUBLISHER'S NOTE

The scanning, uploading, and distribution of this book via the Internet or via any other means without the permission of the publisher is illegal and punishable by law. Please purchase only authorized print or electronic editions, and do not participate in or encourage electronic piracy of copyrighted materials.Your support of the author's rights is appreciated.

Acknowledgments

No woman is an island, and that goes for authors, too. For this—my first completed novel—it has taken a village of loved ones to get me through the finish line.

First, my family. Mami and my sister, Ani, if you hadn't realized I was dyslexic in the first place and subsequently spent countless hours teaching me to read and write, you wouldn't be reading the words in this book today. Thank you both for encouraging me along the way.

A special thanks to my friends (Las THOTSAS, Design Dream Team, and the Roshanitos) you've stepped up and offered support, assurances, and motivation for this project. Your kind words have pushed me to give this my all.

To my phenomenal editor, Eli Raphael: thank you for putting up with me for nearly three years. Your advice, encouragement, and editing prowess on this novel have alleviated much of the anxiety that threatened to overwhelm me. Thank you for finessing my words into intelligible sentences and steering me in the right direction. I learned an enormous amount under your leadership.

To my new Bella Books team: thank you for giving me the opportunity to share this little story. It's been decades in the making. To my new editor, Heather Flournoy: thanks for diving into this story, helping me keep a clear timeline, and keeping the details authentic. This couldn't have gotten done without your diligence.

Lastly, but most importantly, to my wife, without whom I would have never jumped into this journey wholeheartedly. Thank you for reading, rereading, making suggestions, and loving me. This novel would not be possible without your patient love and support.

Author's Note

With this novel, I set out to tell a story steeped in history—our history. The characters, organizations, and events in their lives are fiction. As heartfelt as it was to write about Gene, Isa, Susana, and Martha, their colleagues, and friends, they are all figments of my imagination. So, too, is the novel's local LGBTQIA+ activist group, Equality Miami. Isa's research, developing heart valves with embryonic stem cells does not exist—at least not as of this writing.

However, the backstory about Florida's ban on adoptions by gays and lesbians, particularly the lawsuit Mark Gill and his partner brought forth against the state of Florida to lift the adoption ban so that they may adopt their foster sons, is factual. Their story, their plight is one of many the LGBTQIA+ community continually faces. And unfortunately, we have more hurdles to clear before we achieve true freedom.

After the big win with same-sex marriage, The Human Rights Campaign has kept track of discriminatory legislation that sneaks its way into statehouses throughout the country. There's been an uptick, and now legislators are targeting LGBTQIA+ youth in seemingly harmless "parental rights in education" bills. What these legislative bodies forget to mention is that the only parental rights they're interested in protecting are those of white evangelical heterosexual married parents. But we're fighting back.

Dedication

For those affected by discriminatory legislation. Be vigilant; the fight is not nearly over. And to those who came before me— thank you.

CHAPTER ONE

Gene

"Pampa pampa pampa!" Tito Horacio yells incoherently in my ear. He tries to sing—poorly, but God love him, enthusiastically—over the phone. In the background, Kool & The Gang belts out a cacophonous rumble of the cheesy song from the last millennium as people sing along and glasses clink. My uncle's explosive laughter rolls through the phone, and I hold my BlackBerry away from my ear a few seconds until it dies down. Delightful as it is to hear, I wonder if he's drunk-dialing from a party.

"¿Qué está pasando, Tito?" I yell through the phone, hoping he can hear me. Glancing at the digital clock on my computer screen, it's after midnight in Barcelona and he's carrying on like a college student during spring break.

"Gene. You haven't heard? Parliament passed same-sex marriage this morning." His voice cracks. "Can you believe it?"

"Today?" I say. "No way, not today. I knew it was coming, but I had no idea it'd be today."

While Tito's party guests seem to distract him, I open a tab in Safari and type *Spain, same-sex marriage* in the Google search box. A moment and about a thousand results later, I click on the first link. It's a *New York Times* article by Renwick McLean, and right there, the bold headline with an image of the rainbow flag reads, "Spain Legalizes Gay Marriage; Law Is Among the Most Liberal."

I flip my desk calendar to today's date. Thursday, June 30, 2005. Well, damn. Who'da thought Spain would beat the US at legalizing same-sex marriage? Spain—the country of my parents' birth—a Catholic country, no less.

But it's not until I skim through the article that a few words in the second paragraph catch my eye and momentarily stop my heart from beating. "The bill, passed 187 to 147, says couples will have the same rights, including the freedom to marry and to adopt children, regardless of gender."

"Can you believe it?" Tito's voice seems muddled and far away, or it may be that I'm just stunned as my eyes linger on the words *and to adopt children*. "We can finally get married!"

"What are you going to do?" My stomach twists into an excited knot. I'm half expecting the obvious answer that he's marrying Edu, his partner of more than ten years.

"Me?" he asks with a short sniffle. "I'm going to wait for the three of you to come to Barcelona, so I can officiate your marriage. That's what I'm going to do. When are you coming? We should have a double wedding. Edu would love it!" His jubilation is infectious, and I can't help a smile from creeping on my face as I glance at the photo sitting on my desk of Isa holding baby Susana. *If only.* I don't want to trample on his celebratory mood by talking about my problems at home.

"Es un poco complicado aquí, Tito," I lie. It's not complicated at all. The Defense of Marriage Act, enacted in 1996, gives states carte blanche over recognizing same-sex marriages performed in other states, effectively unrecognizing them all at the federal level. And whether it's only a matter of time until the courts get involved is inconsequential to me. I want to marry Isa. I always have, ever since I was thirteen and saw her across a crowded and stifling school bus. But we live in Florida, and the legislature has banned both same-sex marriages and adoptions by gay people.

I hang up with Tito and begin daydreaming, of course, because that's what I do. If Isa and I got married in Spain, I could petition the courts there to legally adopt Susana as her second parent, and we can finally be a family. Legally! Being a Spanish citizen has its privileges: I can sponsor my wife and daughter, so they can become Spanish citizens, too. If we do all that now, by the time it's legal in the United States, our marriage and my parental rights would be legal everywhere else, including Florida. But how much longer until that happens? It'd be easier if we did it in Spain, now. Then, I wouldn't constantly feel marginalized when it comes to raising my five-year-old daughter. *Big dreams, Gene.*

As I scrub the romantic notion of Isa and I exchanging wedding bands from my mind, I do my best to concentrate on my blueprints. A potential client wants to tear down the house he just bought and build a McMansion on the tiny plot of land, and he wants to see the designs in two weeks. But the newsreels out of Spain are still playing in my head, and I can't change the channel. Ever since Spain's parliament took up the gauntlet to legalize same-sex marriage, the thought has been lingering at the back of my mind.

Because of DOMA and Florida's laws, it doesn't matter where in the world we get married. If we live and work in Florida, it's a no, period. So, you see my dilemma? We'd have to leave the country if we want to get married and live as a legally recognized family. We—as if.

Peering around my bottom-floor office suite, the sun casts its fading rays through the west-side windows, washing the room in a somnolent yellow tinge. Papá designed and built this building in our backyard when we were kids, and he used the bottom floor as his office, as I'm using it now. It's an open-concept floor plan that he designed with a kitchenette and bathroom just off the work area. Off to the right of my desk is a conference room table with eight chairs that has been here since this space belonged to him. Wood flooring runs throughout the suite, and the windows are big enough that I can see our backyard, the patio, and all the way to the back of the house. The upstairs is a one-bedroom apartment that we use when my family visits from Spain. When my parents were alive, Papá used the upstairs as a soccer cave. He and my brother, Lui, spent hours watching all things fútbol—that's soccer in America.

Mamá liked a quiet house. Apart from being a university Spanish literature professor, she was a published Spanish-language novelist. With no TVs in the house, she concentrated on more than a dozen published works. But that seems like a million years ago. Now, we've got a huge TV in the family room that rarely plays anything that doesn't have a singalong rhyme. My family life then, when I was a kid, and the one I lead now, are miles apart. But I've spent some of the best years in this house, both as a kid and as an adult.

The more I think of marriage as the traditional next step for couples wanting to enrich their lives and start a family, the more I think of my own precarious situation in Susana's life, who's my daughter in name only because we have no biological connection. Love is the only thing binding us.

In less than a month, Susana will be five years old. She'll start kindergarten in the fall, but I shuttle her back and forth to a pre-K program now. With a notarized signature, Isa authorized me to drop Susana off and pick her up from that school. Martha, Isa's mom, has the same privilege, sans the notarized authorization. And since I'm mostly the one who takes her to see her pediatrician, Isa signed consent forms there, too. It's ridiculous. A puñetero authorization form is needed everywhere I go where Susana is concerned.

Celebratory music is stuck in my head as I imagine gay and lesbian couples dancing atop tables and singing along to Sister Sledge's gleeful song about being a family. Oh, how I wish I could celebrate with Tito and Edu, and their eventual nuptials. I'm kind of jealous of them.

With all the focus on marriage, the end to my workday has arrived. I shut down my AutoCAD, sign out of my company's network, lock the door to my suite, and walk the twenty paces it takes to get to my house for dinner.

Marriage, marriage, marriage. The idea slams in my head like a speeding volleyball from one of Isa's kills. When I slide open the glass door and walk into the kitchen, it's what I see before me that really sets me off. Isa is bent over the open oven, two juicy chicken breasts (one of them pierced with a thermometer) are laid out in a deep-dish oven pan, sitting on the center rack, and she's poking at the birds, testing their doneness, I suppose. Meanwhile, Susana sits happily in her booster seat, hands, mouth, and dimpled chin covered in chicken juice, kicking her legs to and fro as she chomps down on a drumstick.

"Hey, G," Isa says, peeking up at me, and I'm suddenly pulled out of this Norman Rockwell-ian portrait that's labeled *MARRIAGE*. The only thing Isa is missing is a white apron with a ruffled edge. "I made rice, and the chicken just needs to rest for a couple more minutes. You hungry? I was just about to call you." The words flitter through my brain as I'm sucked back into her reality. Isa meticulously places the two breasts on a slab of butcher block, kicks the oven door closed, then saunters to the sink to fill the pan with soapy water. Routine. It's the only thing in our lives that doesn't change. She lives for it, and I cling to it like a dying Catholic to his rosary because it's what I have left.

"Yeah, that sounds great," I say, but it doesn't. Nothing sounds better than Tito's mirthful voice over the phone right now. The excitement and pride in his tone at what they've accomplished was palpable, meanwhile I stand in my kitchen, paralyzed. I turn my attention to Susana, who finished her dinner as evidenced by the two stripped drumstick bones left on her plate and juicy residue where Isa spooned sauce over the rice. "Susanita, why don't you go upstairs and start washing up. I'll be up to help you in a minute."

Without a word, Susana hops off her booster, walks over to me, gives me the greasiest hug, and smudges a kiss on both my cheeks. I wait until she's safely out of earshot and make a mental note to wipe down the banister, railing, and walls when I go back upstairs.

"Did you hear that Spain passed same-sex marriage today?" I ask, standing a few feet behind Isa. Even over the scent of baked chicken in the air, I can still smell her scent. The ubiquitous aroma of vanilla bean that, by now, seems to be as much a part of her skin as her own pH.

"Yes, I got a news alert on my BlackBerry earlier," she says. Of course she did. Isa turns to face me, leans her backside against the sink, and dries her hands with a kitchen towel. Biting down on her lips, no sign of chin dimples. Her chocolate-brown stare drills into me—waiting. She tucks an errant, dark tress behind her ear. This conversation is an old chestnut. For us, at least. I'd like to be one of those couples who talk about one day getting married if the law allows it. That's the opposite of us. We planned our studies, our life together, and yes, our daughter. But marriage was always one step too far for Isa.

"You know," I say as I walk over to the sink and wash my hands. "Since I'm a Spanish citizen, we could, for the sake of argument, get married in Jerez, or if that's too provincial, we can do it in Sevilla." I pause to wipe the grime off my cheeks with a damp paper towel. "We can live on the vineyard in Jerez with Don Rigoberto while we establish my parental rights over Susana." I rush my words, so I can get them all out and duck when she hits me back with a sharp, *NO*. A heated exchange is coming, and sweat bubbles are already dotting the small of my back. What I'm thinking of doing might seem far-fetched to her, but it's an excellent plan, if only she'd listen. "By the time same-sex marriage is legal in the States, we could either move back here or stay there, in case Florida is the last state in the union to recognize same-sex marriages and adoptions by gay people." This might be the Sunshine State, but it's been putting a damper on my life since I was born.

Isa fixes her eyes on me but remains silent as my hopes seem to evaporate.

"That sounds like a great plan—your best plan, even." She pauses. "But if it wouldn't be legal here, in Florida, where we live and work, why would we get married in Spain in the first place?" she asks, slowly folding her arms over her chest.

"Um…No. I meant that we would live in Spain. Um… If we get married there, the law will protect us. We'd have all the rights afforded to all other married couples in Spain, including adoption. And I would be *somebody* in your life and in *our* daughter's life over there. I'd be her recognized parent if something were to happen to you. And if something happens to me, you'd both inherit my stake in the vineyard."

My maternal grandfather, Don Rigoberto, is the last living owner of the vineyard, Villa Guadalcacín, and Lui and I will inherit fifty percent of it when he dies. Abuela Alba died shortly after my parents were killed in a car accident. The tragedy of losing her only daughter was too much for her weak heart to bear. Although I'm sure he'll live many more years, Don Rigoberto is a strong man, always has been, but he's in his eighties and suffers from vertigo.

He has a vast spread of land in Jerez, a city in the Andalusian region of Spain. There, he grows Palomino Fino and muscat grapes and sells his crop to area bodegas. They make the region's famed brandy, manzanilla, and sherry wines. His finca is only an hour's drive from the capital city, Seville. It's also where Lui and I have our residential address in Spain, giving us the right to vote there.

"G, my work is here. You know I'm in the middle of important research at the hospital, growing human tissue to replace mechanical heart valves. We're building real heart valves with human tissue...in a lab! It takes time." She folds up the towel and places it on the counter, seemingly putting an end to my daydreaming. "I won't leave my research now. Besides I can't. I still have another two years to fulfill my obligation. Remember, they paid my student debt. And anyway, you're a successful architect. Your career is booming. Why would we move from here?" she asks, dramatically raising her hands in the air as she turns in a circle. "And, if something does happen to me here, I signed palimony papers making you Susana's guardian, or have you forgotten? So, for all practical purposes, you'll be her parent."

I hang my head, inching toward the edge. If I fall off, would I survive the drop? I push forward, albeit with some trepidation.

"Yes but 'for all practical purposes' isn't enough for me anymore. You're forgetting that a judge for Children and Family Services has to rule in my favor for me to be her guardian. And that's if something happens to you, but what about now? I want it to be known that I'm her mother, too." My voice cracks. I clasp my hands together behind my back to hide their trembling.

"And," I say calmer, centered. "If something does happen to you and I wanted to adopt her, I would have to lie about my sexual orientation."

"Well, what's wrong with that?" she asks. "Wouldn't you do that for your daughter's sake?"

"Isa," I reply, tamping down the sudden tension headache. The pressure between my eyebrows is digging into my brain. My hands aloft, I grasp my index finger. "First of all, it's illegal to lie on official documents, and you'd better believe that officials for the state of Florida will investigate, but regardless, I don't think I should have to lie to adopt the daughter I helped bring into this world. That's if something happens to you."

I grasp my middle finger. "Second, you are required to be present to give consent for medical care. Remember what happened the first time we rushed Susana to the emergency room?"

I take a breath, trying to wipe the memory away and grasp my ring finger. "Third, I can't sign any kind of legal document for her because I'm not her legal parent."

Pulling at my pinky, sending pins and needles up my arm, I continue, "And fourth, I pay a tax on the benefit I receive from the firm to have both of you on my health insurance. You know, it's a real shame my company is more liberal than this country."

With my chest heaving, head throbbing, and stomach spinning, I give her my final point. "Isa, marriage is about more than just the bond between you and me. There are laws in place that protect the family unit. Why is that so hard for you to understand?"

"Gene, we can't move to another country to get married," she says with cutting finality.

"Isa, we've been together for fifteen years! Living together since college, officially, like most straight married couples. We've created a family. You won't move to Spain so that I may feel secure in my role as one of Susana's mothers?" I keep my voice low, so Susana doesn't hear us argue. A bit clearer than a whisper, but my throat might as well be bleeding from forcing my words through my esophagus without involving any vocal cords.

"We had the opportunity to move anywhere, but you wanted to move back here. And now, because of that, I've already established my research in Miami and must see it through," she says, tapping her index finger on the countertop of the kitchen peninsula, her words biting.

"That's not fair," I say, astonished that she'd even bring it up. "I had no choice. I wouldn't sell this house. This is my house." I pound my chest with my fist. "I lived here with my family. I grew up here, I couldn't let anyone else have this house."

I've got to somehow summon every bit of courage to get through this. But just as boiling water starts to evaporate, so too are my hopes of ever marrying Isa and adopting Susana.

"Gene, we've been living together for the last ten years. Where is the urgency? Why can't you wait until Florida follows suit and legalizes adoptions for gays and lesbians?" she asks.

"Because I know what it's like to lose both my parents and to be unprepared to live without them!" I bellow with a sob. This time, a little louder than before, and the words seem to gush out of me just as the tears sting at my eyes. "But the difference is the state knew who both my parents were. If I die right now, there's no record of whom I loved or by whom I'm survived. Don't you see? I have a birth certificate that says who my parents were. It doesn't say 'unknown' under the word *father*."

"So, you want your name on Susana's birth certificate under the word *father*?" she asks, brows furrowed. "I don't understand how that's going to change anything."

"Because you have no idea what it means to have a child you love, who loves you just as hard, and have zero legal connection to her. You gave birth to Susana, that is undeniable. Your name is on her birth certificate. Mother: Isabel Susana Acosta," I say, making gestures in the air as if Isa's name and title were top billing on a theater marquee.

"I can't do this anymore," I hear myself say, the words leaving my mouth in slow motion and in a deep wistful tone. I drop my arms to my sides and lower my gaze to my Reeboks. The back of my neck is stiff as tears swell in my eyes. "I've given this everything I have, and if you can't at least understand where I'm coming from, then you and I have no business being together at all. I gotta go." I turn and walk out through the kitchen archway, shoulders slouched, feeling as though I'm Yeats's falconer, lost in "The Second Coming" because things are really falling apart. My stomach lurches, and all I want to do is get out of this house before my own center cannot hold anymore.

"Wait, what?" She rounds the peninsula and steps right behind me. She puts her hand on my shoulder, and I turn to face her, shrugging it off in the process. "You're leaving? Leaving us?"

"No, Isa." I point a trembling finger at her. My voice is quivering. "I'm leaving you." Never in a million years did I think I would ever utter those words to Isa. "I will still be in Susana's life, provide for her, and co-parent her with you, the way it states in our palimony papers. I just…I can't live here with you anymore." Shaking my head, I turn back around and make my way to the stairs. Isa calls out to me.

"Gene!"

I turn to face her.

"Be reasonable," she says. Stomach acid churns, melting my insides. "You won't stay here with me if I don't move to another country where we can get married?"

I shove my fists in the pockets of my Bermuda shorts. My head thrashing as if I've just come back from a Mötley Crüe concert. This isn't an impossible task. My own parents moved to the States when the future of their family became untenable in Franco's fascist Spain in 1969. Both sets of Isa's grandparents did the same when they fled Castro's communist Cuba in the early sixties. "Isa," I say to her, after a few deep breaths. "We both knew this day was coming, let's be honest with ourselves. I've loved you since I was thirteen years old, but while you've been playing make-believe, I've been building a family, a home, and a life with you." I pound my chest again, and it's as if my heart has stopped beating. "We've been lovers from the get-go, sharing a house, the chores, the expenses, and a bed. For all practical purposes, as you say, you're my wife."

"But, G, we've been best friends," she insists, and she's being serious, which is what's most astonishing.

"¿Qué?" As my blood blisters, my eyes strain under the sudden pressure, I'm befuddled by her words. "No. Don't you dare say that!" Spittle springs off my bottom lip. "Don't you dare call me your best friend. We are a couple! Best friends don't plan the life we've planned for fifteen years, they don't sleep together, and they certainly don't have children together. Friends don't miss each other so much they practically starve themselves, waiting to be reunited with the other in college! You and I have never been friends, and because you only think of me as such reassures me that I am nothing to you." I stop to give my rapid pulse a chance to ease.

"I wanted more from this relationship," I continue. "From the life we diligently pieced together. The life you planned for us doesn't fit me anymore! But you still don't realize that aside from all the papers we signed, Susana is legally only your daughter. Do you get that? I can write it a hundred times in the air, and it'll still be air and not a legal document." I stop speaking abruptly, turn, and climb the stairs. I need to leave for my own sanity and figure out how I'm going to adopt my daughter.

"Wait. Fuck, Gene, you know I would never take her away from you, if that's what you're worried about!" She's right behind me.

I wait until we're inside our bedroom to turn around. "Really? You won't even marry me; how can I expect you to think of me as her other parent?" As I blurt out those last words, I know I've gone too far and immediately regret them. But I carry on because an apology won't help matters. "Is it really because you don't want to move to Spain that you won't marry me, or is it because I'm a woman?"

"I don't see you like that," she says. "You're just Gene to me."

"Well," I say. "Gene has a pair of tits and a vagina." I grab my breasts and then cup my crotch.

"Gene!" Isa says in a hard whisper. "Don't say that."

"Don't you get it? Susana came out of your body, she shares your DNA. She looks exactly like you." I point out our door toward her bedroom. "I need it to say somewhere that she's my daughter, too." My volume has increased to a raspy whisper, and I mentally throw up my hands as I capitulate.

I turn and walk away, quietly making my way across the hall, leaving Isa to wonder what just happened. Drying my tears on the hem of my shirt, I knock on Susana's bathroom door and walk in to help her wash up.

"Te quiero, Bebé, you know that right?" I hold her pajama top as she pops her head through the collar and then juts her arms through the sleeves. I lead her to her bed, kiss her forehead, and tuck her in.

"Mami is coming in a minute, cariño," I say with barely an inch of voice as I pull the blanket over her. "I love you very much," I repeat. "See you in the morning."

"Te quiero, Mamá."

While I do my best to quell them when I hug Susana good night, I can't stop my hot tears from escaping as soon as I close her bedroom door. Isa is waiting just outside her door. Ignoring her, I cross the second-floor foyer back to our bedroom, Isa's footfalls behind me. Ambling into the dressing room, I grab my suitcase from my side of the closet and open it over the ottoman that sits in the center of the room. I can't stay here one more minute.

"You're leaving now?" Isa asks, closing the door gently behind her.

"I can't stay here with you." Drying my face with my hands, I continue, "I don't want you to worry about anything. I'm temporarily moving into the first-floor apartment down the street and then see what I do for the long term. You and Susana stay here, this is her home." I renovated the vacant apartment in the building I inherited from my parents when the tenants left last year. After the renovations, I'd intended to find another renter, but I guess it'll be me.

"What about the family?" she asks, her eyes two wide brown disks. I stop packing for a second and glare at her.

"We will always be a family, Isa," I assure her.

"I mean, what will you tell the family?" she asks, and it's clear to me she meant the Spanish family. My cousin, Flor, and her mother, Tita Carmen—her confidants. She watches as I continue gathering my stuff from the closet to my suitcase and back again. Of course. Keeping up appearances is all she cares about, even to my family.

"Tell them the truth." I shrug. "I'll be back tomorrow to pick Susana up for school. I don't want to change her routine. I'll take the rest of my stuff while you're at work. On Saturday we can hash out a permanent plan. We'll keep the shared calendar on our BlackBerrys for Susana's events. We'll figure it out."

As I process her comment about the family, it dawns on me that she will always be preoccupied with what others think. Isa worries that if knowledge of our relationship goes public, funding for her research will dry up—she isn't out at work. I know I'm doing the right thing.

Isa stops me on my way back to get more clothes from the closet, puts her hands on my forearms, and pins her eyes to mine. Her fingers on my skin burn as her dark broody eyes press into me. I can't hold her stare for long, but I wait to hear what she has to say.

"Are you sure about this?" she asks, sliding her hands up my arms. I shudder, and her eyes gleam from the natural light in the room.

"No," I say, my own tears deserting me. "But I need to find my own way now." Gazing at her, it's as if no time has passed since I first saw her on the school bus in junior high. Tall but doesn't tower over me anymore; wavy hair the color of molasses with a pair of rich, chocolate eyes to match; her sharp chin with two defined dimples on either side. She's as beautiful today as she was all those years ago. Her grip on me stings. I stare down at her hands, and it's as though she realizes she's lost. Mouth agog, she lets go. I turn around and continue packing.

CHAPTER TWO

Isa

Fuck me! She's gone. I want to run after her, but the gremlins in my ear keep telling me to let her go. I couldn't watch her leave. Instead, I numbly busied myself in Susana's bathroom, spreading her towel over the shower door so it doesn't get musty-smelling because Gene apparently forgot.

When she left, Gene closed the side door so gently, it barely made a sound on her way out. I felt my insides spill all over the bathroom floor.

Across the foyer, I crack open Susana's bedroom door to find her facing the opposite wall, seemingly asleep. The room is washed in a dim yellow hue coming from the streetlight in the alley, but it doesn't bother her. I cross the room and ease onto the foot of her daybed.

"Where did Mamá go?" Susana moves her head slightly toward me, her eyes are two tiny slits.

"It's okay, Bebé." I'm still figuring out how to explain to a five-year-old that her mother is gone. *Will she come back?* "Mamá will be here in the morning to drive you to school. I love you," I whisper and lean in to kiss her forehead. My quivering hands automatically tug her sheets over her little shoulder. "Now, go to sleep."

Susana sighs and closes her eyes.

The steps back down seem endless as I try to piece together what just happened. I tie my thick long hair back with the elastic band I keep on my wrist and dig into the mess left behind in the kitchen.

The dinner I had only just started for us was carefully put on cold burners after Gene stormed into the kitchen from her studio. My day at the lab was too stressful for Hurricane Gene to hit me with her histrionics. I accidentally slam the Hitachi's insert in the sink and the rice flies everywhere. *Mother of fucking pearl!* Taking a deep breath, I stop to ensure there's no sound coming from Susana's bedroom.

Centering myself to the task at hand, I scoop up the mess in the sink and put away the chicken. When that breaking news alert about Spain passing marriage equality came through, I should have known Gene was going to start this up again. But she doesn't get it. She never has. At the research hospital, I'm at the end of an infinite tug-of-war, and the rope is slipping away on my side.

Frustrated and needing some motherly advice, I pick up the kitchen phone, swiftly dialing Mami's number.

"Hola mi niña ¿cómo estas?" Mami says after picking up on the first ring. Her voice is warm and familiar, and it's hard to remember how contentious our relationship was once. She's probably sitting in her plush butaca with her TV table covering her thighs, eating one of her healthier concoctions she bulk-cooked earlier in the week. She did her best cooking wholesome food after the cardiologist diagnosed my dad with a calcified heart valve. But after receiving a bio-prosthetic valve implant, he died four years later. And now that he's gone, she probably has more vegetables on her plate than anything else. I clear my throat before answering to keep my voice from collapsing.

"Hola, Mami," I reply. "How was your day?"

"Oof," she says, making me chuckle silently. "My new client changed the floor plan—again—and now I have to figure out how I'm going to put La Habana en Guanabacoa!" she says in her rapid Spanglish. I let out a guffaw that sprinkles the receiver with my spittle.

"What does he want to add in the house that's so big?" I ask, whipping the phone with my hand.

"Bueno. El comemierda wants me to design a wine room, or a wine vault, or something similar in what used to be the two-piece powder room that was right off the kitchen. The room is barely four feet wide by six. ¡Dios mio! ¿Hasta cuando?" Visualizing her manic hand gestures as she explains, I guffaw.

"Oh my God, Mami," I say. "How many times is he going to change your design?"

"If I only knew," she replies with a sigh. "¿Y tu? How are you?"

"Ay, Mami," I reply with a quivering lip. "I think Gene just left me."

"¿Qué?" she asks, incredulous. "Pero, Isabel Susana Acosta, what have you done?"

I somehow calm my frenzied weeping and answer, "She... Spain...same-sex marriage..." Okay, maybe that wasn't calm at all.

"Take a deep breath and start from the beginning."

CHAPTER THREE

Gene

I walk through the door of the open floor plan apartment, with my shoulders hunched forward and my gaze glued to the floor. The space is cavernous and feels devoid of oxygen. Forty-five minutes ago, I had everything I'd ever wanted. At almost thirty, I had a family, Floyd the mischievous kitty, and a home. But it doesn't count for anything if I have no right to the family living inside.

I close the door behind me and slide down, collapsing on the floor. Clusters of images of our life together mentally unfold like an origami slideshow. My brain conjures a montage of pop culture from the eighties and nineties, and it's all pelting me as if flung off a speeding merry-go-round. Royal blue eyeliner, *splat*; Z. Carvaricci pants, *splat*; Edwin jeans, *splat*; ID shirts, Umbro sportswear, neon colors, freestyle dance music, synthesizer keyboards, and goodness, the Aqua Net hairspray. *Pop, pop, pop, pop.* And all of it moving to "Pictures of You." I'm dancing in my childhood walk-in closet (now Susana's closet), arms out, eyes closed, and feeling every single picture of Isa falling from a box tucked away on the top shelf.

The Cure has been playing the official soundtrack to my life since before I met Isa. The good, the bad, the depressing, and sometimes the strange. My life with Isa is summed up in a nineties' music video.

"Have you ever liked or maybe you thought you might have liked…a girl?" Isa had asked. We were in junior high, and I remember that night as if it were yesterday. It was mere days before Christmas break and our trip to Spain for our yearly visit with extended family, and Isa pops that question. And for the first time, I dreaded leaving because it meant that I wouldn't see her for two whole weeks. That's an eternity when you're thirteen.

That night, it felt as though all the blood from my face drained all over my bedroom floor. How could I answer her? Of course, I didn't want her to think I was a lesbian. If anyone called you that—a lesbian—you were as good as stigmatized as one. And I didn't want it to be true, not then anyway. So, I pretended, and I thought I'd been hiding my feelings for Isa when she asked me that question. The room began to spin as thick cubes of ice slid down my spine.

"Uh," I stammered, in the middle of a math problem. We'd been at my house, studying in my room together, sitting less than two inches apart. The hair at the back of my neck stood as tall as the Sears Tower, my ears burned hotter than white coals. "I, uh…don't know what you mean by that." I totally chickened out, but I knew exactly what she was getting at. I wasn't prepared to admit, *Yes, Isa, I'm totally smitten by you, and would you please go with me to the Valentine's Dance?*

"Oh, no. Never mind, then." She changed the subject so abruptly it was as if she slammed shut a book on my finger as I was reading a complicated sentence. She continued her homework as if she hadn't said a word.

On the last day of school before the break, we'd arranged to meet in the stairwell. I was desperate to say goodbye to her before leaving for two weeks. After the last bell rang, everyone scattered to the football field for our school's annual flag football tournament. Isa was a volunteer water girl, and boy was she as fresh as a fern, decked out all in green, her team's color. Oh, but that smile! The dimples on her chin deepened, and I remember thinking I could stare at those dimples the rest of my life. We locked eyes through the narrow, rectangular glass window of the heavy stairwell doors, her braces-clad grin gleamed through, and my heart was pounding in my chest so loud I was sure she heard it from the other side of the door.

"Sorry I'm so late," she said, her hand over her chest huffing deep breaths, in and out. "I wanted to dump all my books in my locker."

"Why didn't you tell me? We could have met up there." I didn't want to tell her that I had chosen to meet in the stairwell because I wanted to see her privately. And since it was so far from everything, it was the most privacy I'd thought we'd have. But I wasn't counting on everyone scattering out of the building so fast. So, I just shrugged.

"I wanted to give you this," she said, holding out a rectangular box, wrapped in Christmas paper, with a card laid on top.

"Oh my gosh," I gasped. "I don't have anything for you. I was going to bring you something from Spain." I don't remember what I eventually gave her, though.

"I don't care about that," she said and put both items in my hands. "This is for the flight to Spain. My dad told me it takes eight or nine hours." I gazed down at the small box, bewildered, thinking what could possibly be hiding inside? "You're taking your Walkman, right?"

Although dark brown, her eyes shimmered with flecks of gold in them. I'd always wind up smiling like an idiot at her. "Yes! I am."

"I gotta go in a second, but I just wanted to wish you a Merry Christmas and a Happy New Year. I'll miss you," she said with a lopsided grin. And then the hug. It came out of nowhere. She wrapped her arms around me so fast, I didn't have time to react. Back then, she towered over me by at least three inches. When she enveloped me in her willowy arms, my nose digging into her neck, the sweet and musky scent of vanilla bean wafted up my nostrils, plugging into my brain, connecting that fragrance forever with Isa.

In a roundabout way that Christmas, Isa declared her feelings for me through a mixtape of top-forty love songs. The note attached confirmed it. I don't have a cassette player anymore, but the tape is still sitting in my desk drawer in my studio. Mierda, the studio I just left behind.

I outgrew those eighties and nineties songs and fashion trends. The only other thing I own that survived that era is my plastic Swatch that Papá gave me for my thirteenth birthday. I don't ever take it off other than to get it fixed. It's got so many cracks on the original plastic wristband, it's about ready to fall off my wrist. I've replaced the fastener a few times. And the dings! The watch face looks brutalized, but I don't care, I'll never take it off. It's older than my relationship with Isa, which apparently I've also outgrown.

I stop that memory from morphing into more and focus on the bad times. The times Isa cast me aside in public, or when she didn't let me go to Carlos's funeral, all the dinners the hospital board of directors put together. Those episodes grated at me. Every time something similar happened, I added another row of bricks to the wall that eventually came between us.

Snap out of it!

I get up off the floor, put the keys down on the bar top counter of the kitchen peninsula, and roll my carry-on to what's going to be my bedroom. I'll need some provisions for the next few days and, of course, temporary furniture. The last time I bought furniture was when I moved into the off-campus apartment with Isa in Ithaca when I got to Cornell. I peek into what will be my office to measure for my drafting table. Susana's room will be fun, colorful, and easy to update. Martha will make sure of it.

Back in the living area, I scoop up my keys and head out the door.

I climb into the driver's seat and start the engine, determined to get my shit together. With a quivering hand, I wipe my sweaty brow. *Joder! What have I done? I completely changed my life. Where's the undo button for this? Calm down, Gene. Don't panic.*

I convince myself that I would have been miserable for the rest of my life if I hadn't done what I did earlier tonight. *Focus on getting your life in order. Come up with a plan. A fucking plan! Everything in my life es un puto plan.* Taking a deep breath, I close my eyes and exhale so hard I start coughing. To the grocery store I go, a long night ahead of me.

CHAPTER FOUR

Isa

I can barely open my eyes when I hear the alarm clock blaring. Slamming at one of its buttons, I finally shut it off. Moments later—or I think it's moments later—when I drag myself out of bed, my wristwatch says I've nearly snoozed for an hour. *Fuck, I'm late!* I race to Susana's room to find her already in her navy-blue shorts and a Bugs Bunny T-shirt, sitting on the floor and slipping her socks over her feet.

"Sorry, honey, Mami's running a little late this morning," I say as she peers up at me. "I'll run downstairs and get your breakfast going. Mamá will be here soon."

She says nothing as I sprint down the stairs and quickly combine cereal and milk in her miniature bowl and leave it on the table for her—no time for healthier oatmeal. It's nearly seven in the morning by the time I hastily climb back upstairs, and Susana is sitting on the toilet in her bathroom.

"Your breakfast is ready. Please make sure to wash your hands before going downstairs." Silence. Maybe Gene is right, she's exactly like me. I'm not much of a talker first thing in the morning either. Forgoing my morning shower, I hightail it to the dressing room. It's barren with half of Gene's clothes gone. Taking a few deep breaths usually works to settle my nerves, but I'm still a bit of a wreck when I sit at the vanity mirror.

This was Maria's vanity. This was Maria and Roberto's house. We were at Cornell when they died and left the house to Gene. She was nearly born here, in fact. And there isn't an inch of this place that doesn't remind me of her parents, of us. I guess you can say I grew up here, too. *How am I going to fix this?* Focusing on the image through the mirror, I begin applying my concealer over the purple skin under my eyes.

In a clockwise pattern, I rub in the base coat all over my face, but the image staring back at me is nothing short of a disaster. My hair is all over the place because, on top of everything, I didn't wrap it up in my bedtime top bun. My eyelids are as puffy as the floaties Gene insists Susana wear on her little arms before getting in the pool, and my skin, always the picture of youth, is a pale and blotchy desert. Someone would probably confuse me for one of the patients in my hospital. Grabbing the eyeliner, the odiously high-pitched sound of the landline's ring almost makes me lose my shit. *Who the fuck could that be?*

I get up and race to the other side of the room to answer it, tripping over the ottoman sitting in the center, landing in the club chair, face down. I slap my palm down. *Fuck!*

"Hello," I yell after tipping the receiver up and nearly hitting my face with it. My voice is sharp and a few octaves too high.

"Hi," Gene says, hesitantly. "I'm outside. Is Susana ready?" She says it fast, as though I'm going to bite her head off. Truth is, I really want to.

"Why didn't you just come inside the house, Gene?" I reply, righting myself on the club chair. With barely any sleep last night, I need a fucking break.

"I didn't want to intrude," she answers, after a pause.

"I'm trying to get ready for work," I bite back, hating my life for letting Gene fluster me. If she hadn't left so abruptly last night, I wouldn't be in such a foul mood. But I remind myself to inhale and calm down; there'll be time for the firing squad later.

I exhale. "We had a little bit of a late start this morning." My tone is smoother now. "Can you just use your key and come inside? Susana's in the kitchen, having breakfast." Meanwhile, I look like a contortionist on this ottoman. But I don't say that last bit.

I return to the vanity and gaze at myself through the mirror again. Mother of fucking pearl, no amount of concealer can cover up these eight balls. Muscle memory takes over as I apply the rest of my makeup, but I can't stop the gremlins from chattering away at my ear.

The seventh graders wisely chose their seats at the front of the bus. The steamy humidity left an oppressive swelter in the air. It was like glue sticking to your skin and your skin sticking to the vinyl seats in that stagnant tin can. At the back of the bus, I stood up to catch what little breeze trickled in through the open window, two feet above the seat. With only twenty-five cents in my pocket, I couldn't very well buy an ice-cold Coke Damaris, the bus driver, sold for fifty. And I couldn't take it anymore.

"Does anyone have twenty-five cents?" I hollered so that the seventh and eighth graders sitting at the front of the bus could hear me. Most of them turned their heads, but I locked gazes with only one. A lanky girl with long untamed, curly blond hair. Everyone's hair was a mess at the end of the school day. It was mid-August, and the last days of summer in Miami were always hellacious. A little bit of sweat combined with a six- to seven-hour school day frizzed anyone's locks. We were in no way ready for the runway.

The blonde, indigo-framed glasses perched on her nose, peered right at me, cutting into me. I couldn't take my eyes off her. A cacophony of sounds reverberated through the bus, but I didn't hear a thing. Suddenly, she turned her head away from me, and I was stuck wondering who she was, where she lived, and why my heart thrashed against my sternum.

Traffic always went at a glacial pace on the first day of school, but it was at a standstill just then. It took the bus driver almost forty-five minutes just to get to my neighborhood, which was three miles from school. We were near the end of the route with only a few people left on the bus, including the four-eyed blonde. As I made my way to the front and the driver approached my house, I slowed down slightly before walking past the bench the blonde was sitting on. I peeked down to see what she what was so damn interesting on her lap. I lifted my gaze just as I caught a glimpse of her drawing. *So, Blondie's a bit of an artist.*

"Hasta mañana, Isabel," Damaris said as she creaked open the double doors. I gave her a backhanded wave and got off the bus. But just as she revved to drive away, I turned around and caught Blondie staring right at me. It only took a second for her eyes to go from curious to caught-in-headlights. Turning back, I sauntered up the long walkway to my front door wearing a smug grin.

Batting back at the gremlin whispering in my ear, I tuck that memory back in the folder of our junior high years and wipe away a defiant tear before it smudges my makeup. Scooping up my hair in a shabby-chic bun, I pin down the edges and give it a good lacquer. This will have to do. The outfit I picked out last night is waiting on its hanger behind the bathroom door. It takes but a few seconds to slip into it and make my way downstairs. And then, when I hear her voice, my resolve melts away.

"¡Buenos días, cariño!" I hear her say to Susana, but her glee sounds forced. I hadn't heard her come in, but she must be in the kitchen with Susana.

Stopping at the foot of the stairs, I straighten my skirt and brush the sleeves of my silk blouse. My heels clatter against the terra-cotta tiles as I amble through the kitchen archway.

"Mamá!" Susana yells enthusiastically. "Where were you? I was calling for you." My heart plunges to my stomach at the thought of Susana missing her mamá.

"Are you ready for school?" Gene asks her.

"I'm still eating, Mamá. Can't you see?" Susana says with a little more attitude than she should be using with either of us. "I gotta brush my teef after."

How the heck is this situation going to work? Gene oversaw Susana's morning routine because I leave the house an hour before she signs into her firm's network. She's been working from the back building since before Susana was born. And after that, while I was earning my PhD, teaching, and interning at the hospital, Gene would bring Susana into the studio with her. It was much-needed help, but I'd been dreaming of having Susana since I was a teenager.

Gene glances up at me, her eyes run the length of my body. It's been a long time since I felt this naked. Her eyes are like warm hands all over my cold, bare skin. Just as I almost reach for her, I look away to avoid a blush and switch directions to the coffee maker instead.

"Do you want coffee?" I manage to squeal, pouring myself a mug. The pulse in my neck rattles on.

"Please," she replies.

I open the cabinet and remove her *I'm an ~~arcateck arckatect architech~~, I draw stuff* mug I bought for her when she started interning at the architectural firm she works for now. Mindlessly smiling at the happy memory, my hands tremble as I fill her mug with the hot brew. In her usual office attire of T-shirt and shorts, Gene sits back and waits for me to bring the coffee.

"How did you sleep?" I ask, breaking the silent barrier between us. My voice is in tatters. But instead of answering, she shakes her head slowly. I cast my eyes down into my mug. No, I didn't get any sleep either.

The harsh sound of Susana's chair scraping across the floor, followed by her bare feet hitting the tile, shakes us both out of our misery-loves-company daze. Felt chair leg pads might stop that racket, and I make a mental note to get some after work. Maybe I can get Gene to stop brooding long enough to install them. I wish my throbbing headache were as easy to fix.

"I'm onna brush my teef," Susana announces, and drums away out of the kitchen. I let go of a sigh.

Gene and I sit motionless for a few moments, uncomfortably looking at each other. Her usually glimmering hazel eyes are murky and glum, and her incessant morning chatter is as mute as the *Mona Lisa*. But what's left to say after her explosive word vomit yesterday? I'm trying to understand why the fuck she feels the need to move to Spain to get married. Doesn't she understand that I'm in the middle of important research at the hospital? Engineering human tissue for heart valves out of nothing takes time. Well, it's the opposite of nothing. We're using stem cells. Ten years ago, stem cell science was theoretical. Now, everything from Alzheimer's to Parkinson's disease research uses stem cells.

And God forbid Gene understands that my research depends on grants and taxpayer money funneled to the hospital by the government at every level. Dollars, mind you, that are highly coveted by every other research hospital in the nation. And if that weren't enough, this is a male-dominated industry, and I don't want to give the ultraconservative state legislature an excuse to cut my funding because one, I have a child out of wedlock, and two, I live with a lesbian…er, lived with a lesbian.

Besides, gay marriage is bullshit in this country. Congress has left it up the states to decide. A handful of states have made it legal, and the rest have banned it. What the fuck is that? Let's just ignore the Constitution's full faith and credit—that seems like a great idea.

I wish she'd stop looking at me with her forlorn eyes. Those fucking hazel eyes that can be as cold as marble one minute and as warm as a winter's day in the south of Spain the next. A simple glance at them, and I can only get lost. And as we sit opposite one another, I get an unstoppable urge to go to her. It's confusing the hell out of me. And she must feel the same because somehow, we simultaneously stand up and desperately reach for each other.

It's absurd, yet I don't know how we got to this point. Her cottony T-shirt and the warmth of her embrace cling to me like a spider web. We kiss with a desire for one another that has been lacking for a minute. Regardless, I can't stop my arms from hooking under hers and digging my fingertips into her shoulder blades.

It's visceral, this ache in my belly to hold her firmly to me. I bury into her skin through the downy fabric. Gene slides through my lips and finds my tongue, ready for her. I open my mouth and deepen our kiss. She cups my face with her smooth hands, driving us both nuts. Because that's what this is, right? It's a haphazard, fucking crazy-ass loss of reason. If I don't stop now, who's to say we won't end up in the bedroom? Fuck! The bedroom. It was like the goddamn tundra in there last night without her.

She reaches for the nape of my neck, digs her fingers into my skin, and nips at my bottom lip before she abruptly pulls away, snapping me out of the trance as well. The tears can't be stopped any longer. We're both ruddy-cheeked and heaving hot air through our mouths. I inadvertently flipped the hem of Gene's shirt up. When I reach for it, she beats me to it and uses it to dab her eyes dry. My eyes catch a glimpse of her bare stomach, and I just automatically put my hand on her abs. The touch thrills my fingertips, as she wraps her arms around me. She smells of musk and leather and a little bit of the outside from riding around in the topless Jeep. Her smell is familiar to me as I nuzzle the crook of her neck. I know I'm leaving moisture on her shirt collar, but I don't make a sound. I want to stay here forever.

"Why are you doing this to us?" I whimper in her ear. The words fall out of my mouth as if I'd intended to say them all along.

"I can't live in the closet with you anymore," she says.

As Susana's rapid footfalls get closer, Gene breaks contact. She scurries to the sink and splashes cold water on her face, puttering around for a moment while I tear off a sheet of paper towel to dry my eyes. I hand her one, and she shoves her face in it.

"Are you ready to go?" Gene gasps at Susana.

She lifts Susana's backpack from its hook on the wall next the sliding glass door and reaches for my bag on the next one. She stretches to hand it to me, slightly brushing her fingers over mine as I take it from her grasp. Without taking my eyes away from hers, I lug it over my shoulder. Gene focuses on Susana's backpack, holding it while she slides her little arms through the straps. The three of us walk out the side door to the carport, as if nothing had ever happened, nothing at all. As I press the unlock button on my key fob to put my bag in the truck, I can't help shifting my eyes over to watch Gene help Susana get in her Jeep.

The ignition delays for a second before it roars the Jeep into action. Gene backs out of the driveway looking right into my moisture-filled eyes. I get into my red Land Cruiser, and by the time I look in the rearview mirror, she's gone.

CHAPTER FIVE

Gene

Back at the apartment after dropping Susana off at school, a familiar minivan is parked in the spot next to mine. I remove the keys from the ignition and scoop up my wallet from the center console.

Taking a personal day off work today was the only way I'd be able to move my things to the apartment. I called professional movers to help me pack and move my office from the back building later today, all while Isa is at work.

"Hi," I say to Martha as she gets out of her Honda minivan. I walk around to her side and greet her with a tight hug and a kiss on each cheek. Martha's hugs are like Isa's: tight and warm and you just want to live in them forever. They're the kind of hugs I crave after a long day at work, isolated in the back building.

There's no denying grandmother, mother, and daughter are blood-related, either. All three Acosta women have inherited the same chin dimples, dark eyes and hair. I assume they came from some distant relative because I remember Isa's grandparents, and neither had their enigmatic chin dimples. The three share genes that are as dominant as the women themselves.

Martha, at barely fifty-five years old, is elegance personified. Short brown hair neatly straightened and kept gray-free surrounds gold hoop earrings, less than an inch diameter, hanging from her delicate earlobes. She's wearing a pale mustard short-sleeve blouse and a pair of tan herringbone-patterned slacks. On her narrow feet are pair of Weejuns loafers, and instead of the scent of vanilla bean, Martha's everyday fragrance is freesias and lavender. One hug from her and you're skipping through a meadow, stopping to pick wildflowers.

At some point, but not in my memory, Martha was exactly like Isa. Everything from her broody eyes to the commanding way she appears in photographs is every bit the carbon copy of her daughter.

"Gene," she says, the deep line between her eyebrows crinkling with confusion and probably worry, too. "How are you?"

"Isa told you?" I reply. "What did she say?"

"Well, she said that you argued and then you stormed off to hide out here," she answers with a sweeping gesture of her arm toward my building. *That's not exactly what happened*, I want to say but nod instead. "I'm paraphrasing, of course."

Pausing for a moment, I stare into the gold flecks of her dark eyes. Although Isa's mom knows almost everything about us, I've never had to talk about our relationship with her. How do I even begin to explain my side? Because if Isa doesn't understand my side, there's no way she'd be able to clarify it for Martha's sake.

"Are you hungry? I can offer you some coffee. It's about all I was able to get last night at Target," I say, unlocking the front door to the apartment. "That and an inflatable bed, sheets, a little table, and some barstools for the kitchen peninsula."

I walk into the empty living room, Martha behind me. Dropping my keys on the kitchen peninsula, I turn to her, hands on hips, and watch as she sweeps the room for its potential. It still smells of fresh paint, a new place to hang my hat. I make my way into the kitchen and wait for her to finish her assessment. And as if out of thin air, she conjures a brown paper bag in my line of sight. By the heavenly scent of its contents, I'd say it's holding a couple of tostadas and café con leche to-go cups.

"Sos una santa," I say with a sigh and stretch my arms across the countertop for her to hand me the bag. "It's still a bit stark in here, but I'm going to order furniture today. I want this place to feel like a home soon."

"I can help you with that," she says. "If you want, of course."

She walks toward the middle of the living area, mentally measuring, plotting, and placing imaginary furniture. As I remove the tostadas and two Styrofoam cups of café con leche from the paper bag, I can't help but glance up at her as she roams around the apartment. Crumpling up the empty bag, I say, "I'd love that."

"Are you sure about this?" Martha turns to face me. Ambling toward the barstools, she pulls one out and slides over the leather cushion.

"That's a question I don't think I can answer," I reply, tossing the paper wad in the new trash can. "At least, not now."

"I can tell you from experience an empty house can be difficult to get used to," she says. I nod to give myself some time to answer. Carlos, Isa's dad, died when Susana was three. I get melancholic knowing that Susana won't remember the time she spent with her grandfather. Of course, that's after the gnawing regret I already feel because she never had any time whatsoever with my parents.

"I know, I know. It won't always be empty, though," I say with a cheerful lilt, albeit artificial. "Mira, Martha," I continue. "I've been following Isa around as though I were a puppy dog, and she were my rescuer ever since I was in the seventh grade." I set some napkins on the countertop.

"I understand that she doesn't want to make waves at work when she has to petition the government for funds," I continue. "But at some point, she needs to realize that I want to live freely. She's been with the research hospital for almost six years, now. Leading her own team of researchers, she should feel some security. I know this is a competitive area, but her family should come first. We should come first for her."

Walking out of the kitchen, I make my way to sit beside her. I let out a groan, biting into the freshly-dipped-in-coffee tostada. "Aah, this is so delicious. I haven't had tostadas cubanas in a gazillion years."

"I thought you might need a little pick-me-up," she says, taking a bite of her own toast. Martha, true to her Cuban heritage fixes everything with tostadas and café con leche. Any food, really: meats marinated in her special Cuban criollo mojo then oven roasted to a dripping-off-the-bone perfection, or a dutch oven—the diameter of which is the length of my arm—brimming with her savory and soupy arroz con pollo are some of the ways she's gotten me to pep up a time or two. But even her asopado a la chorrera won't fix what's ailing between Isa and me.

"I love Isa," I say after swallowing a mouthful of Cuban bread dripping with butter. "I've always loved her. But you knew that already. I followed her to Ithaca and made Cornell my first choice just to be with her. I don't even think I applied to any fallback schools. That's how determined I was to go anywhere to be with her."

"Yes, and when it was time for her to move back here with you, she did," she admonishes.

"That's true," I retort. "But you know, when she wanted to get pregnant, she didn't exactly include me in the research process. Had she given me a chance to do my own research, talk to our lawyer, or just get advice from other lesbian couples going through the same process, maybe I'd have been prepared to make better decisions."

"What do you mean?" she asks, eyebrows pinched together. "That you wouldn't have had Susanita if you knew it would be like this?"

"No!" I reply instantly. "I just meant that it would've, maybe, been easier to handle if I'd known what to expect, that I'd be playing such a precarious role in my own daughter's life."

"Isa is a single-minded woman. She wants what she wants. You know that already," Martha says, taking a cautious sip from the scalding café con leche. "All I'm saying is maybe you don't rush into moving out completely. Think about how this will affect Susanita."

"Trust me, Martha," I say, with a hand on her left shoulder. "I've thought of nothing else."

"Fine," she says, hopefully putting an end to her plea. "You know I'm here for you and Susanita. For whatever reason."

"I know," I say. Here's a woman who, after my parents' accident, let me stay in her house until I was ready to face the lifeless walls my parents left behind. She helped me cope with my grief when I was knee-deep in my parents' legal papers, and she helped me bring life back to the house I inherited.

"I brought food, too," she says, as if she'd almost forgotten. Sliding off her barstool, Martha pats her napkin over her mouth before removing a canvas grocery bag from her Mary Poppins-esque purse, placing it on the countertop in the kitchen. I'm still sitting on the barstool watching the spectacle. She lifts each container out of the grocery bag and reveals their delectable contents.

"Did I mention you're a saint?" I ask with a relieved sigh. "Thank you."

"I cook in bulk," she says with a shrug. "I don't mind sharing."

"I appreciate it." I wipe my stinging eyes. "How is she?"

"Well, you tell me," she replies. "She called me last night, after you left. So, that should tell you how she is. She isn't exactly thrilled you left."

"We've been separated before," I reply with a shrug. "And she seemed fine then."

"That was different, and you know it," she says, reaching over to put her warm hand over mine. "You and Isa never really separated. You left her in Ithaca after spending the summer with her in Cornell. And then you came back here to finish your last two years of high school."

"We both learned a lot from that," I say, gazing off to an empty corner of the living room.

That summer night in Ithaca was dank and misty. It was how I felt inside, too. The Greyhound bus was my ride to the airport in Buffalo. Isa walked me to the bus stop, just at the edge of campus.

I was like a fiend, trying to get into the architectural program for high school students at Cornell, but it was worthwhile to be with Isa for three more months, although I was in anguish at the end of it. Honestly, it was her fault. Rather than wait for the fall semester, she wanted to get started with her undergrad during the summer term. And, of course, I didn't argue when she suggested I apply for my own summer program so we could be together. But at summer's end, my junior year in high school was calling.

When we reached the bus stop, I checked my Swatch again, realizing I only had ten minutes before departure. I placed my backpack on the bus bench and turned to Isa. It was only August twenty-seventh. The following day was Isa's eighteenth birthday, and I had wanted to stay and celebrate with her, but the fall semester had already started, and life moved forward, with or without me there.

Isa crossed her arms over her chest to keep out the chilly air; autumn was barreling through New York State. The knot in my stomach tightened with every inhale as a sharp breeze ran up my spine, flaring my peach fuzz.

"It's going to be okay," Isa said. Her eyes, glazed over, looked everywhere except at me.

"I know," I replied, almost wailing. My resolve evaded me, and all I wanted to do was get on the bus. That goodbye was worse than an uncertain future.

"We'll follow the plan," she'd said. "We'll write to each other. And we'll see each other when I come home for Christmas," she'd promised.

"I know," I said. What else was I supposed to say? Stopping the tears from gushing down my face just then would have been futile. But I wanted to stop them. I wanted to be strong, but I couldn't hold in the sorrow. She glanced around, making sure no one was near us before she took me in her arms. The moisture on her cheeks rubbed off on my neck, leaving the bad kind of goose bumps.

She released me and abruptly cleared her throat. "I'll see you in December, okay?" she said with her arms extended and her hands planted on my shoulders.

"I'll see you in December," I repeated. My voice was a fragile animal scurrying from danger. A pair of bright headlights slowly approached—the dreaded bus.

Fearing the end of our goodbyes, Isa grabbed me in her arms again and held me against her chest. Her pounding heart synchronized with mine, beating in a deep and heavy rhythm. My palms were clammy, and my world was deliberately becoming unknown to me. And then, something I thought I would never witness—Isa wept in my arms. The back of my sweater bunched up in her fist as she bawled on my shoulder.

"I'm sorry, what?" I ask Martha, who's looking at me quizzically.

"I asked if you wanted to go to the furniture store today," she repeats. "If you have time, I mean."

"Oh, yeah. Let's go," I reply, my head jumbled—and my palms, still a little clammy.

CHAPTER SIX

Isa

The Tylenol I took after Gene darted out the door, Susana in tow, has helped little. Plus, I'm still reeling from this morning's raucous kiss. And now, my headache is further exacerbated by the sharp antiseptic stench that lingers in the hospital's corridors as I make my way to the pathology department. Doing my best to greet the passing hospital staff members, I send them all a fictitious smile they've surely never seen.

My mood cannot get more dismal, and I'm especially disinclined to deal with my inquisitive interns today. They're like little reptiles, adapting to every nuance in their research. But I'm the lead biomedical engineer, so that means our interns are my responsibility; it's a teaching hospital, after all. Thankfully, they're only here until noon, then I can focus on my own work.

The corridor that leads to the therapeutics lab where my office is hidden away seems interminable. It's the same one Tucker Peterson led me through just as I began my sojourn as an intern. The years that have passed since then don't seem like years at all.

"Isabel, let me be the first to welcome you to the Department of Pathology Laboratory Medicine at Miami Research Hospital," the Director of Heart Disease Research, Dr. Tucker Peterson, said, extending his right hand in my direction.

Leading a team specialized in heart disease therapeutics, Dr. Tucker Peterson seemed to be in his early forties. His gray hair, combed back with the help of pomade and thinning slightly on top, didn't quite match his young-looking eyes. No deep lines on his face and no signs of a double chin. But he did have an odor to him, an odd mix of formaldehyde and sewage. It wafted off his body, and the nearer he got to me, the sharper the stench.

His brazen audacity appalled me, too, especially since I'd been twiddling my thumbs in the waiting room near his office for almost an hour. I had to get up to pee twice before he graced me with his presence. Unconsciously rubbing the bump beneath my linen peasant top, I stood up ineptly, reached for his outstretched hand, and gave it a hearty shake. He affixed his beady eyes on my protruding mound with a cockeyed glare. The hospital administrators knew about my due date before they offered me the position—I wasn't due for another three months, and I wasn't about to lie. Anyway, I couldn't hide my belly. I'd signed a seven-year contract, which included my first year as an intern. And, as an extra incentive, the hospital had agreed to pay off my student loans.

"I understand you'll *initially* be with us for three months," he said, making his way through the hallway too brisk for my waddling pace. Mouth shut, I followed nonetheless.

"You're lucky," he continued, with a quick glare over his shoulder at me. "Some of the other chaps who've applied were ready to go the full seven years, with no breaks." I withheld a stabbing comment (one that may have included a *go fuck yourself*) and an eyeroll because I didn't want to irritate my new boss further. "You must have really impressed someone at the top."

He yanked on his retractable key card from his belt, smacked it to the pad next to the door, and, after a slight delay, the double doors to the secure area of the hospital swung open. Another infinite corridor later and he opened the hefty door to the lab. "Ladies first," he said. His irksome grin jarred even the little swimmer doing backflips inside me—I needed to throw up but wouldn't give him the pleasure.

"Thank you, Dr. Peterson," I had said without as much as a flinch. "It's an honor to be working here in the company of such prestigious researchers like yourself." *A little sugar will go farther, Isa, especially if you're working alongside this man.* Convincing myself to do my best, I saw myself tamping down my retorts for the foreseeable future. *Mother of fucking pearl! Seven years of this shit.*

"I'm so glad, Isabel," he said. The saccharin in his voice sent a yawp up my spine. "I hope your husband doesn't mind you working late nights. With the research we're conducting here, our scientists barely take a breather, much less time for lunch. Unfortunately, it's the interns who do most of the grunt work, though." He smiled at me with a mouth full of tiny, crooked teeth, stained from years of coffee drinking and chain-smoking, probably. One of his front teeth was slightly chipped, making almost every word that contained an "S" in it slip through with a whistle and a saliva spray.

"It won't be a problem sir," I replied, feigning a nose scratch as I took a deep whiff into my hand and inhaled a bit of my still-potent vanilla bean hand lotion. "I'm perfectly prepared to make whatever sacrifices need to be made." I was haranguing myself into being pleasant. *Big picture, Isa. Just focus on the big picture. You want to make better functioning heart valves. Hopefully Dad's mechanical heart valve can hold on just a little bit longer.*

As we walked into the frigid laboratory, the icy atmosphere cut right into my joints. But as I glanced around and saw lab equipment, the plastic trays, the tall stools on wheels, I instantly felt at home, even if I was the only female.

"Dr. Acosta," Hearing my name faintly, knocked me out of my daze. I focus my eyes on the floor to center myself and to stop the halls from spinning around me. "Dr. Acosta, the results are in and they're promising," one of my interns says, holding up the report.

"Perfect, Enrique," I reply. "Let me settle in, and I'll go over those results with you."

CHAPTER SEVEN

Gene

Four weeks later, to put her at ease, I invite Isa to inspect the apartment after Martha waved her magic decorator's wand. I've been having a difficult time with the new routine, to say the least, but we're managing to compartmentalize our hurt feelings and go about the business of raising our child in two separate households.

"Hey," Isa says as she takes the step up into the apartment, Susana skipping right behind her.

"Hi," I reply. "Come on in." Unsure how to greet Isa, I'm distracted by a jumping Susana, who wraps her legs around my waist and throws her arms around my neck. I give her a tight squeeze.

"Thanks for coming. I wanted to make sure you approved of the apartment, so you know that I'm providing Susana with a safe environment."

"Gene, you didn't have to," she says, but scans the apartment anyway. "I trust your judgment." She takes a few moments to walk around the kitchen and living spaces. "This looks like it came straight out of Mami's website." Isa chuckles, and it's the best sound I've heard all day. I focus on what she's looking at.

"Let me show you her bedroom," I say as I turn toward the hallway with Susana leading the way. Her bedroom is the last door on the left side, opposite my room across the hall. Susana grasps hold of my hand, pulling me toward her new bedroom. Isa's stare is burning a hole at the back of my head as she follows behind us. My heart seems to have made a bed for itself in the hollow of my throat as I turn my back to my bedroom door. *The things we can possibly get up to in there.* I wait for Isa to enter Susana's bedroom, and as she inches past me, her vanilla fragrance clings to me. Nothing stops me from taking a whiff.

"This is really cute," Isa says of the space. Martha helped Susana pick the colors to create a fun kid's space complete with hues of purple and periwinkle splashed throughout. Two beanbags—one bright purple, the other periwinkle—sit on the floor. To keep things consistent with what Susana has at the house, Martha had a similar brass-framed daybed made and covered it with a My Little Pony quilt to match the colors. On the other side of the room, Martha placed a wood storage desk that her handyman painted in periwinkle. She kept the walls white, though.

"Oh, man, Mami did a really great job in here," Isa says as she rolls the violet miniature office chair from under Susana's desk. Isa squeezes in it and moves her gaze about the room, mentally scrutinizing all the safety items: rounded corners, plug protectors, and a doorknob that doesn't lock.

We head out into the living area, and I catch Isa surreptitiously inspecting the rest of the apartment with her critical eye as if examining every electrical outlet, every table corner, and every possible non-toddler-friendly area of the apartment with a magnifying glass. She flags nothing. From floor to ceiling, wall to wall, I took extra care to ensure the apartment is as safe as possible for our five-year-old Tasmanian devil.

"The apartment looks great," she says. "Safe. Thank you for showing it to me." I just nod and walk them out. If she thinks this is easy for me, she's wrong. I watch as she lingers. She clasps her hands together in front of her, then folds her arms across her chest, then puts one hand on her hip and scratches the back of her neck with the other. And now, I'm staring at the nape of her long, luscious neck.

"Okay," she says, turning to face me. "Well, we should… we should go." Putting a hand on Susana's shoulder, she guides her out the door, and they both saunter off. Staying put on the sidewalk, I watch them walk toward the house with a pang of regret gnawing at my heels. *Run after them!* Each footfall cleaves a chasm that gets harder to close with every step away from me.

So much has happened since we conjured her up, as if from thin air. How it happened seemed to have been magic.

It was my official first day of work as an architect. Although I was heartbroken that Papá never got to see me follow in his footsteps, I was proud to have finished, and with Isa's support.

Just before finishing my master's degree, I had secured an internship with Ibarra Group, a small urban planning development firm with offices nearby. They gave me a permanent position after I received my M. Arch. Previously, I had apprenticed under their lead architect while I prepared for my Architectural Registration Exam. It was no easy feat, but after a couple of years, I became a licensed architect.

Isa was more than a quarter-way through with her PhD program, doing all her research, studying, teaching, and writing during the day. Then, at night, the two of us were like a married couple. Isa and her parents were all the family I had. They were all the family I needed.

It'd been a grueling day at the office, but all that melted away as soon as I walked in and smelled the familiar scent in the air. When we moved into my parents' house, Isa immediately took custody of the kitchen. I didn't mind that one bit. As hard as Mamá tried to teach me, I was never into cooking, but I did all the cleaning afterward.

Isa had filed all Mamá's handwritten recipes into a binder that she'd reference. That night she'd pulled out an old favorite of mine, and the smokiness of the paprika in the albóndigas hit me as I walked in the house. But it was the scent of the pork and chorizo meatballs cooked in its special tomato sauce that hit me the hardest. Instead of being exhausted from learning the ropes at work, a second wind had joyfully energized me. We lived happily together.

I wandered into the kitchen, with a smile the size of the Hoover Dam on my face. To boot, the table was already set, weird because we always ate in the family room while watching the evening news. I'd glanced at Isa happily fluffing the rice, humming along to some retro freestyle song of which she was so fond.

She'd made this dish before, and she preferred to combine the Andalusian favorite with white rice. I guess Isa's way was a Cuban thing because Mamá used to serve it tapas style with sherry wine and nothing more.

Floyd was scurrying through the kitchen, running after some imaginary prey, and a cackle caught in my throat when he slammed into my ankles. I plucked him up and gave him a little nuzzle before he squirmed in my grasp. He resumed his imaginary spy games when I released him.

We grinned stupidly at each other as she approached me and pressed her body into mine, welcoming me home with a sensual kiss on my lips. It was as if I'd been inside a black-and-white TV set. I played the role of the husband coming in from a long day's work, while Isa was playing the doting wife. *I love my life.* That night, though, Isa was more purringly affectionate than usual. But the bedroom was the only place she showed her desires for me, though, so I'd have to wait to get the purr out of her.

"I hope you're hungry," she said. "Because I made your favorite. I hope it's as good as Mimi's," she said. And it struck me that when she referred to Mamá, she used the nickname she and Martha had given her a thousand years ago. I took a deep breath, closed my eyes, and swallowed the ache of nostalgia. I'd also kept the roil in my stomach at bay by watching the cat's crazy antics.

"It smells divine in here. How can I help?" I asked, clasping my palms together.

Isa ignored my question while she plated the food. Indeed, the meal was nothing short of amazing as I devoured every morsel on my plate. Honestly, it was better than Mamá's.

"Keep feeding me these delicious dinners and I'll have to figure out how to add more miles to my morning runs," I said, getting up for seconds. I gestured to take Isa's plate and she nodded.

"I do my best to keep you fit when we're alone," she said with a crooked grin. Her chin dimples electrified my nipples.

Isa served me a second glass of a Ribera del Duero she'd opened, which was unusual because we'd rarely drink during the week. It was delicious and tantalized every single tastebud as I swished the red wine around in my mouth. Having any kind of wine always reminded me of Don Rigoberto's vineyard. He'd let us kids sip certain sherries but then say that the brandies were for the adults. My parents were wine enthusiasts, probably because Mamá came from a grape-growing family. They left us an ample collection of old-world wines, including the one we were drinking.

"I want to talk to you," Isa said, putting the wine bottle back on the table. I put my fork down, swallowed the last bit of meat in my mouth, and gazed in her eyes.

"I'm all ears," I said, taking another sip to wash down the last bit. I sat back in my chair, replete.

"I'll be finished with my dissertation in a year and a half," she began. "And while I'm still teaching at the university, I'll also start my internship at Miami Research Memorial. I'll be at the hospital only two days a week for now." Isa was anxious to make a real breakthrough in the biomedical field. I shared her enthusiasm. She amazed me. As teenagers, I envied how quickly her mind processed information. She had been in the top ten percent of her class in university only after being the valedictorian of our high school.

"That's spectacular, Isa," I said, encouragingly. "Have they given you a start date for the research hospital?"

"Yes, it's all settled," she said with a wry smile. She sat back in her chair a bit smug at her accomplishments and sexily glanced at me over the rim of her wineglass. Those chocolate eyes were the first thing I had noticed about her. Big, deep, and dark, but it was her chin dimples that had reeled me into her clutches.

"Well?" I asked.

"The Department of Pathology wants me to start in seven months," she said with the sparkle of teeth. "I'll be working directly with physicians, developing new treatments and devices to meet the needs of heart patients and address heart disease. I can't wait." To hear her talk about the biomedical industry was as intoxicating as the wine I had been enjoying.

She licked her lips slowly and the scent of the Ribera on her tongue was sending tingles through my scalp. She made me thirsty as she licked her lips.

"That's wonderful!" I said after clearing my throat. I placed my hand on hers and squeezed tightly. She interlaced our fingers and stared at our clasped hands for a second. There was something else she'd been holding back. "What is it, Isa?"

"There is more," she admitted. "I'm ready to start our family, and I want to get going with the process before I start at the hospital."

¡Olé! I wanted to scream. We were going to be a family. There was an ecstatic little Snoopy inside my chest jumping for joy.

"Here," she said, grabbing a legal pad she'd been hiding on the chair next to hers, holding it out for me to take.

Isa had done all the research—where to find the sperm donor, which procedure to get, where to get it done. Every detail had been meticulously written down on twenty sheets of a yellow legal pad for me to read. It was all very scientific, all so very Isa, written in her perfect block penmanship. I looked at the wad of pages she gave me, then set it aside.

"Isa, I don't need to read a proposal," I explained. "I'm all in. I told you that already. I would love nothing more than to start a family with you. Just tell me when you want to start."

"I made an appointment with a fertility clinic for tomorrow morning."

A humid breeze rolls through the air and stirs me from my reverie. Before it starts raining, I run back inside the apartment.

CHAPTER EIGHT

Isa

Going through a stack of paperwork nearly a foot high, I'm at my desk thinking that the farther up the career ladder I climb, the more paperwork I fill out. My team has succeeded at growing human tissue, but it's not sustainable enough to replace a mechanical heart valve—not now, anyway. The biomedical field is a tedious process of trial and error. But, of course, without it there is no medical advancement. And, since I have another two years on my contract, I might as well make the best of it. We did, however, learn what it takes to make the human tissue viable. The next step is to get it to survive longer than a hundred days. Way longer.

"Isabel." Breaking my concentration with a startling knock at my doorjamb, Dr. Tucker Peterson leans into my office. His thinning hair flutters under the air vent, leaving me to wonder if he changed to a weaker pomade. Taking a deep breath, I glance up at him. "I have a dinner meeting with a prospective donor tonight. Do you want to join us and explain why we're not getting anywhere with the human tissue?"

"With whom?" I ask, ignoring his snide remark.

"Patrons of Mercy," he replies, tugging at his shirt cuffs from inside his blazer sleeves.

"Dr. Peterson, isn't Patrons of Mercy a religious organization?" I ask, not mentioning that the name seems to imply it's a military mercenary group. "Why would they fund our research when we're using stem cells to grow human tissue. Aren't they against 'the taking of innocent lives'?" I ask, gesturing with air quotes.

"They came to me. But I'd be happy to tell them you're not interested in their cash," he replies.

"I am," I assure him. "I'm just wary of these organizations. I don't want our work further politicized than it already is."

"Let's see what they have to say before we reject their money. Shall we?" Just once, I'd like to wipe that supercilious grin off his fucking face. "Are you coming or not?"

I give my wrist a shake to glance at my watch face. It's nearly six and I need to get out of here. Admittedly, I would go with him, as I often do, if only to accurately describe my research, but it's my first night to be with Susana in a week. "Sorry. Can't. I'm late to pick up my daughter. Then, I'm going home to make dinner."

"Ah, not the husband's night, is it?" I force a grin but say nothing. He must realize he's not getting anything further from me and leaves. *Asshole!*

I stare after him in case he decides to return. My eyes drift from the door down to the picture frame on my desk. Gene had beautifully captured a candid image of Susana and me playing in the pool. I was teaching her to hold her breath underwater, then I'd lift her up in the air and she'd reward me with thrilling laughter. I hadn't even realized Gene had taken the picture. I reach for the frame to wipe off the dust. Susana was a baby in this photo. A sudden stinging catches my eyes as I think how much happiness she's brought to my life.

We had just come from celebrating my PhD at my parents' house. That's the night Gene gave me the Mont Blanc Star

Legacy Automatic. She even engraved it with, *The future is hours.* She thought it was a little cheesy, but I didn't. I don't take it off, just like my high school class ring I wear on my right ring finger. I wasn't due to give birth for another two weeks, but I'd been feeling some contractions throughout the week. My obstetrician insisted it was normal, so I ignored them. When we got back home, I was downstairs making us tea. G doesn't like tea, but she never declines when I offer, so I always offer. She'd had a few things to finish up in the baby's room before going to bed, so tea mugs in hand, I climbed the stairs to deliver G's tea.

The crib looked nearly finished to me, and she was about to attach the piece that doubled as a headboard to use as a transition bed when the baby grew into a toddler. I'd been staying out of her way while she built the furniture—God forbid I told her something was crooked. She almost bit my head off when I asked why the changing table didn't have its drawer knobs affixed.

I waddled my way up to the door and placed her mug down on the dresser. "Here's your tea, honey."

"Yeah, thanks. Just leave it on the dresser for now," she said without turning to see I'd done just that. Just as I planned to say something sarcastic, she glanced up at me and was about to say something when a glob of clear-ish goo fell out from between my legs and splashed against the wood flooring. Well, it was more like a splat; some of it landed on my feet and the hem of my nightgown.

We froze. Our eyes were focused stupidly on the wet floor. I knew what was happening, but I was still flabbergasted. We'd created a birth plan we called The Baby Plan. In it, we wrote down everything we were supposed to do when the time came, but it hadn't accounted for the knot of dread butting up against the baby. In that moment, I'd forgotten everything in the fucking plan, including where I had put it away. It didn't matter.

"Fuck! That was my water!" I said like an idiot and gently placed my mug on the baby's dresser next to Gene's untouched one. I don't even know why I put my hands under my belly—I guess it was to prevent her from falling out?

Gene leapt to her feet and padded quickly to the room I'd been using for my dissertation work, carefully moving around the pool of goo at my feet. She snatched the receiver from its phone cradle on the desk and called Dr. Audrey Hernández's emergency line. As I stood there, a monument of incredulity, she hung up with the obstetrician's service and called my mom, who was supposed to drive us to the hospital.

Once we got there, Gene dashed out of the van and into the hospital's main entrance and bolted out in less than two minutes, it seemed, rolling a wheelchair out through the automatic doors. She sprinted back to the car Mami had parked under the portico, opened the front passenger door, and gave me her hand to help me out of the car. Gene was under a determined spell, or something. She wheeled me through the hospital's sliding doors, and we were all whisked away to a sterile suite in the maternity ward. The room was so frigid, my nipples were two thick and sensitive pyramids of hard nerve endings.

My contractions were getting more frequent, but I wasn't in much pain—a five or a six, tops. By one in the morning, my cervix was fully dilated, and the baby was doing fucking back flips inside me.

"Whoa," I groaned suddenly. Then a wailing, "Ahhhh." I grasped the bed railing for stability because the pain intensified. Gene jumped out of the plastic recliner next to me and pounded down on the call button for the nurse. I took a deep breath, let it out, and began heaving in and huffing out. I didn't know what else to do. I heard the shrieking, squeaking sound of my obstetrician's sneakers hitting the linoleum floor before I saw her. Moments later when she appeared, I was already prepared to claw my baby out of my body with my own fingers. Nurses filled the room, wheeling in dozens of mobile machines. The room transformed into a disorderly array of people in masks, high-pitched beeps, lots of murmuring, and Gene holding for dear life to my hand.

"Am I getting a shot?" I asked anyone who'd listen.

"I'm afraid it's too late for that," a masked nurse said. *Oh. Shit!*

I squeezed the bejesus out of Gene's hand. The pain was as severe as unimaginable abdominal cramps—the kind that keep you crouched over on the toilet, practically touching your toes, for hours. Or, as though a dozen colossal kidney stones, lined up, one larger than the next, were languidly making their way out of my tiny urethra. The medical team moved things around, turned the bed into a birthing table, and ready or not, the baby was crowning. That was the part where my insides felt as if they'd been ripped from my body.

"Okay, Isa, *push!*" Audrey screeched. Oh. My. Fucking. God. The pain! I pushed as hard as I could muster, letting out a multitude of farts and shit, probably. Sweat barreled down my spine, fell off my forehead, pooled in every crevice, everywhere. After the second push, everything else happened like the wind. Audrey pulled the baby out of me with such ease, it seemed, as though she'd been dipped in baby oil. It prompted a ridiculous thought in my exhausted brain: *Is that where baby oil comes from? Birthed babies?*

Our daughter was born at two thirty-five that morning, a midsummer baby. We'd been so preoccupied by her arrival that we neglected to choose a fucking name for her and include it in The Baby Plan. Oops! Clearly, it was nothing but a mediocre plan.

All the superficial doubt I felt, all the angst about parenting drifted into the background. I was numb to all that. Our baby girl was a healthy, wrinkled little mound of hair.

I stirred in my hospital bed to find Gene holding the baby in her arms. I wish I had a photo of that, but no one else was in the room with us to take it. When she realized I was awake, she reached to put her hand on mine.

"I'm here," she said. "Martha and Carlos have gone home to rest." My dad had just suffered another minor heart episode.

"Susana Maria," I said, my husky, sleep-deprived voice pushing it out in a low octave. Gene glanced up from the baby to me with a smile. She settled the baby between her crossed legs, watching her with adoration. "I thought we could name her after both our mothers?" The two names sounded good together. My and my mom's middle name is Susana, and Gene's mother's name was Maria. It was the perfect combination.

"Susana Maria Pérez-Acosta," I said with finality, shifting my gaze to the baby, then to Gene. She closed her eyes tightly, trying to prevent tears from falling. Gene was such a softie.

That was six years ago. As I let the memory sink back into my subconscious, my eyes are still stuck on this picture of Susana and me. And because she snapped the photo, I think of Gene whenever I glance at it. It's been nine months since she left the house, and I can't say it's been breezy. It hasn't. Gene was my partner in everything. I miss her, but those last words she said to me before she left—"I need to find my own way now"—have stuck with me. She's right; Gene needs her space. Maybe this time apart has been good for her. Meanwhile, I'm still having bouts of insomnia.

"Dr. Acosta." My assistant Camila startles me as she peers at me from my doorway.

"Mother of fu...uh...pearl, you nearly stopped my heart," I reply with my hand over my chest.

"I'm sorry," she says with a chuckle. "But you'd asked me to remind you to, how did you put it? 'Get me the heck out of here' at six." She glances at her watchless wrist. "It's five fifty-seven."

"Gosh, thank you, Cami. I don't know where my head is at."

"Huh. Before you go," she says, coming closer to my desk. I shut down my laptop and pack it in my bag.

"Yes?" I glance up at her.

"The other day," she begins. I settle back down in my chair, as this sounds like it's going to take a while. "When we had lunch together in the cafeteria?" I motion for her to continue. "My cousin saw us, and he's...well...he's curious about you."

"Curious?" I ask. "Why curious?" Folding my arms over my chest, I let her proceed.

"He said you piqued his curiosity. That's how he said it, anyway," she says tentatively. "And he asked me if you were single. You've never talked about anyone in your life, but I know you have a daughter. I mean, she's the only one you actually talk about. And you don't wear a wedding ring. So, I always just assumed you were, uh, single or divorced or something." She gets through the last bit briskly, and I can't tell if she's finished.

"I don't like talking about my private life, Camila. I'm sorry to keep you wondering," I reply, evading her assumption and hoping that closes the matter.

"Well?" she asks, persistent.

"Well, what?" I've been careful to make sure my colleagues don't know anything about my personal life, especially because I don't want it getting back to Peterson.

"Dr. Acosta!" she whines. "Okay. Look, my cousin's a…well, he's a nerd and has a hard time with adjectives. He found you attractive and wants to ask you out. Even if it's for a cup of coffee here in the hospital."

I relent and say, "Who's your cousin? And does HR know you have a cousin working at the hospital?"

"Oh, neither of us knew we'd end up here. It was a coincidence. We were hired at the same time, unbeknownst to either of us. He's in pediatrics, far away from pathology."

"Oh. I see."

"Actually, he's a pediatric heart surgeon."

"Ah. Impressive," I say with a pause. "Camila, I'm trying to get my life together right now. I don't want to get involved with anyone."

"Oh. I see," she replies with an abashed smile.

"What have you done?"

"Well, since I wasn't sure about your situation, I told him he should stop by sometime and meet you in person. I figure if sparks fly, you can decide how to proceed."

"Oh, Camila!" Flustered, I grab my bag and storm out of my office. *The fucking nerve.*

CHAPTER NINE

Gene

If I had to be honest with myself, I'd admit that I thought Isa would break down and ask me to come back home within the first month. It's been a year since I left the house and there's no sign of that happening. At all.

In the kitchen, I'm preparing a small snack for Susana because now that she's almost six, she's a bottomless pit. I glance at my Swatch to make sure it's the perfect snack time.

"What are you cutting, Mamá?" Susana asks, hands on the edge of the counter, barely tall enough to see what I'm doing.

"I'm cutting up a melocotón, so you can have it with some yogurt." At her look of utter horror, I stop slicing and pick up one of the juicy quarters. My left hand is sticky from the drying nectar when I dug out its pit, I hold out the piece of peach for her. "Here. Try it." Eyebrows cocked in skepticism and lips askew, she opens her mouth and, with her eyes closed, almost takes my fingertips as she gobbles up the flesh morsel. "Do you like it?" I ask before she's finished chewing.

She nods as she chews and makes a gesture for the bowl of yogurt in which I've been tossing the small pieces. With a spoon, I fold in the fruit and hand it to her.

Movement at my front window draws my attention while I wash my hands. I glance up, and Isa is about ready to ring the doorbell. *Hmm. She's early.* I toss the kitchen towel I'd used to dry my hands over my shoulder and make my way to the door. Susana twists her torso to see who's at the door.

"Mami! I'm having a mellow cotton," she yells. *Hmm, maybe Carlos was right. It's time for some proper Spanish classes.*

"Hola mi amor!" The enthusiasm rolls off her tongue.

"You're early," I say, closing the door behind me.

"Yeah. I'm still having my snack," Susana chimes in.

"I can see that." Isa snickers and bends toward our daughter. "But I have to talk to Mamá for a minute before we go home. Go to your room and finish your homework so we can talk. Okay?" Susana glances in my direction, eyes as doleful as Bambi's.

"You can take your snack into your room," I assure her. Instantly relieved, Susana jumps off the barstool, collects her bowl, and skips into the hallway.

"Don't make a mess. Okay?" I call out to her. But all I hear is her bedroom door slamming shut. This causes a little laughing exhale.

I turn back to Isa. "What's up?" And then quickly mind my manners. "Do you want something to drink or eat? I haven't made myself dinner yet, but I have melocotón," I say, showing her the halved fruit. She waves away my offer with a flick of her wrist.

"No, I'm fine. Thanks." She sets her heavy bag down on one of the club chairs. "Shall we sit?"

"Ah, it's one of *those* talks." I have no idea what's coming, but sitting down is never good. Her face gives nothing away. I sit in the other club chair, facing Isa, sitting on the couch. Isa pulls out her BlackBerry, tossing it in her hand a few seconds before glancing back up at me. My hands are palms down on the arms of the club chair, imagining them creating big, round sweat stains. Isa seems to be taking her sweet time. That, or what's unfolding before me is just happening in slow motion. She looks at her phone and taps a few buttons. My heart quickens.

"Can you take Susana on Wednesday night?" Her question is a bit vague. Which Wednesday night does she mean? The day after tomorrow, next week, every Wednesday night?

"Why?" I snort. "Do you have a hot date?" And just as I pronounce the last word, I want to suck that question right back into my mouth and down to the pit of my stomach to smolder in its gastric acid. *Stupid, stupid, stupid!* My eyes are locked on Isa as her face drains of blood and expression. Heat radiates from the tip of my scalp, and languid droplets of sweat form at the base of my spine. I bite down on my bottom lip, immediately preventing any more words from mistakenly slipping past my lips.

"Oh," I murmur before she even has a chance to utter another word.

"I wasn't sure how to bring it up." It's all she says. And it's as if a drop door underneath my chair has swung open, and I begin a dark descent toward emptiness. I wait numbly a few seconds, physically unable to speak. My saliva catches in my throat, sweltering as I try to swallow it down. *Keep it together!* "He's a colleague. From the hospital. A surgeon." I caught that: he. And Isa's use of fragments also means she feels as much dread as I do. I just nod. "The cousin of my assistant. He's thirty-nine and he's, uh…from Argentina." *Stammering, too?*

I feel as though I'm on one of those planes carrying skydivers up. And that song, the "Top Gun Anthem," is playing in my head, the slow one, where he's prepping the plane before he takes off. I'm the very last passenger to jump in a long line of reluctant first-time skydivers, waiting for my turn to die—I mean dive.

My legs are numb, and as I rub life back into them, I slip my hands under my thighs to stabilize their incessant shaking. But her watchful eyes catch me. Shifting back deeper into the club chair, I roll my hands into fists and wedge them in the opposite armpit. *What do I do?* I draw my right ankle over my left knee. This isn't comfortable, so I switch legs and draw my left ankle over my right knee. Not good either. I remain with both feet cemented to the floor and stretch my arms over the chair arms like Lincoln's stone, cold position in Washington, DC.

"We've only seen each other at the hospital a few times. Our schedules haven't synched until now," she replies as if I'm asking questions—I'm not. In fact, I don't want to know any of this. Forced to work out the math in my head, I figure out about how long she's known this guy versus how long ago we separated—a year, maybe. Who knows? There's insufficient information. *This isn't helping.* I hold my breath so the tears don't unwittingly burst out of my eyes and just nod like an idiot. *Is this why she's here so early? To tell me about this man she's dating. This old man... because she's barely thirty-one years old.*

"Roberto," I think she says.

"I'm sorry, what?"

"His name is Roberto."

Joder. Why did he have to have my own father's name?

"Yes. I can take her on Wednesday," I say to shut her up.

"Which Wednesday would that be? This week, next week. All the Wednesdays?" As the sarcasm seeps out with my words, I can't help but move this little meeting along. I get up and smack the cushion I was just sitting against a few times and head for the kitchen.

"Well," she says, looking at her phone. "This Wednesday, since next week is already your week."

"Mm-hmm," I hum and nod idiotically. I must look like one of those ridiculous bobbleheads who's been flicked over the head a couple times with my arms folded against my chest. Behind the peninsula bar, I remove a blank notepad and pen from the junk drawer, and, with a tremble, I unnecessarily jot it down, knowing full well I won't forget. *Please get out.* I want to scream, but I can't. My daughter is still in her bedroom, probably painting her walls with yogurt.

"Let me get Susana, I'll be right back," I say instead, putting my pen down and marching toward the hallway. I need to be in a room that isn't simmering in vanilla bean. As I cross the threshold, I glance back to make sure I'm out of Isa's sight and lean up against the hall wall to take deep breaths as quietly as possible. Folded over, my hands perched on my knees, I quietly heave. *No tears, please!* After a few seconds, I take my last breath and right myself with my left hand holding the wall as if it's about to fall on me, or maybe I on it.

As I tap Susana's door, it slowly opens. I clear my throat.

"Cariño, Mami's ready to go. Are you ready?" Susana is already packing her little schoolbooks and homework dittos into her backpack. She zips it closed and saunters past me. She skips down the hall—ignorant of the torment playing out inside my belly—toward her other mother.

After Isa leaves with Susana, I'm nauseated. *Or is this shock?* The air has all gone to my head. I leave the kitchen spotless and jet to my bedroom before I lose my cookies in the hallway. Tumbling through the bathroom door, I lance myself to the floor and lift the toilet lid. But the only thing coming out are hot, salty tears.

This scene is as ridiculous as those videos of monkeys scratching their butts and fainting after they've smelled their fingers. When nothing comes out of my mouth, I get up, throw myself on my bed, and nuzzle my face in the crook of my elbow. In a gush, the tears just fall off my face.

An hour later my phone buzzes abruptly in my front pocket. I dig in, pull it out, and feebly place it on my ear. I don't even bother to look at my screen before fumbling for the call button.

I exhale a cracked, "Hello," my face buried between the comforter and my left arm.

"Gene?" Only the sweet sound of Martha's heavily accented English can bring a modicum of pacification to my otherwise dismal disposition.

"Martha?" I sniffle, my voice drunk with anguish.

"Where are you?" she asks.

"In my bedroom," I whisper in a ten-year-old's voice.

"I spoke to Isa." That's all she needs to say before I double down on the tears. "I've been ringing the doorbell. Can't you hear it?" And just as she says it, I hear the high-pitched chime, singing off-key as though it needs a battery change.

"I'm coming." I don't try to get up. No. I merely slide myself off the bed and crawl toward the doorway, unable to walk to the hallway. If I get up, I might collapse, so I opt to crawl the rest of the way to the living room and stretch my arm up to reach the dead bolt.

"I unlocked the door." I bang my head on my side of the door. "Can you pull on it?" Martha gives the door a hard tug, toppling me over the first step. All I see are a pair of tidy black loafers.

"Ay, Gene," Martha says, staring down at me like disappointment is rushing through her veins. She makes a popping sound with her teeth, like that of a frying egg sizzling in oil. Martha crouches down and pulls me to sit upright. I put my head in her lap instead and continue my sobbing. Her soft caress of my hair is just right. *Get up! Get up!* I talk myself into straightening up because the mother of a six-year-old child is stronger, can take this kind of news, and move on with her life.

Leaning on my elbows, I lift my torso into cobra. And seeing as my head feels fine, I bring my foot close to my palms, plant it down on the floor, and pull myself up, using the doorknob for support. Martha holds on to my waist during the whole warrior-two-to-mountain-pose flow.

"Come on," she says. "Let's go to the couch." But I make sure to sit on the opposite end of the couch from where Isa had been sitting earlier. I don't want to relive those tense moments. Martha sits between me and where Isa had been sitting, shielding me from that other end. I place my head on her shoulder.

"I've lost her." That's all I can say. "I've lost her now, for sure." Fifteen years of a relationship, and it's over.

CHAPTER TEN

Isa

"Enrique, this is excellent work," I say. "You've made subtle improvements to this procedure, but improvements nonetheless."

"Thank you, Dr. Acosta. I appreciate you saying so," he replies, cheeks rosy.

"Make sure you make a note of the changes you've made for your peer review." As I turn away from Enrique, the shriek of my first name being called out in the lab rouses my attention.

"Am I catching you at a bad moment?" the shrieker asks, as if he gives a fuck.

"No, Dr. Peterson, I was just heading back to my office. What can I do for you?" I really should try calling him Tucker to see how he likes it.

"Funding," he says. I raise an eyebrow and wait for further explanation. "Patrons of Mercy has committed to donating eleven million dollars to fund stem cell research."

"What?" I ask. "That's an unprecedented amount of money, especially from a religious organization."

"It turns out the group is led by a wealthy conservative whose mother is living with Alzheimer's disease, or dementia, or something like that. She wants the bulk of the funds directed to Alzheimer's research, however she's willing to fund the entire program." His delighted visage seems unnatural.

"May I ask how much of that will fund my team's research?" It suddenly dawns on me that this might have a negative impact on my team if the Alzheimer's research group gets most of that award.

"The department will get a detailed report of all that. But for now, Isabel, a win for Alzheimer's is also a win for the whole department. So, put a smile on that beautiful face," he says, tamping down the ten wisps of hair flittering over his scalp. He pats my shoulder and walks away. *Gross.* Putting the thought that I should take my lab coat to the cleaners on the back burner, I'll have to look for better ways to fund my research. Especially now that Dr. Peterson has made it his mission to circumvent my request for more resources.

With a sigh, I check my vibrating BlackBerry for an incoming text.

Roberto: Can you meet up for coffee in five minutes?

Isa: How about ten?

Roberto: OK.

Roberto: Can I order for you.

Isa: No thanks, I can order for myself.

Roberto and I are busy professionals. He more than I, of course. Since our dinner a few weeks ago, we haven't seen each other outside the hospital. He gets away from his wing in the hospital to come see me in pathology, but there hasn't been a consistent time block upon which we've been able to agree. Either he's in surgery or I'm running to pick up Susana, which, if I were being honest, is fine with me.

He lives twenty miles away from me and commutes to the hospital on the Brightline. But there's a lot to like about him. He's handsome with his thick, dirty-blond curls and wide grin. I'm not used to his dry sense of humor yet, but he's mature. He's divorced but, oddly, has no children. Didn't he want children when he was younger? I haven't told him about Gene. If this gets serious, I'll have to tell him about our arrangement at some point.

Gene, with her crestfallen face, stares blankly at me in my memory. Disbelieving, bewildered. It broke my heart to watch her stifle her tears as I told her about Roberto. That's why I asked Mami to check on her.

This wasn't what I wanted. Not at all. I was happy with our simple, little family. But she wants to live in a world that I can't inhabit. Lately all she talks about is gay rights and volunteering and making a difference. She wants to fight a fight I don't see us winning. It's too hard. And there are too many people against LGBTQ rights.

At work alone, I'd lose my funding if they knew that I'm unmarried and that my daughter has two mothers. That's too much for the politicos in charge of signing the checks to understand. It's too much for anybody to understand same-sex couples, much less same-sex couples with children. I wish we lived in a world where no one cared what you did in private. But they do, they all do, and it affects everything from politics to the workplace. It sucks, but *this* is the world in which we live.

I'll admit that I was naïve to the state laws against gays and lesbians adopting. Well, laws against gays and lesbians in general. That was the furthest thing from my mind when I was researching ways to get pregnant. I desperately wanted to be a mother; I always had. And I wanted Gene to share that experience with me. It never dawned on me that she would have no parental rights, or that she would feel alienated because of it. Parental rights were the last thing I thought about when I was giving birth. No one said anything to me. Not my fertility specialist, not my gynecologist, no one. In fact, Gene accompanied me everywhere I went throughout my pregnancy. All my doctors, nurses, and medical personnel, everyone received Gene with open arms it seemed, until Susana was born. That's when the problems began.

Susana wouldn't stop crying. She was only six months old, so it wasn't as though she could tell me what was wrong. It had been that high-pitched wailing that you hear sometimes when you're at a restaurant, the grocery store, or worse, on a plane—where the mother (it's always the poor mother) moves heaven and earth to quiet the baby down. Susana would inhale for five seconds, then exert her best, most agonizing howl. The neighbors down the street must have heard it, I was sure.

I'd done everything I knew to do—troubleshooting, as Gene called it. Her blaring was unbearable, and the last thing I did was sit with her to see if my presence would calm her. It did not.

Gene had told me she'd be in meetings all day, so I didn't want to bother her, but I was going to go mad if Susana didn't stop screaming. With no idea what time it was, I propped the glider Mami gave us against the crib so Susana could clench her little fist around my thumb. It didn't quiet her down, but clutching my finger let her know I was there, feeling her anguish. I guess it's called bonding. Only a Big Gulp full of wine would've made me feel better.

"What's happening?" Gene yelled over Susana's enraged outcry. I hadn't even heard her come in or run up the stairs.

"She won't stop CRY-ING!" I whimpered, breaking the word in two for emphasis. I was at the end of my rope.

Susana had been fussy for the last few nights. Rocking her in the glider helped some but nothing I had done for her worked that day. Gene walked up to her crib to find her a crimson-faced mess. She checked her diaper, but it was fresh—I'd changed her twenty-two minutes ago. She put her finger in her mouth to see if she was hungry and nothing—did that twenty-four minutes ago. Susana seemed to immediately reject anything we put in her mouth, including her pacifier. Gene put her hand on her forehead, no apparent fever—no shit, I did that eighteen minutes ago. Picking her up made things worse, and Gene was dumbstruck. She turned her face to me.

"I've done all that, smartass." I stared up at her, my ears already used to the inharmonious sound. "I also tried to soothe her in the glider to no avail. So, I gave up and put her back in the crib. I thought I'd just stay here and wait it out with her."

"Why didn't you call me earlier?" Gene asked.

"Because you told me you'd be in meetings all day." I raised my voice a few decibels to be heard over Susana's pitch. I wiped away the sweat on my forehead. "Besides, I'm pretty sure she has colic, and there's nothing to be done for that.

"Pero, Isa, the firm gave us two new BlackBerrys," she said, walking over to the little red phone on the table next to the glider. She held it up. "For to text," she said and put it back down. "I'll always answer later if I'm busy, but at least I'll know something's wrong."

"I just couldn't concentrate anymore over her racket," I replied.

"Okay." Gene relented, her hand massaging the back of my neck. Her cold fingertips were heaven. "We should take her to the hospital in case it's something more serious than colic."

"Fine," I said as I rose to my feet. "Let me get into something more decent." Tugging at the collar of my old Cornell T-shirt riddled with baby vomit stains, I got up and left Gene in the nursery.

In the time I got changed, Gene had packed up Susana's baby bag and put her in her car seat, all tight and secure, as if she'd used duct tape. I opened the passenger door of our SUV and settled into the seat with a heavy sigh. Trapped in a tiny space with a screaming baby was the highlight.

It was the longest five-minute drive to Coral Gables Medical Center of my life as my daughter got increasingly shrill. Gene backed into a corner space, and just before she put the car in park, I was on the pavement. Dazed and just short of a migraine, I waited in front of the SUV for Gene to finish scooping Susana out of her car seat.

The medical center was a small community hospital, where the reception desk was merely two paces from the entrance. The glee I felt when we walked in to see no one in the waiting area was akin to getting my first car as a gift for my sixteenth birthday. As the exhaustion was oozing out of my pores, my vocal cords seemed to quit working. Gene took the lead and stepped up to the desk with Susana still red-faced, mouth agape, and reeling from her horrible pain, clutching onto Gene's shoulder with a viselike grip.

"Our daughter hasn't stopped crying all day, we don't know what's wrong with her," Gene said, unusually terse. She must have been at her wit's end, too, and she'd only been experiencing it for a half hour at most. The receptionist stopped what she was doing on her computer and glanced up at us, puzzled.

"Name," she said curtly.

"She's Susana Pérez-Acosta," Gene started to say, before the receptionist cut her off.

"Which one of you is the birth mother?" The lady glared at both of us with disgust.

"What difference does that make?" I said, hands gripping the rounded edge of the Formica countertop she hid behind. I eyed the stapler next to her mouse and considered throwing it at her face.

"Only the birth mother can make medical decisions for the infant," she clarified robotically. I dropped my forehead in my hand with my elbow propped on countertop.

"Isabel Susana Acosta, I'm her birth mother. She was born here." I carefully enunciated each word methodically, as if it was the only way the receptionist would understand me. Gene remained silent.

"Thank you," she replied. "Do you have an insurance card for her?"

One-handed, Gene removed her wallet from her back pocket and swiftly slid the card out with her thumb. The lady grimaced at the card and snatched up the phone.

"I'll have to verify her coverage, Ms...." She elongated the title while she read Gene's full name. "Eugenia Maria López-Pérez." Oh boy, and the lady pronounced it in English, with the hard *G* instead of the Spanish *H*-sounding one. Gene's face was a scarlet sheen of composure, which was admirable. I'd have yelled out the proper pronunciation of my name if she'd butchered it the way she had Gene's. She hated her given name and went by Gene when I met her. I'd told her a thousand times to legally change it already.

But Gene ignored the gaffe as she rocked our daughter in her arms, walking around the sparse waiting room trying to comfort her. I waited for the receptionist at the counter.

"The doctor will take you now," she said, and I gestured to Gene to come back to reception so we could go inside.

"You can't go in there with them." The woman barely stood up to give us a scowled warning. Had she been a dog, she would have snarled at us, canines out ready to devour us.

"Only the biological mother can accompany her child to see the pediatrician on call." I'd had about enough and turned to Gene, eyes rolling, as I grabbed Susana from her clutches.

"Don't worry, it'll be okay," I whispered in Gene's ear, trying to soothe the hurt at least a little.

"I'll be right here, in case you need something…uh, from the bag," Gene said as I slid through the closing automatic door.

"The pediatrician said she has colic," I told Gene later. It had taken more than an hour to tell me what I already knew.

"The doctor also assured me that the colic will eventually go away, we must be patient, loving, and caring. Can you believe that bullshit?" I was a belligerent bitch to him, but Gene didn't need that information.

"What about the crying?" Gene asked. There was an inkling of hope in her eyes that maybe the doctor had prescribed Susana some baby version of NyQuil. No fucking luck.

"Didn't you hear me?" I was close to tearing her a new one at this point. "There's nothing to do. No hay nada que hacer!" I repeated it in Spanish to be sure she got it.

"I'll start the first shift," Gene said to me after putting Susana, who had continued her crying throughout the fiasco and showed no signs of stopping, back in her crib. "I'll look in on her every hour."

"Okay," was the only thing I could say. And I added a shrug for good measure. "I'll get one of her bottles. Maybe that will pacify her." Just as I was headed down the stairs, Gene stopped me.

"Let me do that," she said. "You go get some rest in the back building. Don't worry. I've got this. I'll come get you in the morning."

My heart sank. Gene had been treated as though she were a nobody, but she brushed it aside and showed me more humanity than I'd shown her during the whole ordeal. I felt horrible. But I got a few restful hours.

CHAPTER ELEVEN

Gene

"Thank you all for coming to our semiannual gold-and platinum-level donor's brunch and silent auction," Jay Bato, the Executive Director of Equality Miami, says into the microphone. Jay is the kind of lesbian who wears spiffy bow ties, seems to have them in all sorts of colors and patterns for all occasions you can imagine. Once, when I volunteered at the EM headquarters, she started her day in a brilliant purple, blue, green, yellow, orange, red gradient bow tie, and by the time she left the building, she had changed into a dramatic cyan one festooned with yellow polka dots. Her short, dark hair is shaved closely to her scalp at the back and sides and styled at the top like a glistening Toblerone chocolate prism.

As she explains the rules of the silent auction, I take a moment to sweep the room. Eight- and ten-top tables packed with mostly male couples and only a sparce scattering of women. Unfortunately, that seems to happen in these organizations: men are the dominant driving force. I guess when lesbians couple up, they nest and forget all about the world outside.

Jay returns the mic to the singer and walks off the stage to linger around the silent auction table I organized. The auction will help us through to the next quarter, where we will need more than half a million dollars.

The entertainer, a bossa nova singer, has remade Chris de Burgh's "Lady in Red" into a silky, throaty, and syrupy-sounding rendition. Her deep, melancholic tones are mellifluous, sounding like what diving into a vat brimming with thick Valor chocolate might feel all over your skin. The singer seems to be boring her gaze into the attractive blonde sitting, seemingly by herself, with an older couple. But as my ears twitch to the sultry stimulation, I think about Isa, my own lady who favors red anything. Except she's someone else's now. A pang of agony scratches at my heart, thinking of her and What's-his-name. *I wonder how that's going.*

A lesbian executive chef owns the ornate Asian and Cuban fusion restaurant in which we're hosting the brunch. I guess holding it at her swanky restaurant was Amada Lanza's contribution to this upper-crust doner event, but I can't be sure, since I wasn't involved in that part.

Meeting new people petrifies me, and since I've never actually been to one of these brunches before, I'm hesitant to network with strangers. But I chose to join this LGBTQ organization because they're working to expand on our fledgling gay rights. Just a few years ago, the Supreme Court struck down sodomy laws. And I'm here to join the fray to fight for my parental rights. I should make the best of it. Maybe…find the courage to talk to that lady in red before the end of the brunch.

Sitting at the bar, sipping on what's left of my Bellini, gazing romantically at the crowd, I spot Jay walking toward me. The board president introduced us a couple of months ago at a phone bank fundraiser at headquarters. Cold-calling for donations is probably the hardest thing I've ever done, but I volunteer because I need to help. That's what I do on the lonely nights when Susana is with Isa. Honestly, I do whatever they ask of me, whatever it takes.

"Jeannie?" Jay calls out to me from a few feet away. She thrusts her right hand at me to shake.

"Gene," I correct, hoping to hide the tension in my shoulders. I take her hand after glaring at her with a fake-ish smirk.

"Oh, sorry," she says with a glint of embarrassment. "I wanted to thank you again for joining the organization. I know phone banking isn't the best job, but we need more volunteers right now. Aside from consistent cashflow, of course."

"Of course." I smirk. "How have you been?"

"It's been busy, to say the least." As she shoves a hand in the pocket of her slim-fitting jeans, I take the pause to assess her. She's sort of petite; I'm easily three or four inches taller. And I'm in Oxfords, which are flatter than the clunky wingtip brogues she's sporting. Dressed in a crisp lilac shirt, purple paisley fifties-style smoking jacket, and matching paisley bow tie, she's putting my own outfit of skinny pants, T-shirt, and blazer to shame. I wasn't sure what to wear to this brunch, and I'm not ashamed to say I plucked this outfit right off the J.Crew website.

"We're working with three couples petitioning the state to let them adopt their foster kids."

"Oh, yeah?" My ears suddenly perk up.

Fearing that the anti-LGBTQ rhetoric coming from the current president's administration will inspire more discriminatory legislation, I all but gave up hope on the possibility of legally adopting Susana in Florida, especially. We haven't had a Democratic legislative body or governor since I graduated high school. And even then, they were part of the Old South Democratic base and switched parties during the great migration of Democrats to the Republican Party in the nineties.

Before moving out of the house, I had been secretly contributing to Equality Miami for some time because I'd read about their partnership with the ACLU on several LGBTQ-rights issues. They get things done and pay the legal fees for people who can't afford them. So, after Isa's strategically placed bombshell last month, I decided to get off my ass and do something to change my parental predicament.

"Yes, that's why we're tapping into top-tier donors so much lately," she says with a perfectly toothed, guilty grimace. As Equality Miami has done quite a bit of tapping into my finances, I smile but say nothing. "Thanks, by the way." She lifts her Champagne flute in salute.

"I don't mind," I say with a chuckle. "This issue hits home for me, too."

"Really?" She gestures at my Bellini flute. "Can I refill that for you?" I glance at the drop of Bellini left, then at Jay.

"I'd better not," I say and push my flute toward the inside of the bar, for the bartender to collect.

"Oh, come on," she says. "Live a little." She grabs the bartender's attention and orders two Bellini cocktails. "So, what's your story?"

"It's simple," I say, looking right in her hypnotic copper eyes. "For all practical purposes, I'm a recently divorced, nonbiological mother who wants parental rights to the child she helped create."

"Well," Jay says, taking the fresh Bellini flute the bartender serves. We clink glasses. "Here's to expanding LGBTQIA+ rights everywhere." I'm toasting to the possibility that Florida will recognize me as Susana's second parent one day.

Jay takes a sip, smiles at the Bellini flute, and says, "Mmm… damn that's good. Gay adoptions, that's right up our alley. And your ex? Is she against you adopting your kid? Are you sharing custody?"

"We share custody," I say after a delectable sip of my own. "Isa, my ex, has been great throughout our separation and co-parenting. I'm sure she'd support me adopting Susana. In the end, it'd be more convenient if we could both make important decisions on Susana's behalf."

"You know." Jay gazes at me with a gleamy honeyed eye. "You should join the board. You'd be in the front row of history, and once we win—and I'm confident we will—you'll have participated in something bigger than *us*. This is for the future of LGBTQIA+ families." We clink glasses again. This time, I feel it at the back of my neck.

I'd be lying if I say her words don't motivate me into action. Joining this organization has given me hope when I thought it was lost. In Spanish, the word *hope* translates to *esperanza*. The root word of esperanza is espera, meaning "to wait" in English. I know these things take time, and I will wait. I just hope the laws change in my lifetime.

CHAPTER TWELVE

Isa

From behind the sliding glass door, I watch as Susana splashes water all over Silvia while she balances over a paddle board. Her swim lessons are her favorite part of the weekends when she's with me. And Silvia, or "the Venezuelan Olympian," as Mami refers to her, is a dynamic instructor. Watching them wistfully reminds me of Papí—he'd initially paid for the lessons as a gift for Susana's second birthday. But by the time Susana was three, she no longer had a grandfather to play with in the pool.

I wipe the thought away and focus on the enormous task I have ahead of me. Reorganizing the binder I made of Mimi's recipes into a Word doc on my computer so I can always access them has me nostalgic. Mami offered to help—menos mal because there are dozens of handwritten recipes.

"Here," she says, handing me another tattered, fold-creased piece of paper. Maria would only jot down methods when she'd test her own mother's recipes, not the ingredients list, because of course she already knew them. Sifting out a legible list from her scribbles, I'm also converting her metric to our imperial measurements from her handwritten paragraphs. "This one is Mimi's famous huevos a la flamenca. It was one of Gene's favorites. ¿Te acuerdas?"

"Sí, Mami. I remember." I have to suppress a sigh every time she mentions Gene. Gene's mom, although looking nothing like Gene with her dark silky hair and dark broody eyes, was as introverted as Gene. A quintessential Andalusian woman, her accent was a bit more polished than most, though. She was a force, an alpha female, who Gene utterly loved and revered. She adored her father, Roberto, too. He was a bohemian. An artist. Aloof, Mami would say. They were an odd couple, more so than even Gene and me. When I met him, he wore his blond curls short and well kempt, but his beard was a scruffy shrub. There are pictures in this house of them as young college students. His hair was bushier and his beard even scruffier. Mimi always wore her hair long and silky straight. It was the late sixties when they met, after all; ungroomed hair was all the rage.

After they immigrated to the US, Mimi became a Spanish professor at Florida International University, helping me with my own AP Spanish classes during high school.

"What does this say?" Mami asks, pulling me from my memory fog. I glance at the flimsy paper she waves at me. I lean in and try to decipher if it's ajo or ají. If it's an *I*, it's a stout one. But between garlic or a bell pepper, there's a huge difference.

"I think it's garlic." I resume my own decoding and typing.

"So…" Mami starts. I mentally roll my eyes because I think I know what's coming.

"How are things going with *Roberto*?" She says it with a slant, and for a second there, because of my recent musings, I think she's talking about G's dad. But then I realize, of course, she must mean El Argentino, as she sometimes calls him.

"Fine," I reply without missing a beat in my typing.

"Have you two…?" She stretches the word. Martha is bold, and so am I. But my mom has an extra audaciousness about her; she'd ask if the pope ever raped an altar boy—*to his face*.

"Have we…what?" I ask, eyebrows squeezed together.

"*Sex*, have you had sex yet?" She lets out a heavy sigh.

"*Mami!*" I don't know why, but I knew this question was coming, just as I'd known she wouldn't appreciate me dating a non-Cuban. Although Gene is Spanish, in her book Spaniards are part of *La Madre Patria*. Motherland or not, this conversation is disturbing to say the least.

"¿Qué? You should feel comfortable talking about these things with your mother. I have experience that you lack," she says with a wry smile. *Mother of fucking pearl!*

"Fine, yes, we've had sex." I leave out that I strategically placed a moan here, a groan there to help speed things along. I also didn't mention how I showered immediately afterward to scrape his remnants and those of the sticky latex off my body. Apparently there's a three-date rule to having sex. Ours happen to have been three months later—but who's counting?

"And?" she asks.

"And what?" I stop my typing and fix her with a glare.

"And how was it?" Oh. She's good with that coy smile of hers.

"Mami, it was *fine*, and that's all you're going to get." As I get up, the scraping of the chair on the floor startles her. But it doesn't shut her up. I cross the kitchen and place my water glass under the refrigerator door's water dispenser. I stare out the window while my glass fills.

"Well, do you like him? You don't seem to see much of him," she asks just as my glass overflows. I suppress a gasp and remove my glass.

"We're both busy. But it's fine. We get along well. He's a good-looking, interesting guy. And he has a fascinating career." I grab the dish towel and dry up the little puddle I created on the floor. Returning to my chair, I resume typing.

"I see," she says, sifting through the pile of recipes. "Have you told him about Susana?"

I halt my typing and stare at her. "Yes, of course I told him about Susana." I pause for her next query. My eyes beating down on her.

"And have you told him about *Gene*?"

This time I don't suppress my sigh. Gene and her clear hazel eyes, dirty-blond curls, flawless smile, and sporty legs. Gene. A woman who has the power to frustrate me and love me till I'm completely satiated. Sex with Gene was anything but banal.

For the third time I paced the living room, my eyes darting from the door to the wall clock. I paused, thinking I heard a knock, and opened the apartment door to find it was nothing. I waited for Gene to come through my front door after almost two years of her absence in my daily life. I hadn't been home for the last few breaks between semesters because I was feverishly finishing up my junior year at Cornell. Since I'd been planning to complete my PhD program just as Gene was completing her master's in architecture, getting the extra classes in, here and there, to complete my undergrad was imperative. That way we'd both have been able to start our careers simultaneously. I always dreamt about living together somewhere in the northeast, where architecture and biomedical engineering jobs were in high demand, which I know was lofty at the time.

I had already made room for Gene's stuff in the off-campus apartment I lived in since junior spring semester. All that was left to do was wait—and wait. And then, just as I sat on the couch, the doorbell rang. Then, again…and again. I raced to the door, turned both dead bolts, and swung the door open. There she was. Standing at my door, almost hesitant. Our gazes met, and I launched at her, scooping her slight body into my arms. Her hands were in my hair instantly. They were like icicles, but I didn't care. I closed my eyes, hoping it wasn't a dream.

"Gene," I squealed, barely able to push the words out through my oropharynx. "You're finally here."

Easing our grip on each other, I cupped her face in my hands, wiping away errant tears from her hollowed eyes with my thumbs. "I missed you so much. Where are Mimi and Roberto?"

"I made them wait downstairs. I needed to see you first—before we started bringing my things up." Her sigh was high-pitched. Her tender gaze lowered to her hands which she'd been wringing like a tattered rag. I pulled her back in my arms and enveloped her tighter, barely able to hold back my own tears. The wait was finally over. We stayed like that for a few minutes before going downstairs to help her parents haul all of Gene's things.

We unpacked all her things and after her parents drove away, I had Gene all to myself. I had no idea where to start. What I wanted was to take her to our bedroom and ravish her. But I was a bit squeamish, as though we needed time to reacquaint ourselves. Here was the woman I'd been pining after during my first two years at Cornell while she was in Miami. I had been so lonely without her.

I closed the front door, leaning my back against it. "Alone at last."

I looked everywhere around the room except at her. My heart inched its way up to my throat and a stinging heat rose through me. But it wasn't until I finally fixed my gaze on her and ambled to her in the center of the living room that I noticed the effects of our separation. Her eyes, cloudy and downcast; her cheekbones, chiseled and pronounced; her skin, blotchy and ashen. This was a different woman to whom I'd said goodbye at the bus stop two years before.

Gene glazed at me with those sleepy, hungry eyes. "I want to be with you."

She snaked her hands around my waist as my heart feverishly thumped against my ribs. When she eased her lips over mine, I wrapped my arms around her neck. I couldn't help myself. I pushed my tongue into her mouth as her fingertips ran up my back, her touch igniting my skin. My fingers pressed through her tendrils and as if on autopilot, my nails dragged over her scalp. She'd cut her hair to shoulder length, and it was lighter but still thick sliding through my fingers. I clasped down on her unruly curls, twisting them back away from her face and into a tight ponytail. When I let go, there was a rolled-up ball of pent-up adrenaline in my stomach ready to unleash havoc.

This woman had always driven me crazy, but I'd managed to maintain my senses and tamp down my arousal because she was two years behind me. I thought I'd get skinned alive if I tried anything with her while we were in high school together. But this time…this time, I was in a heightened state of frisson. I wanted to rip Gene's clothes off that instant. Fortunately, she wasn't wearing much, a tank top and a pair of cutoffs. She'd already taken off her basketball shoes.

We danced toward the bedroom, leaving a trail of clothes behind us.

"I can't believe we're finally here," she squealed out with her husky voice.

"I know, I couldn't wait to get you alone." I backed her naked body toward the bed. I'd seen her naked before. How could I not? Traveling all over Europe together with our parents, they'd put us in the same room. And while we never went all the way, I did get my share of glimpses of her taut skin and the way it wrapped around her corded, athletic body.

She suddenly tumbled back over the bed, taking me with her. I covered her body with mine, and the warmth of her velvety skin hit a pinnacle for me. Instinctively, I placed my thigh between her legs. And she snaked her leg around my hip, sliding along the back of my thigh. It was exhilarating. She oozed moisture and it pulsated against my thigh as I pressed closer and deeper against her pelvis. Then, as if fighting against her own fury, she flipped our positions. Her fingers slid down my body and cupped my center with such initiative that I gasped and almost lurched forward.

"Oh, fuck," she huffed, seemingly by accident because I'm the potty mouth. "You're so wet."

I closed my eyes because I couldn't focus on her face while her fingers were inside me. I tilted my head back into the pillow, giving her free rein of my neck. She placed light kisses down the front of my throat, licking the dip between my collarbones, slowly inching her way down my body, prickling my skin as she went. My pulse hammered everywhere; I was sure she heard it.

Gene took a nipple between her thumb and forefinger and put her hot tongue over the other one, sucking lightly as if were a mouthwatering ice cream cone. I was so delirious, I hadn't noticed her creeping lower over my body. Feeling a little helpless, I ached to touch her, and I wasn't about to wait.

Pressing her head down into my pelvis with both hands, I luxuriated in her charged focus. Sometimes, while pulling an all-nighter at the library, I'd take a break and rummage the dinky LGBTQ section. Pulling paperbacks off the shelves, I'd open them about halfway through and read the illicit bits of the two lovers wrestling with their passion and each other. Usually, I'd get lucky and wouldn't have to read much before getting to the naughty bits. Of course, when the librarian asked if I needed help, I'd toss the books back on the shelf and dash back to my study cubicle.

Gene and I were ungraceful at first, trying to dominate each other. It seemed that she, too, had been doing her fair share of research.

Leaving her hands on my swollen breasts, I couldn't help but contort my neck to watch her. I placed my hands over hers and squeezed, pressing her hands down harder on my breasts. She drove a wet, titillating tongue right into my slit. I couldn't stifle a moan as she lapped at my sex. Glancing down at her, we locked eyes, hers hazy but piercing through me, hypnotizing me. I licked my bottom lip in anticipation of her next move, nodding as her hand caressed my inner thigh. She eased higher, gripping my thigh right at the crease.

She rubbed her thumb over my outer lips, and I dug my heels into the bed, the friction causing them to burn. Parting my inner folds, her thumb pushed past the slippery parts. As sweat trickled down my chest, my eyes were busy watching Gene. She slipped her thumb inside me, eliciting a pleased whimper. She pulled back and entered me with another finger…I'd lost count. I disappeared to the rhythm of her jutting digits.

"Oh. God," slipped out of my dry mouth, panting and ready to throb. "Harder." I groaned, breathing into it, begging her for more. Gene thrusting, licking, and I…I arched my pelvis into her. Then came the release inside her mouth, and I stopped moving. I was agog, my pulse reverberating in my ears. But she kept her tongue heavy on my clit and fingers inside me, holding the pressure because by this point, she knew I liked it. I eased my hips back down on the bed, but my breathing was still erratic. She pulled out of me with a languid ease and slipped her finger up my labia, pressing lightly on my engorged clitoris. A jolt of electricity made me quiver once more as a tense release escaped my muscles.

Gene waited a moment before crawling back up my body. I took a few deep breaths, easing the panting. A violent shudder come over me. Moisture stung at my eyes. Gene seemed to be feeling it too because she wrapped her arms tightly around my torpid body, squeezing me nearer. I held her against my pounding chest. The rawness of our sweaty embrace filled me with such joy, I didn't want to let go. We remained like that for a few long moments as I began to absorb our reality. The distance was gone, the loneliness, the pining. It was behind us.

When Gene eased off me, I didn't hesitate to flip her on her back and pounce on her, filling her as she did me. She grunted and tried to wrap her muscular legs around me, but I wanted none of that. I grabbed both her wrists and pressed them to the bed, spreading her legs with my thigh. The friction between our centers made my hair tingle. Slowly licking a line from her belly button up toward the center of her chest between her breasts, I wrapped my tongue around a nubby nipple, biting down softly, easing off her wrists.

Everything we did to each other was an experiment in discovering how to take the other over the edge. There was nothing she did to me that didn't thrill me. Her humid body, her slick arousal, her intoxicatingly musky scent made me lose whatever focus I had on her stare. Then I placed my tongue inside her, and I almost swooned. The sweet, salty taste of her made my mouth salivate. The taste of her was even better than I had ever imagined. I was desperate for more, but when I gazed up at her, she'd closed her eyes.

"Look at me," I demanded in a whisper. Gene opened her eyes.

I sat up to straddle her. "Come here," I said, gesturing with a wet finger.

Gene engaged her core and torso to meet me in a sitting position. Then, she opened her legs wide enough for my ass to fit between them. Grabbing her wrist, I guided her toward my entrance and placed my other hand on her sex. Mother of fucking pearl, she was wetter than before. She understood what I wanted and mirrored my moves as I stroked her with my middle finger. Panting, the pulse in her neck was at full throttle as we gaped together, locked into the other's embrace, experiencing another new sensation. This time, the tears escaped Gene's eyes from the magnitude of our situation. She knew she was safe. I was with her, caressing her back with my free hand. Hers, at the back of my neck, gently squeezed, our foreheads pressed together.

"It's okay," I whispered. "We're here together and nothing is going to change that." I soothed her with my lips, my mouth, my tongue until we both froze together, holding still our hands. I pressed her closer as she groaned and recoiled. Once, twice, we trembled together.

"Well?" Mami asks. Gene's satiated, goofy grin dances before my eyes as I grab my glass of water and nearly down it in one gulp.

Clearing my throat, I ask, "Well, what?" I slam the glass back on the table and look at my mother.

"Have you told him about Gene?"

"Not yet."

CHAPTER THIRTEEN

Gene

After months of volunteering—and tamping down my skittishness about strangers—I accepted an invitation to join the Equality Miami Board of Directors. We've been preparing for our biggest legal battle to date. After securing the necessary funding, of course, we partnered up with the ACLU to sue the state of Florida to lift their ban on adoptions by LGBTQ people. I'm pulling my hair out with this lawsuit. But with Jay Bato leading the charge, we'll ensure no one goes through unnecessary legal hurdles while family planning. Witnessing this bit of history excites me, and it would be so sweet if the state allowed me to adopt Susana.

This doesn't happen in a vacuum, so to thank the volunteers, donors, and EM's two full-time employees for their hard work with fundraising, canvassing, and daily office work, we organized a family picnic—a day of gaiety, so to speak.

In the park across the street from the apartment, we set up a bevy of activities for the families. Isa and I used to make fun of my brother, Lui, like formidable mean girls for losing many soccer matches here during our teenage years.

"Gene!" Someone calls my name. I'm busy placing chafing dishes on a gingham-covered folding table, sorting cutlery, and stuffing plastic napkins inside heavy utensil holders. I turn around, hands clutching stacks of napkins, as Jay and her jiggling bits speeds toward me in a golf cart. She's dapper in a pair of lime-green Bermuda shorts patterned with crossed tennis rackets, a navy polo buttoned up all the way, and a lime-green bow tie snakes around her neck. "Hey," I say, smiling at her sprightly outfit as she squeezes my torso.

"Is everything ready?" she asks.

"Yes." I gesture to the catering manager. "Michelle and I were just building the buffet table."

"Great," Jay says. "Do you need anything from me?" She fans her face.

"Nope, we're all set,"

"You have your speech ready?" she asks.

I pat the back pocket of my khaki Bermudas. "Everything is all here."

"Yes, I guess it is." She wiggles her eyebrows. I shake my head and walk toward the park exit. "Right! Okay, see you later then." Jay gets back in the golf cart and zooms over the bumpy terrain.

Since it's Isa's week with Susana, she is letting her spend a few hours at the picnic with me. Pulling my phone from my front pocket, I scroll through our text messages and type a quickfire, *two minutes out* to her as I walk toward the house and press send.

At the front door, my fingers seem to want to avoid the archaic door knocker. Its heavy, cast-iron handle squeaks as I lift and bang it against its base. It's as though I'm knocking on the door to my past. While I wait, I look up at the balcony to what was once my parents' bedroom, then our bedroom, and now it's Isa's for her to do as she pleases, with whomever she pleases. I knead away the soreness over the left side of my chest with my index and middle fingers. Hopefully the Tasmanian devil is ready to go.

"Hi," Isa says after she opens the door. Susana shoots out from behind her and snaps onto my legs. Catching my balance before I topple over the stoop, I kneel to give her a proper hug and kisses on both cheeks.

"Hola, Bebé! You're getting sneakier every day!" I glance up at Isa and force a smile. "Hey, what's up?" I try for a cavalier tone.

"Good. Everything is good." She nods. I nod, too. "Can we pick her up at three thirty?"

"Yes! Yes…that's fine," I say as I straighten to face her. I bite back a sigh, a grimace, and twitch at the word *we*. Wearing what's probably a stupid grin on my face to clench away my feelings, I dig my thumb into my chest to massage the knot bulging underneath.

Susana and I make our way to the park in time to give my speech. She zooms ahead of me and directly to the playground, joining the other kids. As families jostle for their space in the gazebo and adjacent canopied area, I saunter to the deejay and grab the mic he stretches out for me. *Deep breath.* I memorized my speech, but instead of a benevolent group of people, the growing crowd might as well be a riotous hate group—pitchforks and torches at the ready. My palms itch and my chest throbs. As I stare out into the group of about fifty families with rowdy children, my hearing becomes muffled and I can only hear the thump, thump, thump of my escalating pulse. *Deep breath.*

I utter the first word, "Family," and my throat is attacked by fire ants climbing up my esophagus. Family, family, family, I mentally repeat. *What comes after family?* Nothing. I give in and remove my written speech from my pocket. Tapping the mic a few times might make everyone think there'd simply been technical snafu and not that I'm petrified standing up here. I try again, and this time I ingurgitate the fire ants and proceed.

"Family!" I say a bit raspy, plastering on a grin, nonetheless. "We have so much for which to be thankful…"

My voice repeatedly catches. It's as though my own words are taunting me. The crowd bursts with applause and whistles, unaware of what lurks within me. I gulp down whatever saliva I have and wait another second as if the crowd were a menacing giant, peering at me with gnarled teeth. "This has been a long time coming..." I forge ahead with my speech, uninterrupted for the rest of it.

At the end, I give Michelle the thumbs-up. She nods and unveils the lunch buffet to the crowd. The deejay slides on his headset and immediately Sister Sledge's drum riff to "We Are Family" blasts from the speakers. The song reminds me of the day I left the Isa. I've come to loathe it, with its snickering lyrics and joyful meaning. Susana and her new friends ignore the food line and continue their hijinks on the jungle gym.

I remain behind because I don't feel like eating and find a suitable spot at a picnic table, shaded by the canopy of ficus trees. Climbing on the bench seat, I sit on the tabletop, facing the jungle gym while the kids play. My head is still spinning, and I rake both my hands through my scalp for a little respite.

The two other kids Susana's been playing with are about her age. One is a cute, curly-haired boy in denim overalls, the other a girl in a long yellow shirt draped over pink leggings. They're like untamed beasts, climbing up the slippery slide.

Watching the kids at play, a woman in white cutoff shorts and a loose racerback tank comes into my sight line. Heading toward the little boy, she kneels and gives him a drink from something that looks to be a plastic sippy cup. She wipes his mouth with a rag and puts both items back in the backpack slung over her shoulder. The woman straightens and saunters to my bench. Alarm bells ring off in my head as she steps closer, my brain shouting, *stranger approaching, stranger approaching!*

The sun behind her baseball-capped head draws a shadow over her face. But as she walks, her thigh muscles stretch and tighten into a long, sleek line and her smooth skin shimmers under the midday sun. My eyes dart from Susana to the woman's stealthy legs, back and forth, moving to the rhythm of her shuffle.

"Is this seat taken?" she asks, her English drenched in the Miami Hispanic lilt imported from the Caribbean. She gestures to the spot next to me on the table.

"No." My smile disappearing quickly. "It's all yours." She plants her backpack down with a thud, takes off her cap, and removes the elastic band from her mussy blond ponytail. I sneak a glimpse at her face. Her eyes are brown, lighter than Isa's. Isa has two dark chocolate medallions for eyes, littered with specks of soft gold. This woman's eyes are brown, just brown.

"Is that your kid?" I ask because the silence, once she sits, is like fleas frenzying on my ankles.

"Oh, no. Christian is my nephew." She's pointing at the overalled boy.

"He's very cute." My heated face blisters like a lightbulb.

"Thank you!" Her beaming smile catches me off guard. "The outfit was a birthday gift, and I was so happy when my sister-in-law dressed him in it."

"Which one is yours?" she asks after a moment. I draw a sweaty finger toward Susana who, as if on cue, slides down the tongue of a giant plastic dragon and into Christian's waiting arms.

"The little girl sliding into Christian's arms," I say. "That's Susana."

"Is she your daughter?"

"Yes, she's mine." My reply is confident. "I share custody of her with my ex," I add. Ex. The dreadful word that rolls off the tongue with the same ease it would if I'd just bitten down on a spoon piled high with peanut butter.

She nods but says nothing else, then heaves herself up on the table.

"I'm Gene," I say, hands clasped between my bent legs.

She juts a dry hand toward me. "I'm Viv." I stare at it for a moment, then wipe my hand over my shorts. My fingers wrap around her palm and with a hesitant shake, I retreat my hand between my legs. We gaze at each other for a few seconds before my eye wanders back to Susana.

"Are you from around here?" I ask.

"Yes and no."

I perk up an eyebrow and wait.

"I was born in Cuba," she continues. "But I've lived in the Gables since I was five." Her accent does have a tinge that resembles Martha's lilt. "I take my nephew sometimes to give his parents a chance to be human."

"Oh, I understand that." Martha would look after Susana when Isa and I needed some private time. But I don't mention that to Viv.

"Where does he go to school?" I ask curiously, pointing in the little boy's direction.

"He goes to Coral Gables Academy." She turns to face the street and points in the general direction of the school.

"Really? Susana goes there, too," I say, tamping down my ecstatic smile.

"Ah," she murmurs. "Do you think they know each other from school?"

"Susana is a little social butterfly. Whether she knows him from school or not, she'd still play with him," I say, chest out like a proud hen in Susana's direction. That's how Isa was when we were kids.

"I see," she says. Another drab silence falls between us, and I don't know what else to say. "So, what do you do?" she asks. Sitting with her elbows on her knees, she rests her face in her palms, eyes focused on her nephew.

"I'm an architect with an urban development firm, Ibarra Group," I say. "I saw you the other day." The words just slip out of my mouth. But now that I've gone this far, I might as well go all the way. "At the brunch. You were wearing a red top and the lounge singer was singing to you?" I grin stupidly, the muscles in my neck growing sore from protruding.

Viv looks at me with pursed lips. "Hmm. The lounge singer?"

"Yes, at the donor's brunch a few months ago. You were in a red top and...uh..." I stop myself before she thinks I'm a stalker. "Never mind," I say and hang my head.

"Do you mean Eva? The bossa nova singer?"

"Yeah, the bossa nova singer."

"Oh, she...uh...commented on my top and told me she had the perfect song for me. I'd never met her before, but I think she was just trying to get a tip out of me."

"Oh, I see." I stop talking and home in on Susana.

As we watch the kids play, I take advantage of another silence to think of questions I'd want to ask her. *Okay, just repeat her questions.* I don't even remember how to make friends anymore.

"So…" She elongates the syllable. I shift my gaze back to her. "Your ex. Is this a long-time-ago ex, on-again-off-again ex, or you-just-split-up kind of ex?"

I look at my Swatch, which doesn't display the date, and answer, "I moved out of my house just about a year and four months ago."

"Ah." She arches both her thick eyebrows. "Does that mean you're never getting back together again?" It's a question, I know, but it comes off as if it were a reprimand.

"Well," I say, trying for a cocky grin, "Seeing as she's been dating someone else for the last four months, I highly doubt it."

"I see. I'm sorry, I only ask because I've been burned a few times by indecisive exes."

"Oh." As the flames engulf my face, I rub the back of my neck. "Well, it turns out, women weren't her cup of tea after all."

"Damn." She shakes her head. "Damn. I'm sorry. So, she's dating a man." I just nod. "How long were you together? If you don't mind my asking."

I do, but I answer anyway. "Nearly seventeen years." Moisture spikes over my eyes at the thought. I hang my head slightly because our seventeenth year would have been tomorrow. I straighten and pretend to watch Susana.

Isa started dating him almost a year after we split up, but I just never really thought she'd date anyone at all, and maybe she'd figure at some point she couldn't live without me. But the opposite has happened. And as if the world has turned against me, the guy's name is Roberto. Of all the names in the Spanish language, why did he have to be a Roberto? And, as Isa mentioned the other day, he doesn't like to be called Rob, Bob, or even Robert. Nope, he goes by Roberto. Papá only went by Roberto. Mamá only ever called him Roberto. I frown at the thought.

"I know I'm a stranger," Viv says, cutting into my internal monologue. "But do you want to talk about it?"

Shaking my head, Isa's boyfriend is the last topic I want to discuss. Ugh, that word, boyfriend. Even thinking it makes me want to shower with rubbing alcohol. It's enough that I constantly type out horrific stories in my head about those two.

"Oh. Because you're going about a mile a minute there." She suddenly puts her hand over my bouncing knee, forcing me to stop shaking. I hadn't noticed, and when Viv doesn't immediately remove her hand, I sit back a little, stretch out my legs, and cross them at the ankles. Her hand slides off my knee, and she shifts to grasp the tabletop.

"They say it takes a month per year of a relationship to get over an ex. If that's the case, I might be a little early to this party," Viv says, puckering her lips.

I look at her, eyebrows pressed together, but before I can reply, I catch Susana and Christian running toward us. I flip my wrist over to peek at my Swatch, but it's only been a few minutes since Viv came to sit with me.

"Uh-oh. Looks like the jungle gym is boring our little terrors," she singsongs.

"Mamá, tengo hambre," Susana whispers in my ear while she rubs her tummy. I glance at Christian, who looks ravenous, too, and then at Viv.

Viv pounces. "Tell you what, how about I pick up a pizza and we can continue…" She lingers for a second. "Chatting somewhere private?"

I glance down at my Swatch again, three thirty on the dot. Just as I return my gaze to Viv, Isa appears in the background. My living, breathing metronome, Isa walks casually toward us with a man beside her. Roberto, I assume. The relief off my brow that they're walking arm-distance apart is palpable—at least to me, because my head is pulsing.

"Uh. It looks like my ex is coming to pick up Susana." I glance in the distance behind Viv's shoulder. She turns her head to face the approaching pair.

"Damn. Perfect timing," she whispers. "I can get out of your way if you want."

"Nah. Isa is just coming to collect Susana and be gone. I noticed they came in a car, so they might be going out together." When I say it, my stomach gives a thunderous growl. The skin on my shoulder blades prickles, my belly twitches, and blotchy circles bounce on the edges of my eyes.

"Maybe you and I can enjoy the pizza with Christian…" Viv begins in a whisper.

"Cariño," I say, eyes tethered to Susana. I point over to Isa and Roberto, who are getting closer. "Look, Mami is already here to pick you up. You'll eat with them. Okay?" Susana turns her head and jets off for her mother. Isa stops, takes a knee, and gives Susana a full-body hug. The image stings, and I'm forced to look away. Susana looks up and is cautious to wave at the stranger. Meanwhile, I don't feel my heart beating. Everything around me is motionless, the air stifling.

Isa is introducing Roberto to us today. Why she wants me involved is more than baffling. She called to talk about it a few days ago. That's what Isa does. She plans and organizes events to coincide so that no one, especially Isa, is inconvenienced. I had this picnic scheduled, and I wanted to bring Susana along. So, what does Isa do? She decides today is the day Susana and I would meet Roberto. Except that watching them for the first time together, rhythmically walking next to each other, is nothing but inconvenient.

I get up from the picnic table, brush imaginary dirt from my shorts, and straighten out my Pride flag T-shirt. My hand trembles as I comb my fingers through my curls. I don't walk more than two steps from the table when Isa, holding Susana's hand, and Roberto step into my space. We're facing each other as if we're in a boxing ring. It's high noon in front of thousands of hostile spectators, and we're about to go ten rounds, but the referee is explaining the rules of engagement first.

"Hi," I croak, my breath rattled. My hand rolls into a stony fist behind my back. A covert eye runs the length of Roberto's towering figure. His mere presence is like an anvil slipping down my back. This man, this interloper Isa has brought onto *our* field, could have been Papá's twin, except he has no grungy beard, and his eyes are more azure than even the sky on the clearest day in Madrid. He could have been related to me, but he's not. His pale, peach complexion is weathered, dry, and tired-looking, but that only adds to his rugged handsomeness. He's in a polo, shorts, and sockless loafers. I stand up straighter, as if that would give me the extra four or so inches to equal his height.

"Hi," Isa replies. After her half wave, she drops her right hand into her left, wringing the fingerprints off them. Her shorts are moderately short, and her sneakers are the trainers I got her our last Christmas together. She's wearing a white V-neck that flows on her body as if she hadn't been up all night planning her outfit. When she realizes I'm waiting for her next word, she shoves her fists in her pockets and shifts her torso toward the man. Her head tilts in my direction.

"Roberto, this is Gene López-Pérez," she says. Her voice husky, as if she'd just woken up. Sexy. It's the voice over the phone that kept me up past midnight when we were teenagers. She swings her hips back in line with her legs and casts her gaze on her trainers.

"Ah, Gene. Encantado, I've heard so much about you," he says in singsong Argentine-accented Spanish. I manage to stop my automatic eye roll as he hesitates to stretch his hand in my direction. Stretch, retract. He does it again until I relent and offer up my clammy paw. Our hands are clenched together, and as the moments elapse, I narrow my eyes at him. Peering through me, his villainous gaze, as though saying, *I'm going to put my name on them both*, gradually raises all the fuzz on my body. Viv's warm hand on my shoulder breaks our contact, and I take back my hand, as if scorched by searing coals.

Christian joins us, wrapping his shoulders with Viv's forearms. I don't know what compels me to do it, but I draw my arm around Viv's unfamiliar shoulder and say, "This is Viv." No last name, I just leave it at that. She pulls her hand away from Christian's clutches, and Roberto greedily takes it in his.

"Hi." She looks at Isa and takes her hand next. "Vivian Pascual. And this little guy here is Christian." She withdraws her hand and clasps it over Christian's shoulder as she peers down at him.

"Pleased to meet you both," she adds casually. Christian nods.

We stand for an instant, silent, until Isa chimes in. "Well, we're going to take this one to get something to eat. You haven't fed her, have you?" Isa fixes me with her dark, broody eyes. No sign of chin dimples.

"No, she wasn't hungry, so she hasn't eaten anything. But she's hungry now, she just told me." I stop babbling and motion toward the buffet station. Most of the picnic guests are now sitting and eating at tables scattered under the shade.

With a short wave from Isa and a warm embrace from my daughter, they turn and walk away from me and toward a bright blue Porsche. It's been idling on the street behind three properly parked cars, hazards flashing. The pain in my chest resumes. Whereas before it was dull, it's a blunt stab to my heart now. And as my eyes threaten tears, I turn my face away from Viv and yank my keys off the table, brushing my shoulder across my right eye. But then, I hear Viv behind me, rummaging through her backpack. She says nothing but hands me a wet wipe. I take it from her with a nod, and I clean my face with the moist towelette. Wringing my hands with it, I glance at Viv with a sheepish smile.

"Are there any adult beverages in those coolers?" Viv points toward the lined garbage cans that are full of soda, water, and maybe a few beers.

"There might be a Mahou Cinco Estrellas left in one of those bins," I reply.

"Mahou? Is that a beer?"

"Never mind." I usher her toward the buffet.

We take our places on one of the benches off from the rest of the crowd. It's the only one left unoccupied, near the buffet table. I fish out two small, pull-tab Mahou bottles from the beer bin, open one, and hand it to Viv.

"Here, try this beer. It's from my motherland." I hand her a bottle and carefully peel the top off mine. I take a long, refreshing sip.

"Oh," she says. "I've never had it."

"It's especially refreshing during a hot picnic," I say with a smirk.

"Is that where your family is from? Spain?"

"Yes. Mamá was born and raised in a small town in Andalucía." I continue after another delightful sip, "It's been almost nine years since they died. Died. As if. A car wreck killed them. My mother's whole family is from all over Andalucía, mainly Sevilla, Jerez, and Málaga."

"Oh. I'm so sorry about your parents," she says, raising both eyebrows. I shrug it off. "I hadn't realized you had a Spanish accent. Were you born there?" She reaches for her Mahou, takes a sip, and nods. I don't even notice when I'm speaking in Spanish anymore. But I guess when I talk about or even think about my parents, I instinctively switch to Spanish.

"No," I say, clearing my throat. "My parents immigrated to the US from Spain just before my brother was born. He's five years older than me."

"Oh, so he's an anchor baby?" she asks with a grin. Heat rises from my neck to my scalp. I'd never heard him referred to as that before.

"Uh…" I stammer. "I mean, my parents…Uh…Yeah, unfortunately the United States treats European immigrants differently than those coming from Latin America." I shake my head. "It's probably a cliché to say they were escaping fascism when most Latin Americans are running for their lives to the US, escaping some form of governmental corruption for a better life."

"I was kidding." She taps my shoulder with the beer in her hand. "You know? Because I'm Cuban and we have certain privileges coming here."

"Anyway," I say. "My father's family is from Madrid and Barcelona. My uncle lives in Barcelona now, but he's the reason my parents immigrated here in the first place. Tito Horacio was a university student in the seventies and had been advocating for gay rights in Madrid. For a long time in Spain—especially after the civil war, when Franco became Spain's dictator—authorities arrested homosexuals, sent them to insane asylums, and tortured them.

"Because my uncle had been such a vocal dissident, my grandparents were afraid he'd get arrested. So, my parents dropped everything and fled Spain with my uncle. My father had been in his last year of his master's in architecture and my mother had been earning her master's in Spanish literature. The three of them applied for student visas and were accepted to their respective programs at UM."

"Oh wow! That's eerily like what happened in Cuba when we came to Miami on the Mariel boatlift in 1980." She stops and takes another sip.

"Yeah. But I think the Castros are going to surpass Franco's dictatorship."

We talk and eat as Christian gobbles up all his barbeque, mouth outlined in the sugary brown sauce. I'm distracted by the movement around the tables. People picking up their garbage, Michelle closing her food station, and Jay talking to the deejay as he packs up his equipment. The crowd is thinning out and I want to follow suit.

We've cleaned up our bench and Viv scoops up her keys and asks, "Let me see your phone for a second."

Handing her a wet nap packet I found in the napkin bin when I served myself, I comply and brandish my BlackBerry from my pocket, holding my breath until she uses the wet napkin. When she does, I exhale. She takes the phone and swiftly presses various keys on it. Then, as she hands it back to me, she says, "I put my number in there. Call me if you ever want to get together again. I had fun today. Maybe we can do something fun without the children."

I swallow hard but only nod.

"Great." She winks. "So, I'll hear from you?"

"Yes," I assure her. I walk Viv and Christian toward her car, and as she pulls out of her spot, I turn around and walk to my front door, alone, turning my head toward the house as a tear slides down my cheek.

CHAPTER FOURTEEN

Isa

"No rice," Susana says, perusing her menu.

"No, my dear," Roberto replies, putting his menu down. "Argentinos don't eat rice."

"But I eat rice," she says. I'm staring at the words on my menu, but they're a blurry blob, missing the mark.

I'm somewhere else...lingering at the park, cold sweat running all over my body. My mind scrutinizes every movement, every word, and every time Viv put her hands on Gene.

"Mami," Susana says with a firm grip on the crease of my arm. "I don't know what to eat here." I put my menu down and tilt hers with my thumb and index finger so I can see it.

"Let's see," I say dragging a finger down the column of empanadas. "You'll like the beef empanada."

"What's chichimimi?" she asks.

"Chimichurri," Roberto corrects. "It's like God's homemade sauce." Susana's blank stare only serves to intensify the impasse. "It's a sauce made with perejil y aceite," he explains after a moment.

"What's perejil?" Susana asks, wrinkling the right side of her top lip in a tiny bunch.

"It's parsley." I take her menu abruptly. "You like parsley. You've had chimichurri before. It's a marinade for meat and other things. In this case, it's for the beef empanada. You had it the last time we were in Madrid with Mamá, and we went to an Argentine steakhouse." And just as I say the last words, I wish I could swallow them back. Roberto shifts in his plastic chair with a grunt, hiding behind his menu.

"I don't want that." Susana squints at me. My eyes dart up and catch Roberto's piercing glare.

"Okay," I relent. "What do you feel like eating?"

"Mamá lets me eat pizza sometimes on Saturdays."

"So, you want pizza?"

Susana nods.

"They make a margherita flatbread. You'll like that," I say.

"I don't like margherita."

"Yes, you do." I lower my voice and tamp down the urge to take her home and feed her to Floyd. "It's cheese with tomato sauce."

"Oh. Well, why doesn't it say that instead of *magarita*?" I stifle a snicker but shoot her my best Martha Acosta warning stare.

"Because that's how they do it here," Roberto says, teeth clenched.

"This place is dumb." Susana wraps her torso with her arms. A red flag suddenly waves before my eyes. This is someone else's daughter.

I turn to Susana. "Let's go wash up." My voice is saccharine, but my face hurts from forcing a smile. Turning to face Roberto, I ask, "Can you please order the margherita flatbread for her and the ham and cheese miga for me? We'll be right back." I don't wait for a reply. Instead, I wrap my fingers around Susana's wrist and scurry with her into the bathroom.

"What's going on with you today?" I ask as soon as the door to the bathroom firmly shuts. I drag her to the double sink and open the faucet for her. "You've never been rude to anyone before. Why are you being insoportable with Roberto?"

"Why are we eating with him?" She puts her little hands under the soap dispenser. When it shoots down slimy soap, she slips her hands under the water.

"Because he's my friend," I say, peering at her through the mirror. She's busy watching how the water and soap make suds. "I thought Mamá was your friend," Susana says. I slowly inhale and turn my faucet off. "Why don't we ever go out together with her?"

"Mamá has her own friends now." That comes out of my mouth hurried and thoughtless. "I meant that Mamá and I are both making new friends." Or at least that's what it seemed like Gene was doing.

"Well, I don't like your new friends." Susana runs to the paper towel dispenser. She reaches up and grabs a wad of brown paper, dropping a few on the floor, and roughly pats down each arm. I squeeze the bridge of my nose while she wads up the paper towels and trashes them. Gesturing for her to pick up the ones she threw on the floor, I stop her before she runs out the door, pressing my thumb into her shoulder.

Squatting down to her level, I say, "Listen to me. Whether you like our new friends or not is not my concern. You will treat everyone you meet with kindness and respect. Do you hear me?" She gives me a terrified nod, eyebrows stretched to her hairline, eyes gleaming.

With Susana's hand in mine, we march back to the table, where a miniature grill sits, sizzling with several cuts of meat. Nothing I asked for is anywhere on the table. Roberto sips on a brimming glass of red wine.

"Hey." I hold out Susana's chair and wait for her to sit. A whiff of charred meat wafts up my nose. I sit down and take inventory. "What's all this?"

"I ordered us a parrillada with some of my favorite cuts of meats. I thought you'd like this better than a ham and cheese sandwich." He looks pleased with himself.

"Oh. But I'm not really hungry for all this…this meat."

"Ché, it's all so delicious, try it." He picks up an overcooked chorizo and pops it in his mouth. His use of the word *Ché* has stunted my appetite. I never believed that word was actually still in use today.

"Did you order her flatbread?" I glare at him.

"Oh, yes. That's coming. But I was starving, so I ordered this. I can order your miga if you want."

"No." This lunch is stretching my patience as if it were a chorizo's casing. "I'll just have a few pieces." There's nothing more off-putting than a horde of greasy meat crammed together on a tiny grill. And then having that grill left broiling in your face the entire time you're eating. I say nothing, though.

My heart soars as I catch the food runner heading our way with Susana's flatbread. *Ah, a little bit of peace.* She places the long plate at the center of the table. Larger than I had anticipated, I take Susana's plate and serve her two square pieces. "Cuidado, Bebé, it's hot. Okay?" She nods, and I add two pieces of the flatbread to my plate.

Susana digs into hers, picking out the basil leaves and discarding them on its original plate in the center. Roberto stabs a few pieces of sausage, examines all the sides, and adds the more charred pieces to his plate. He repeats this method with the churrasco and the strips of vacío.

"How do you eat so much red meat?" I ask, befuddled. "You're a heart surgeon."

"I operate on babies, not on adults," he says, cutting more meat off the grill. That piece looks to be a piece of stomach. "Most of my patients are born with heart defects that I fix for them. Besides, I keep trim by eating more protein and less carbs." He jabs at a piece of meat with his fork and holds it up. It reeks of death.

"Yeah, my dad kept trim by eating more protein and less carbs, too. He died of heart disease," I deadpan, focusing on cutting up Susana's larger pieces of flatbread and adding them to her plate. I take another piece for myself.

This last piece has gotten cold and tougher to run my knife through easily. Hacking into the flatbread, the thought of Viv casually placing her delicate hand, fingernails tipped in red, on Gene's shoulder and the way she gingerly took my hand when

Gene introduced us sends an ice-cold bucket of water down my spine. Or, it could have been how close she'd been sitting to Gene on the picnic table that's got me in this irritable mood. The kid was adorable, though. What was his name?

"Mami!"

"Isabel?"

"What?"

"You're cutting into the plate there." Roberto points at my knife, which is now shrieking against the plate. The two flatbread slices have fallen off to the side. Grimacing, I pluck a discarded slice off the table and throw it in my mouth.

"The flatbread is delicious. How's yours?" As Susana nods her assent, Roberto frowns.

"I'll take the rest to go," he says, unperturbed, slicing pieces of vacío on his plate.

Later, Roberto pulls up to the house and cuts the engine. But before he moves to open his door, I press down on his forearm.

"Thank you for dinner," I say in a smooth monotonous tone, as if I'm reading off a list of summer books for Susana to read at home.

"Can I walk you in?" A smile creeps up to his eyes, and I stop breathing.

"Better not," I reply quickly, pointing to the back seat where Susana is almost certainly feigning sleep. "I gotta get this one to bed."

"When can we go out again?" *We? As in the three of us, or as in you and me and no one else?* I think but don't say.

"Why don't you come by my office on Monday afternoon? I have an early morning department meeting," I say, thinking better than to let him down easily. I know that my schedule is fully packed that day, but he doesn't need to know that. "I might be able to get away for a quick coffee?" I haven't had so much coffee since the last time we were all in Jerez together. The Spaniards love their coffee, morning, noon, and night.

Roberto pulls out his BlackBerry. "I have back-to-back surgeries on Monday." He rolls the gear wheel on the side of the gadget, skimming through his week. "I have some free time on Friday at about two in the afternoon. I can pass by then."

"Sounds like a plan," I say with a sparkle on my front tooth. But when he leans in for an intimate moment, I hold his chest back and gesture with my head toward Susana, still motionless in the back seat. Oscar worthy. Roberto nods his agreement.

"I'll see you next week, then." He twists, contorting himself in the limited space of the driver's seat. "Do you need help with her?"

"No. I'll get her out of the car, and she can walk up to the house on her own. She'll fall asleep as soon as I change her into her pajamas. Kids," I say with a shrug.

"Gotta love them." He rubs his hand over his expressionless face, scratching at his clean-shaven jaw.

I get out of the passenger side, figure out how to pop the seat forward, and scoop Susana in my arms. Carrying her is like wearing lead boots, but I manage.

"Mother of pearl, you're getting heavy, Bebé." Susana shifts in my arms and wraps her arms around my neck and hitches her legs around my waist. Well, at least I'll be able to open the front door easily. I slam the passenger side door with my foot and stagger up to the house. Roberto drives off as soon as I close the front door behind me.

Susana jumps off me and flashes a wry smile. "Home! Finally." She runs up the stairs, leaving me to rethink my situation. I saunter over to the foot of the stairs.

"You'd better be all washed up and ready for bed when I come up to read to you."

"Okaaaay…" comes her muffled reply. I don't step away until I hear the slam of her bathroom door, though.

With a sigh, I walk through the kitchen arch and pick up the mail I'd dropped on the counter earlier today. Junk, junk, oh, shit, the pediatrician! Scooping the BlackBerry from my back pocket, I scroll through my calendar for Monday. Damn it, I'm supposed to take Susana for her yearly checkup because Gene has an important meeting.

Without hesitation, I tap Gene's number. As it rings a third time, my breath quickens. Could she still be with that other woman?

"Hi." My breathing normalizes when I hear her croaky voice. It makes the hair on my neck stand at attention. Imagining her in bed, I close my eyes. Maybe she's reading.

"Hi." I open my eyes and remember why I'm calling.

"Did you get Susana off to bed?" she asks.

"She's upstairs washing up. Seems like she had a great time playing with…Christian, was it?"

"Yes, that was Christian."

"And…Viv…" I have no idea what to say about her, so I rush out, "Is very pretty."

Gene is doing exactly what you're doing. Leave her alone, the gremlins in my ear admonish.

"Yeah. We struck up a conversation while the kids were playing together on the jungle gym at the picnic."

"Well, I guess this is what you wanted, isn't it?" Jesus, I'm all over the place today. She's ruffling something, shifting in the bed? Maybe she's putting her book on the nightstand. She used to sleep on the right side here, and I wonder if she still does.

"Isa, I just met her today." There's a tinge of melancholy in her voice. But why? This is what she wanted. She left me. She left this house. The house she loved so much she wouldn't consider selling after her parents died. The house she was determined to move into, with or without me. She left it all. And for what? Because I won't hold her hand in public? Because I didn't want her coming to my father's funeral—although I never told her that. Being gay is her thing, not mine. I just wanted to be with her, not because she was a woman, or because I'm…a…lesbian or anything. It was just Gene. I just fucking wanted to be with Gene.

"Yes," I say. "But you're attracted to her. I can tell by the way you watched us when we were greeting each other." *Nice, Isa.*

"She's nice." Ugh, I hate when she's evasive. "But we were just talking."

"Is Christian her son?" I move on to the boy because Gene sparking a relationship with someone else can't be the last thing I think about tonight.

"Her nephew. Hey, Susana has that appointment with the pediatrician on Monday," she says with a terse tone I've never heard her use. "Did you find out if you can take her, or should I? I don't mind taking her."

"I...uh...that's what I actually called you about," I say. I don't want her thinking I called her to see if she's going to be seeing that other woman. "It totally slipped my mind, and when I riffled through the mail, that's when I saw the reminder notice. Peterson scheduled a last-minute staff meeting first thing Monday. I'm sorry, I don't know where my head is at."

"It's okay, I can take her," she says. Always so reliable. Gene would be a better mother than me if...but I don't have time to continue that thought when she says, "I'll swing by to get her then." She cuts me off and puts me on speaker. It sounds as though she's typing in the information. "I'll just set a reminder to rearrange my meeting in the morning."

"Yeah, okay," I whisper.

"I'll call you when I'm on my way," she says.

"Good night," I say and rush off the phone. I set the BlackBerry on its charger and leave the kitchen. Susana is waiting.

CHAPTER FIFTEEN

Gene

I pull the old Jeep into the driveway, ready to pick up Susana. When she rides in the Jeep, she make-believes she's on a Youth Fair ride, especially when we go over speed bumps. Even now, at almost seven, she throws her arms in the air and shouts, "Weeee!" and then, "Go again!" Papá left me his Jeep. It wasn't in the will the way the house and the apartment building were. No. He'd given it to me on my sixteenth birthday, way before the wreck that killed them and totaled Mamá's sedan. The Jeep was bare-bones when I got it, and by the time I came back from Cornell, I was driving it regularly.

I've added a few things to it. A stereo system with a USB port, a backup camera—I didn't know that was an option until I did the research—and an airbag-equipped steering wheel. These were my perks. Everything else is original, down to the driver's seat, frayed with years of Papá's driving posture. I could afford a new car—even a new Jeep with all the bells and whistles—if I wanted one. But this one, this 1984 Jeep Wrangler, has his built-up grime, sweat, and memories. Papá's fingerprints are all in the details: the sun visor, the gearshift, even the door handle. And this is what he used to teach both Isa and me to drive one summer. It doesn't belong in a junkyard, or worse, in someone else's garage.

I glance up at the house, another relic of my childhood happiness. It, like this Jeep, would never belong to anyone but me. And somehow, that house, with its Spanish arches, colorful ceramic tiles, and dark brown wood trim, drove me away twice. First, when I followed Isa to Cornell, and second, when I left her and Susana and moved into an apartment for which I have no magical attachment. I was never going to live in my house without my parents and without Isa. It was something I'd known since my parents' death, and that's why I gave it to Isa in our palimony papers.

I snatch my phone from the console, unplugging it from its charger, and dial the house number.

"Hey," I say. "I'm outside. Is Susana ready?"

"Yes, I saw you pull in, she'll be outside in a few seconds," Isa says before disconnecting. Maybe she was on her way from the stairs to the kitchen when she saw me through the living room window. Or maybe she was watching me through what used to be our bedroom window, upstairs above the living room. I sit back with my eyes closed, mentally going over my to-do list for the day, and sigh with relief when I don't see the pretentious blue sports car.

Susana pops out of the house and sprints down the stoop and across the grassy front yard. Like an ecstatic chimpanzee, she hauls herself up into the Jeep. A boisterous laugher comes over me, watching her work her way into her booster seat, then reaching for the seat belt and locking it place.

"Ready to go, Bebé?" I ask with a wide grin. Susana giggles and sends me a salute with her cherubic hand.

"Vroom, vroom, Mamá!"

Stepping on the clutch, I slide the gearshift in reverse and focus on her smile as I twist to check the street behind us. I hit the gas, loosen the clutch, and back the Jeep onto the street. There's a slight dip that always gets Susana giggling as the Jeep jumps onto the road. Her laughter magnifies when I hit the brakes, stopping us mid-inertia. Movement at the front door catches my eye, and when I look out the passenger side, Isa is leaning against the doorjamb, arms crossed with a grin bright on her face. I wave at her and imagine her vanilla scent wafting in the Jeep the way it used to when she'd ride with me. I snap back to attention but wait for the dizziness to subside.

Children are nearly crawling up the walls at the pediatrician's office. Susana pays no mind to that, instead making a beeline for the play area and finding a friend. Meanwhile, ringing the chime button at the check-in window, I fight the urge to repeatedly press my thumb on it. I look around the window ledge for the sign-up clipboard, but it's missing.

When I turn around to check up on Susana, she's busy explaining something to a bewildered little boy. A smile worms its way onto my face as I think how integral she is to my life. I didn't take meticulous care planning every aspect of having our daughter. That was Isa. Everything had been decided when she was ready for motherhood. The right donor, the impregnating procedure, and her birthing plan were items on a list she checked off. It's how she's planned her whole life—*our* whole life. But for Susana, I was merely invited to participate in the living. I held Isa's belly when Susana kicked, massaged her feet when they were swollen like balloons, and made love to her when it was right. Truth be told, she wanted a baby, so I wanted a baby. And here we are, seven years since all that. I'd do it again in a heartbeat.

Despite being an Isa replica, Susana has taken on many aspects of my disposition. She stomps her feet when she's mad, acts out sometimes, and talks back—all Isa's doing, of course. Yet she's mindful of others, is gentle with animals, and thinks through her tasks—of course, all my doing. And she adores her grandmother. Martha is the only other adult she's ever been with, apart from her teachers and swim instructor. And now, *him.* The thought makes my skin crawl.

The sliding of the acrylic window startles me, and as I turn to face whoever is peering through, I notice a familiar face.

"Funny seeing you here," Viv says. Her face is fresh, eyes wide and restful.

"Hello," I reply. "Susana's here for her yearly checkup. You work here?" She'd mentioned something about being a nurse on Saturday at the picnic, but I scarcely remember.

"For now," she replies, the edges of her lips curling. "I'm a traveling nurse, remember, so I go wherever I'm needed. I started at this practice a few weeks ago, replacing the NPs on maternity leave," she clarifies.

"Oh, yeah. That must be Betty," I say. "She talked with Isa about wanting to get pregnant the last time we were here."

"You haven't called me," she says, exaggerating a lip pout.

"I was getting around to it," I reply, shoving my fists in my pockets. "I wasn't sure what to say."

"How about, 'Hi, it's Gene, wanna chill?'"

"Uh…I would never say 'chill,'" I say with a grin but give myself a mental lashing.

"All right," she says in a whisper. "I'll wait for you to call me. Any time after seven today."

"Susana Pérez-Acosta," another nurse calls out from the door that leads to the examination rooms. I stick my hand out for Susana to grab and guide her to our destination. Once inside, I notice Viv at the counter, writing in one of the patient files. She glances my way, and I wink at her as I pass. Yes, I think I will call her.

Sitting in the Jeep after dropping Susana off at school, I grab my phone and search through the contacts to find Vivian Pascual. I highlight it and tap on the send message option.

GLP: Want to order in tonight?

I hold my breath while I wait for a reply, and just as I'm about to start the Jeep and drive off, my phone beeps twice.

VP: That's more like it.

VP: Sure, what time?

I hesitate, thumb on the number seven. Before I can type in my message, another two pop up from Viv.

VP: Don't be shy.

VP: I get off work tonight at 7, how about that?

I push away the nausea that creeps up and an inkling I'm committing adultery to fire off my reply.

GLP: Sounds good, my place?

I follow with my address, then sit back and wait for her answer. When nothing else comes in, I set my BlackBerry down on the center console and drive. My phone beeps twice more while I'm on the road. Finally, back at the apartment, I feel a dank breeze on my face. A tentative glance up at the sky tells me I'd better cover up the Jeep or else risk losing my new sound system.

My front door is a mere three steps away, so I dart into the apartment, race toward the kitchen, and paw my way through a hard-to-reach corner cabinet for the Jeep's full body cover I have for emergencies like these. I finally grab it and race back to the vulnerable Jeep, unfurling and throwing it over the vehicle, running back and forth getting it neatly tucked under its protective vinyl cover. A thunderous crack breaks the sky open, unleashing a downpour. The back of the Jeep is the last part of the cover I tug down, saving it from the rain. Brushing the wet, flattened wad of wilted curls from my forehead, I stretch the material with everything in me, pull at the draw rope that lines the bottom seam, and finally secure the whole Jeep. It should hold through the rainstorm, at least until I can install its soft top.

Climbing the steps of the portico, I linger just outside my door, when it dawns on me that I left my BlackBerry on the center console, under that tarp that soaked me through and through. A sigh escapes my nostrils as I flit back to fish it out. I'm a dripping, drenched mop, but I have my phone.

Not for the first time, Mamá's voice sounds loud and clear inside my head telling me to wait while she brings me a towel, jarring other memories with it. The front door slams shut with a howl, and I'm left inside a freezing apartment, sitting in a puddle of despair. I can't help the sobs, the gasping for oxygen either.

My head leans against the door, his smiling, clean-shaven face taunting me. I wrap my arms around my bent legs, hugging them tighter to my chest. A shiver runs down my back, reminiscent of my first night here. The stark emptiness, the unfulfilled dreams, the life I left behind.

My beeping phone rattles me. I scoop it out of my wet pocket. It's a message from Martha.

MA: Hi. How are you?

It curls my quivering lip into a smile.

GLP: I'm okay. U?

Then, I switch to Viv's message thread.

VP: Yes!

VP: Looking forward.

I leave all my drenched clothes by the door and race to the shower in the buff. Putting myself back together will take time, and time is what I have.

Work distracts me from the memories. I receive the go-ahead from the project manager on a house I'm designing. Now that the first stage is complete, and with the client's approval, I can bring my engineers into the fold. Architecture is like life. There's more planning involved than is necessary, more people get involved than you'd like, and sometimes, the outcome suits someone else's expectation.

For a moment, a little bit of dread builds in my stomach as I glance at the photo sitting on my desk of Isa and Susana in the pool. I took it years ago, just after that pool was built. I had two pictures framed. And since I don't appear in it because I'm behind the camera, it was the perfect family photo for Isa to put on her desk at work. "No one will know," I had assured when I gave it to her.

My phone vibrates on my desk as I shut down my computer. I check my Swatch—it's only six, so I grab the BlackBerry and scroll through the messages. Viv.

VP: No more patients...

I shrug. Then another message pops up on my screen.

VP: Do you mind if I'm a little early?
I take a moment to answer, then fire off my reply.
GLP: Not at all. Come over.
Putting the phone back in my pocket, I get up from my desk and close the door to my office behind me. Walking into the living area, I run a cursory eye over the room, making sure nothing is out of order. No rogue bras hanging around, no shoes under the coffee table, and no toys in the living room.

The doorbell is like an out-of-tune trumpet that blares for a second then dies down. I make a mental note to get batteries. Before opening the door, I smooth the front of my polo and shorts with both hands as if brushing away who I once was. On the other side, an all-smiles Viv, carrying two brown paper bags, is waiting.

"I brought dinner," she says and walks in. "And adult beverages." I turn around, closing the door behind me, and watch her hips swing up and down as she walks toward the kitchen. Isa carts around a plumper bubble butt, but it'll do. I slap the thought of Isa's ass out of my head and follow Viv.

She turns back and asks, "Do you mind?" pointing to the kitchen.

"No, go ahead," I reply, following.

Viv steps into my kitchen and unpacks two wine bottles from the first sack and a medium-size aluminum to-go container sealed with a white, cardboard lid. It all smells delicious, but I have no idea what it could be.

"I brought arroz con pollo," she says.

I've never had anyone's arroz con pollo other than Martha's, so I'm holding my applause until after I get a taste. Putting two place mats down on the countertop, I set each with a paper napkin and utensils. The aluminum container almost singes my fingertips, so I cautiously remove the lid using the spoon I took out. Scooping two heaping servings of the chicken and rice on each plate, I set them down on each mat.

There's no getting Martha's motherly smile out of my head as she serves me up arroz con pollo. I wonder if Isa has this many flashbacks of our life together when Roberto does something that reminds her of me. Sixteen years is sixteen years. I move around the peninsula and sit on the barstool next to Viv.

"Oh. We forgot the wine," she says while chewing on her food. A cringe creeps up my right shoulder as I stand and step back into the kitchen. Yanking the corkscrew from the junk drawer, I hastily grab the wine bottle and knock it over. It doesn't break, thank goodness, but everything shrieks as I drop the metal corkscrew back in the drawer, preventing the wine bottle from falling.

"Sorry, that was loud," I say with an innocent shrug and roll the bottle my way. I right it and attempt to remove its cork.

"We didn't drink much at the house," I say, twisting the corkscrew into the cork and immediately wanting to cork up my own mouth.

"Who's we?" she asks around another mouthful.

"Uh…never mind," I reply, placing the bottle between my thighs to give myself some leverage. The squeaking sound of the moist cork against the glass grates at my spine, and I do everything I can to keep it from being the only thing I hear.

"You mean, you and your ex?"

"Yeah," I reply, serving a glass for Viv and one with less wine for myself, then return to my barstool.

I mix the rice on my plate, which looks more like takeout fried rice from the Chinese restaurant down the street than arroz con pollo. The chicken, cut up into tiny cubes, looks more like greasy tofu. They used long grain rice instead of Valencia, and to top it off, it's dry. This is not the way Martha makes hers at all. Martha cooks hers with Valencia rice and adds all the liquid from the cans of vegetables she adds to it until the rice swims in a thick, savory broth—it's better when it's wetter. This one has some flavor, but it tastes as if it came out of the frozen aisle at the supermarket.

"Mmm," I hum, careful to keep my mouth shut and chew. "This is great." I smile, nearly choking on the words. I've never been rude.

"It's yummy, right?" she asks. I hide my dismay at the word *yummy* and let her continue. "The place I got it from is only open until six, so I got in just under the wire tonight. I've been getting lunch there since I started working at the pediatrician's office."

"Ah," I murmur, making a mental note never to eat at that cafeteria. "Do you do that often?"

"What? Work at the pediatrician's office?" she asks. "Well, the thing is..." She pauses and takes another forkful. "My specialty is in pediatrics."

"Oh?" I ask, eyebrows cocked. "But what exactly is a nurse practitioner?"

She swallows the rest of the food in her mouth before she replies. "I'm a midlevel practitioner, which means that I can assess patients' needs, order and interpret lab work, diagnose some common diseases, and create treatment plans for my patients."

"Oh," I say. "So, today you were running the lab work?"

"No, I've been assessing patients, which is what Betty does," she clarifies.

"I see. Where else do you work? Other than at the pediatrician's office, I mean."

"I work at Research Memorial, too," she replies. "Under Dr. Roberto Ruiz's surgical service, specifically."

I choke on my rice and aspirate a grain or two. Now it's stuck somewhere inside my nasal cavity. The coughing fit I'm having is burning my face. Viv runs around the peninsula, grabs my wineglass, dumps its contents, runs it under the faucet, and pours a fresh glass of water for me to drink.

"Gosh, I'm sorry," I say after gulping down all the water. My face is probably a tinge of red because I can feel the fire down to my collarbones. "Thanks."

"Yeah, just breathe. Sounds like you choked on a grain," she says. And I use the coughing fit to push away my plate, get up from my barstool, and serve myself more water.

"I don't know what happened," I say, voice hoarse.

"I'm sorry I mentioned it. I don't work that service often, so it was a surprise to see him the other day."

"But he didn't seem to know you," I croak.

"He doesn't know me, know me," Viv explains. "He's the top surgeon, so he only comes in to operate, nothing else. We assess the patients and determine the course of action. When Roberto needs to intervene, he does. He's a busy guy."

"Apparently," I say around another cough.

"That's how it is for most surgeons. They're either in the hospital doing rounds, going to medical conferences, running continuous education, and studying for recertification," she explains.

"Where else do you work?" I ask. "In the pathology lab?"

"Funny, no."

"Wow, so he really doesn't know his own team?"

"I didn't actually say he doesn't," she replies. "Look at it like this: I work on the outside, if the patients I assess need his intervention, he takes care of them in the OR. So, we never see each other because I'm not part of his surgical team. That's a very specialized service."

"Tell me about it," I say.

"So, your ex is the one he's seeing," she says as if it's locker room fodder. I nod. Up from my barstool now, I gather the dishes into the sink. Replacing the lid of the almost-full rice container, I pack it back up using the same brown paper bag Viv brought and set it aside for her to take when she leaves.

"I see this still bothers you," she says.

"Why do you say that?"

"Because you seem distracted."

"I have a few things on my mind, that's all," I reply. The question, as annoying as a circling gnat, sticks in my craw, especially now that I know Roberto and Viv work together. But yes, I'm worried. I spend too many hours thinking that Isa is going out with a thirty-nine-year-old man who might want to start his family by adopting my daughter. This is my worst nightmare.

"Here, you wash, and I'll dry," Viv says, sneaking up behind me. I let out a little gasp as she grabs the kitchen towel hanging over my shoulder. Her touch singes me, and I practically flinch.

"Thanks for dinner," I say to Viv as I usher her to the door.

"No," she says with a smile. "Thanks for letting me crash your evening." I step out of the apartment and hold the door open for her. Viv steps down and comes closer to me. I assume she's going to kiss my cheek, so I reach down with the side of my face, but it happens in a blink. Viv nips the corner of my mouth, and now I do recoil.

"Oh, sorry," she says, pulling back. "I may have read that wrong." I space out for a few moments before saying anything. How do I tell her, without hurting her, that I just want to be friends?

"Viv," I say, clearing my throat, still raspy from my coughing fit earlier. Running my fingers through my tussled curls, I bow my head and pinch the back of my neck. "I don't...I'm not looking to start anything." That was probably a cop-out, so I continue, "I mean that my state of mind is all wrong to date anyone. I had a nice time with you at the picnic and tonight, but what I really need right now are friends. I don't have many." Right about now, Martha is my only friend.

"Friends, huh?" She sighs. "Okay, I can do friends. Do you want me to introduce you to the lesbian underworld?"

"The lesbian what?"

"I'm willing to take a different tack, and since you said the other day that you and your ex never went out, I can take you around the Lesbian Happy Hour Network," she says, eyebrows shooting up.

"I've never heard of that."

"Well, there are no more lesbian clubs, no ladies-only bars, and bathhouses have been outlawed. There are a few underground places that are promoted through word of mouth, and then there's a Facebook group that sets up a networking happy hour every other Thursday. We can start there. They're called the Lesbian Happy Hour Network. They choose different venues around Miami. The group posts the information on their Facebook page the Monday prior. It's a lot of fun, and you don't always see the same people. Plus, you know your ex would never go to one of those, so you'll never bump into her."

"No, I guess I wouldn't," I reply dryly.

"The next one is a week from Thursday. Do you want to check it out?"

"With you?"

"Well, yeah. As friends. You say you need friends, but you need to meet people to have friends. And I love donating to and volunteering at Equality Miami, but you're not going to meet any hot lesbians there." She chuckles.

"Yeah, okay. That sounds good. Are you sure you're okay with just being friends?"

"You might be smoking hot, but I think I can keep my hands off you," she says with a wink. She reaches up and places her lips on my cheek. There's no spark as her lips touch my skin. She turns and walks away.

CHAPTER SIXTEEN

Isa

"Hola, maja!" The unexpected but cheerful sound of Flor's Spanish accent from more than four thousand miles away forces me to stop packing up. G's cousin has a nose for calling when I'm itching to talk. I glance at my watch and run a quick time conversion for Madrid.

"Flor! It's great to hear from you, but it's nearly midnight over there, what are you still doing up?" Although the Spaniards tend to have later work and life schedules, midnight is pushing it, even for Flor.

"Well, with the time difference, the day got away from me, and by the time I called Gene to see how she's doing it was almost eleven here. We talked for like an hour, so blame her if I'm calling you too late." Sounding as though she's shifting the phone from one ear to the other, the water running in the background distracts me.

"The life of a Spanish movie producer," I reply, curling my lip.

"Ha! I wish it was that glamorous," she says. "If it were, would I be washing my own dishes?"

"Yeah, good point. Anyway, how did she sound?" I ask, fixing my tone. "With the anniversary and all."

"Ya sabes. La pobre. Nine years is a long time, Isa." Flor's voice breaks a little.

"Yeah. The day got away from me, too. I'm shutting down my computer and heading to the apartment to pick Susana up and to see how Gene's doing. It was her week with Susana, and I haven't gotten a chance to check in with her today." The phone is wedged between my ear and my shoulder as I straighten my desk.

"How's everything with you? Roberto?" She lingers on Roberto's last syllable.

"Uh." I'm trying to come up with something to say as I pack my laptop in my bag. I sit back in my chair, drawing a long squeak from it as I lean back. "Actually, Gene met him last month."

Her lack of response makes me rethink what I want to say next. Maybe Gene has already mentioned it to her. "Susana was a little bitch during dinner, but nothing I couldn't handle."

"How did Gene react when she met him?"

"Um, she didn't say much. Well, she didn't say anything at all, at least not to me. Has she said anything to you about him?"

"Mm-hmm," she hums. Ah, I've just come to the crossroads between friendship and family. I love Flor. And when we met, ages ago on my first trip with Gene and her family to Madrid, she and I hit it off instantly. But for the Lópezes, family comes first, regardless. "She has, but the one thing that stuck with me was that she seems to think he looks exactly like Tito Roberto."

"He does not!" The comment flies out of my mouth terser than I intend. How could Gene think he looks like her dad?

"She said he's tall and has thick curly blond hair."

"Yes, well that's true, but he's nothing like Roberto. Your uncle, I mean. He's Argentine, for crying out loud." My volume shoots up a bit, and I look out my office door to make sure Cami can't hear me talking about her cousin.

"Right." There's a long pause, and I can tell Flor is measuring her next words. "So, he doesn't remind you, even a little bit, of Roberto?"

As I move my office chair from side to side with the tip of my stiletto, images of Gene's dad come to memory.

"I'll have to think about it and let you know."

"Mmm."

"Listen, my friend, I've gotta let you go. I texted Gene that I was heading out just before you called." I'm flustered by the thought that Gene might be right about the two Robertos.

"Ah, yes you wouldn't want to be a nanosecond late." Her laugh puts me at ease. "Te quiero prima."

"I love you, too."

"Hey," I say when Gene opens the door. Inviting myself in, I stroll directly to the kitchen peninsula, place my laptop bag down on the countertop, and turn to face her. She looks a bit gaunt, but that could be from spending the last week running after Susana—her relationship with Susana is a bit more physical than mine is.

Gene closes the door and walks over to me, leaving a gap exactly three feet between us, but the separation is considerable. "Susana is just picking up her stuff. I think she's finished with her homework. She only had to read for forty-five minutes, and then connect a few words to their definition. No math today."

I nod. "And how are *you* today?" On instinct, my hand reaches for hers and gives it a tight squeeze. Her eyes, dim and sunken, are darker than their usual gleam of soft honey. The darkness under them tears at my heart.

"What can I say? It is what it is, right?" She shrugs and wipes away a bit of moisture from her cheek. "It's been nine years, but sometimes I can still hear them. It's weird."

"It's not, weird," I say gently. Still joined, our hands feel right clasped together. When I let go of her, I turn around to force back my own tears.

"I spoke to Flor," she says.

"Yeah, she told me." Pulling myself together, I face her hapless hazel eyes, wishing for a switch to turn this all off. Her parents were so young, barely midforties. "What are you doing later? It's Art Basel after all. Are you catching any galleries?"

"I'm supposed to meet up with Viv at a lesbian networker. But the prospect of getting stuck in Art Basel traffic is horrifying. I might crash later." Her voice is clearer, but still a little shaky.

"Oh," I say, and almost cover my mouth so it doesn't regurgitate my thoughts. "You should meet up with her. I guess that's as good an idea as anything else you could possibly do tonight."

"Yeah, I guess you're right." She stands in front of me, so forlorn, her thick eyelashes damp, her fists in her pockets. She crosses her bare feet at the ankles, and the movement draws my eyes to them. Her narrow feet and long, perfectly groomed toes, the curve of her high arches, the smooth ball of her heel. My eyes scan the length of her muscular calf, her defined quads. But the hem of Gene's shorts stops further inspection of her long legs. "Hello?"

Lost in her haze, I look up at her. "Sorry, what?"

"I was saying that tonight's networker is at one of the satellite art shows, showcasing the work of an artist I've been wanting to see."

"Yeah. It'll be good for you to get out," I reply, glancing past Gene toward the hallway. "Susana?" Oh. God. Now I'm yelling.

"I'll go get her." And before I can protest, she turns on the balls of her feet and disappears into the hall.

Mother of fucking pearl! My head is somewhere else. Running my hands through my hair, I massage my fingertips into my scalp. The pressure is soothing, even for a second. A door in the hallway slams, and I give my hair a quick shake. The rapid patter of Susana's feet gets louder as she approaches, and I feign being caught off guard and draw her into my arms.

Gene watches as Susana wraps her arms around my waist. Nearly four feet tall, her head is almost at the height of my chest now. I bend a bit to give her a good squeeze, and a long whiff at the crook of her neck smells fresh like lemon infused with wisps of ginger. The fragrance lingers in this apartment, too. And I guess since Susana's been here for the past seven days, the sent has melded to Susana's body. A whole new aroma for a whole new Gene. I can't help but wonder if it's Viv's doing.

Susana makes a break for the door as I scurry to grab my bag and keys from the peninsula. I turn to face Gene one last time before leaving, and when our eyes meet, a montage of hundreds of snap moments we experienced together plays between us. And as if we never separated at all, least of all for almost a year and a half, I find her hand, interlock our fingers, and place it on my heart.

"I miss them, too."

Letting her go, I turn around and walk toward an impatient Susana, waiting with her hand on the door handle, and give her the okay to open it and flee.

Stirring the sauce for dinner, I take a long sip from my wineglass. My in-laws had left us an ample collection of red wine tucked away in an air-conditioned pantry. Roberto and Mimi especially loved Spanish varietals. This one is a Ribera del Duero I found wedged between two Riojas. If Mimi taught me anything at all, it was how to enjoy a good wine. I won't drink the whole bottle tonight; I can barely manage one full glass. But I've been craving something tart and bold, with hints of currants at the end of the palate, especially after leaving G alone to deal with her anguish. Well, she won't be alone for long, anyway.

Off to my right, in the corner, under the kitchen table, Floyd is still sleeping in his plush kitty bed. I left his food and water close to his bed before I went to work this morning, but he's barely touched it. He's been with us since we found him in the park across the street from the apartment building Gene inherited. That was before Susana was even born…I think we'd just moved back down from Cornell.

Gene and I would go on long walks around the soccer field. It was how we coped with the sudden upheaval. Our plans changed in a snap—her parents' lives lost forever.

Gene heard him first. Walking around the bend on the track field, we heard a continuous little squeal. I hadn't paid any attention to it, until Gene stopped us and dragged me toward the decorative boulders at the edge of the park. We'd waited for the shriek again and followed the sound to a teeny kitten. He was stuck behind one of the boulders, tethered to a dingy rope, the other end wedged under one of the heavy stones. He was a scrawny thing with crusty, infected eyes, riddled with fleas. It was a pitiful sight.

We brought him home with us, and while Gene bathed him and ran a plastic comb through his fur, I ran out to the pet store and begged one of the employees to help me. Having never had a pet in my life, I had no idea what a cat needed. Kitten kibble, a litter box and kitty litter, a bed, a pet carrier, all this stuff I would have never found on my own. Gene named him Floyd, after her father's favorite architect, Frank Lloyd Wright. He's been healthy since, for at least eight years.

Today, when Susana and I got back from Gene's, we found little piles of cat vomit like breadcrumbs leading to the kitchen, with the last bit just in front of his bed, where he's been lying listless since.

Later, in the kitchen, comparing this week's tissue growth results from last month's findings, I stop to watch Susana parading in front of me in a new set of pajamas.

"Oh, those are cute," I say of the Disney-cast-studded pjs. "Did Mamá get you those?"

"No," she says looking down at her top-and-shorts combo. "Mamá said that Viv dropped them off the other night for me."

"Oh. Viv." I can't help the icy lilt coming through in my voice. Ugh, I can't stand myself.

"Floyd doesn't look good at all." Susana ambles over to him. I set my work aside and close my laptop before peering in their direction. She's sitting cross-legged next to Floyd's bed. Getting up from my barstool, I regard them for a moment. Water bowl full, food dish full, he hasn't eaten or drunk anything for hours. I grab my mini flashlight from my bag, walk over, and crouch down. Feeling his little square forehead, I pet behind his ears to see if I can get him to open his eyes. Nothing. His nose is dry and warm, all while his little belly moves up and down, but thankfully it's not distended.

"Can you call Mamá? Maybe she'll know what to do?" I glare at Susana with distain, but she's not facing me. As if. I'm the one with the PhD.

I get back up and grab my BlackBerry off the charger. If Susana wants her mother here, she shall have her mother here. Opening our message trail, I pop off four quick words.

ISA: Something's wrong with Floyd.

That's a bit cryptic, so I send a better follow up.

ISA: He's listless and has been on his little bed all day since yesterday.

"Okay. I sent her a text."

My phone rings three minutes later.

Gene and I walk into the kitchen, and the scene is just as I'd left it a moment ago to open the front door: Susana lying on the floor next to Floyd's little round bed.

"Yeah, he looks bad," Gene deadpans after petting his face. "I can take him to the vet in the morning, if you want, but I'll have to tell him what Floyd has gotten into." She peers up at me from her crouched position. She looks fantastic in her relaxed-fit hip-huggers, white V-neck T-shirt half-tucked in the front, and brown leather sneakers. It's been a while since I've seen her dressed up.

"He was out in the yard for a few hours yesterday. Maybe he ate a lizard, or something equally disgusting," I say.

"But you don't know for sure."

"No, Gene. I have no idea what he could have gotten into out there. Last night, he was howling in front of the sliding glass door, so I let him out. But then when he came back in, he was different. He went directly to his bed." I shake my watch face forward to check the time. "Since eight thirty last night. Then tonight, when we walked in, past all the barf I found on the floor, I noticed he hadn't eaten anything since yesterday. Susana begged me to call you, and here we are." Susana's eyebrows press together as she fixes me with a set of brown beady eyes.

"Has he thrown up?" Gene asks.

"Weren't you listening?" With a deep breath, I continue, "Yes, when we got back from the apartment tonight, there were a few small piles of cat vomit. And he was in his bed by the time we came in."

She touches his belly. "It's not tight or swollen," she says as I stare down at her, arms crossed, eyes rolling, foot tapping. "He's just warm, and his nose is dry. Animals usually have wet noses." *Yeah, no shit!* I purse my lips and chew on the inside of my mouth.

"It's nine thirty now. I can come back after dropping Susana off at school tomorrow morning and take him to the vet, unless you think he's too sick to wait," she says, giving Floyd a scratch under his chin, to which he responds with a yawning purr.

"Uh. I guess we can wait," I reply.

"Keep an eye on him tonight, and if he's not better by the time I get back from dropping this one off, I'll take him." Gene bobs her thumb in Susana's direction.

CHAPTER SEVENTEEN

Gene

"Roberto has asked me to marry him," Isa says. She and I are sitting side by side on the top bench of the hard aluminum bleachers, watching Susana's Saturday soccer game in the park. "He also wants to adopt her."

My heart beats furiously, and I start falling forty feet toward the ground. As I try to grab onto something, I stretch my foot, hoping to soften the landing, but with a violent jostle, I fall back in my bed, eyes wide open, heart thrashing in my throat. Eyes darting all over the room, I'm looking for something familiar, something grounding to fix my gaze on. Then I realize, with icy sweat trickling down my brow and my back, the thumping in my chest easing its pulse a bit, that I'm in my bedroom and not in the park. It was just a dream.

My visit with Isa to check on Floyd last night must have triggered this nightmare. Alone in my bed with no one to soothe this vitriol, I reach for my phone, and the display signals a blinding five thirty. Although I had less than a flute, the effects of last night's Champagne at the art show, before Isa's harried text message, is digging into my head with a screw the size of my arm. And since I promised Isa that I'd check in on Floyd this morning, I get out of bed and start my day.

I'm a little earlier than usual as I drive into my old space behind Isa's Land Cruiser. I scoop up my BlackBerry and call her, not wanting to intrude on their morning routine or run into a barely dressed Isa. When I get the okay from her, she opens the door and no one other than Floyd is bouncing off the floor, running to greet me. He's quick and scurries off when he decides he's done with my amorous petting, though, and makes playing with his tiny soccer ball his next amusement. It jingles as he slaps it toward the wall just outside the living room. A cackle escapes my lips at his seemingly speedy snapback.

"He threw up everything he's ever eaten in his life this morning." Isa points toward the kitchen. "When I got up, it was all over the kitchen, and I almost slid in it," she says with a shiver.

"Ah, so I guess it was something he ate."

"Apparently!"

"I better get going. I've got a ton of things to do when I get back to the apartment," I say after I hear Susana running down the stairs. I bend slightly at the waist to get a full hug from her. Never one to shy away from affection, she squeezes me tight.

"Ready?" she asks.

"Always."

To make up for ditching her at the art gallery last night, I promised Viv my homemade marinara sauce for dinner tonight. Between the hypnotic stirring and the aromatic scent of basil infused with tomato acid, plus the oregano I just threw in, my mind drifts to last night. The cat, my sympathetic daughter caressing his little beer gut, and Isa with her chin dimples, her sorrowful eyes, and enticing legs. How could I have forgotten those legs? Those powerful legs squeezing my head when she's had enough, walking toward me, walking away from me, straddling me…

The doorbell's brassy ding startles me from my somnolence. I run my hands under the faucet's icy water, then dry them on the dishtowel ever draped over my shoulder as I peer through the window to find Isa standing on the other side.

I open the door enough to invite her inside. "Hi." Her vanilla scent overpowers the tomato and basil odor in the apartment. It stirs my senses, and I'm pulled behind Isa as though I were a butterfly, conspicuously fluttering about, waiting to feed on her pollen. I inhale deeply, filling my lungs with the nectar that spills from her. I've forgotten all about Viv, the sauce, and Susana, tucked away in her bedroom, busy with homework. My only focus is what I have before me. Isa in her office clothes—a navy pencil skirt, a silky yellow chiffon blouse, and her weighty red laptop bag she'd rather die carrying than leave in the car. The clicking of her heels makes me wish I were spread over the floor instead of the herringbone-patterned wood flooring. She gently places her laptop bag on the barstool and turns to meet my eyes.

"Let me get Susana," I say as my arid mouth longs for a sip of something refreshing. Lemonade comes to mind.

"You're making your marinara?" she says, peering into the kitchen. Stretching on the balls of her feet, calves bunching up, her heels sliding out of her stilettos. Those stilettos.

"Mm-hmm." I leave her and amble through the hallway.

"Susanita," I whisper from her cracked door. "Mami's here."

Susana glances up at me and with her index finger, gives me the "be right there" sign, so I disappear back into the hall and check on the sauce.

A moment later, Susana shoots out of her room and almost crashes into an expectant Isa.

"I have to pick up my room," she says to her mother, bypassing a proper greeting. I'm a bit embarrassed by her informality, but that's how Isa grew up, too. Nothing to do with how my parents raised me. It was always "yes, Mamá" or "gracias, Papá," and always with the highest respect for each.

Isa ignores Susana's impertinence as she vanishes into the hall again. Disregarding her watchful eye, I turn into the kitchen, check to see that the sauce is right, and begin dumping cooking utensils in the sink, making a holy racket in the process.

Isa sidles up to the peninsula. "Is your friend coming over? Making a Valentine's dinner?" Her ability for snide, sarcastic comments she inherited from Carlos. He was always a shrewd businessman, and while he did well for himself, his blunt nature always irked me. Regretfully, he passed this trait all the way down to Susana, who views tact as a waste of time.

I don't lie to Isa. Why should I? But I just nod my assent. Isa remains silent, eyes lingering toward the hallway. Conversations between us have been limited to details of the house, the cat, and Susana. We've disconnected our lives from each other, neither wishing to know the minute details. I certainly don't. The only thing I know about Roberto is what Isa has told me, and that they've been dating for the past seven months.

"Susanita," Isa hollers. "Let's go, Mamá needs to prepare for the company she's having."

I stop everything, dry my hands on the dishtowel, and throw it on the peninsula.

"Let's go outside for a second," I say with a blank stare, placid as a flat lake.

Before joining Isa outside, I march up to Susana's room to find her straightening the little mess she'd made with her homework, drawing a smile on my face. Before I forget why I'm here, I say, "Mami and I are going to be outside. Just come out when you're ready to go home, okay, cariño?"

When she nods, I make my way back into the living room, catching Isa through the window, already outside, lugging her laptop bag. She glances at her watch and folds her arms over her chest. I step outside and touch the door to its frame.

"This is really none of your business," I say. "But Viv and I are just friends. She's been nothing but kind to me, and I'm giving this friendship a chance to flourish. When I meet someone who I'd like to date, and I'm ready to introduce her to Susana, I'll let you know. For now, all I ask is that you give me the same space to have my own life as I've given you."

As I utter my last words, Susana dashes out the door, taking Isa with her. "Let's go, I have to finish my homework."

"Hey," I call out to Susana. "¿Adios, no?" And just as I lean over a bit, Susana thrusts herself in my arms for a wholehearted goodbye hug and kisses.

They walk off and Isa turns back to face me, contrite. Susana tugs at her hand, and with a wink and a chuckle, I yell, "That's your kid."

To subdue my thirst, I take hefty gulps of freshly poured ice water. The pasta sauce is done and simmering, so I busy myself drawing the front elevation for my next project. The county has changed its code, again, ergo county hall needs a fresh façade. It's up to me to come up with something good, pretty, and cheap—if only life were as clear-cut.

Just as my eraser devours yet another ill-placed line, the doorbell yelps to life. It's past eight, and I'm starving. Five minutes isn't going to kill me, but it'd be nice if Viv would be punctual, even if it's only once. Her wide-eyed grin clutches at my heart when I open the door. Grasping a brown paper grocery bag in the air, the aroma of freshly baked bread, if my nose is correct, wafts in the air.

"I baked bread," she touts, holding the bag aloft for me to take, a Cheshire cat grin spreading over her face.

"Thanks?" I cock an eyebrow and take the bag, whose iconic La Pasteleria logo is emblazoned on the front as she strolls inside with a perfunctory air about her.

"I'm kidding!" she says. "I ordered it from the bakery nearby so it would be ready when I was finished at the hospital. Where's the wine I brought the other night?" Dashing toward the kitchen, Viv opens the junk drawer and extracts the corkscrew. I stand bewildered at how quickly she's managed to feel at home in the apartment. *I haven't even started feeling at home here.* I shuffle my feet getting to the wine and hand Viv the bottle.

"Glasses?" she requests. I take a step to the other side of the kitchen, grab the wineglasses, and place them on the already-set dining room table.

"Fancy." She gestures with her chin toward the table.

"Anything else you can think of that we might need?" I ask.

"I think this about covers it." She rips open the bag containing the hot bread, toasted fennel seeds perfuming the air.

We eat in tepid silence as I do a bit of mental spelunking for an explanation of my disappearing act last night. Jay had been there, too. And when I received Isa's texts, Viv had gone off somewhere with the artist. I'd left word with Jay to relay to Viv, whose terse message this morning had been anything but understanding.

Interruptions aside, Viv's been doing all the questioning, and I've been doing all the answering, but for now, I'm still figuring her out. I'm curious to know what she thinks of dinner, as she takes her time rolling the pappardelle on her fork, gently slipping the flat pasta in her mouth. She smiles, happily chewing.

"This is delicious," she says, before swallowing. "What exactly are we eating?"

"The sauce is a basil and oregano marinara, and the pasta is pappardelle. I just call it pappardelle marinara."

"Well…it's so yummy," she says, chewing on another forkful.

"Thank you." I try not to cringe. "The sauce usually takes a few hours to make, so I started cooking feverishly as soon as I got home with Susana after school."

"Is she here every day?" Viv asks.

"Yes."

"But she doesn't actually stay overnight every day?"

"It depends," I say. We've never talked about my routine with Susana. "We alternate weeks. So, she'll stay over starting next Thursday through to the following Thursday afternoon. But I pick her up after school every day and bring her here to do her homework. Then, on Isa's week to have Susana, she picks her up here after she gets out of work."

"Wow, that seems complicated."

"Having lived in a household with both parents myself, I wanted to make things as seamless as possible for Susana when Isa and I separated. It was difficult at first and certainly now that Isa has apparently moved on with her life it's tricky, but I'll put up with all of it to see my daughter every day.

"That's what's important to me. So, if it means that I have no choice but to see my ex on the days I don't keep Susana, so be it. Anyone I will eventually date will also need to get used to the routine."

Viv takes another bite. "You're a great cook. Do you cook every day?"

"When Susana stays with me, we cook together. The nights Isa picks her up, I eat leftovers. Isa likes to cook for Susana when they're together. But sometimes when she works late, I'll make enough food for all of us and then pack up their portions, so they can have dinner together at the house."

"That's another mouthful."

"Sorry, am I talking about Isa too much?"

Viv continues rolling pasta on her fork, avoiding eye contact. "No, it's fine."

"It's important to me that there's peace when we interact," I continue. "Especially with Susana around. I don't want her growing up thinking that her parents hate each other. We never had before, so why would we start now?" I draw my fork to my mouth. Viv quietly chews, tearing off a piece of sliced bread.

"You know," she says, mouth full of dry bread. "I've met women who have wanted to start a family and women who were adamant about not having one at all, but I've never known anyone separated with kids."

"Yeah, me either."

Viv snaps up her wineglass, twirls it, and takes a sip. "How did you come up with this tidy custody plan, if you don't mind my asking?"

"Well," I say, picking my own wineglass. "We drew up palimony papers in case we ever broke up, and our lawyer set up a trust for my assets and a will for Isa. Her will gives me guardianship over Susana if anything happens to her. The trust makes Isa and Susana inheritors of my estate."

"You're not her biological mother, I take it?" She takes another sip.

"No," I reply. "And before you ask, yes, not being related to her puts a damper on my situation."

"Are you afraid that the doctor will want to adopt her if he and Isa get married?"

My knee automatically starts bouncing under the dining room table, the balls of my feet propelling my heel. The nightmare, where Isa tells me she's marrying Roberto and he's adopting Susana, is an almost nightly occurrence.

"Look," I say. "It's occurred to me. I'm not naïve. Months turn into years, and couples move in together and establish a family. It's all I've been thinking about for the last seven months, since Isa told me about the doctor." Blood slowly drains from my face and I'm getting a bit lightheaded.

"But you're not on her birth certificate, or anything, are you? Because I read somewhere there's a couple in Orlando hoping to add both their names on their kid's birth certificate."

Happy to be talking about something other than Isa's love life, I barrel forward. "We're helping three couples with adoptions. We have a gay couple petitioning the state to adopt their two foster sons—they were married in New York. Then those two lesbians you mentioned, they were married in Massachusetts, but they live in Sarasota, Florida. They got pregnant by intrauterine insemination—the same method we had used for Susana—and want to add both their names to the birth certificate. The last one is a lesbian couple from Destin. One of them had a daughter through IVF when she was single. By the time she met her partner, her daughter was two years old. They got married in Ontario and are hoping to petition for second-parent adoption."

"And where do you fit in all of that?" Ice burns the length of my spine as I imagine a world where I *fit* perfectly.

I sigh loudly. "I'm not sure where I stand right now. Isa didn't want to get married when same-sex marriage became legal in Spain. Since I'm a Spanish citizen with a legal residence in Jerez, it would have only been a matter of signing some papers to get a second-parent adoption approved over there. The wait is only a few months, I think. The only caveat being that we would have had to live in Spain while we waited.

"I lost all hope that she would ever marry me, so I left and decided to fight for my equal right to parent Susana. But the key difference between the couples Equality Miami is supporting and my case is that they were all legally married somewhere. In states where same-sex marriage is legal, most married couples can get parental recognition when they adopt or when one of them gives birth and the other is the nonbiological parent." I take a sip of wine. My shaking leg comes to a stop.

"The hope is that once marriage equality becomes law in all fifty states, all the rights and benefits associated with marriage would also apply to married same-sex couples. But don't forget, there's a ban on adoptions by gays and lesbians in this state, so we're trying to lift that first. And then we'll focus on marriage equality. We want the Children and Family Services department to reject each petition for adoption so we can sue the state for infringement on equal protection. It's the only way a judge will rule the ban to be unconstitutional. And then the state will have no choice but to lift the ban in the legislature and allow gays and lesbians to adopt children."

"Wow, that sounds like a lengthy process," she says.

"Yes," I reply, my eyes darting around the room. "It is and the wait has been unimaginable. But we've been working hard to get to this point, and I believe it's only a matter of time."

After dinner, Viv helps me store the leftovers, load the dishwasher, and wipe down the countertops and the dining room table. With all the cleaning done, Viv follows me, with both wineglasses, to the couch. I take the left side, close to the corner of the couch, and Viv wedges herself between me and what's left of the corner. Instinctively, I inch over the other way to give her—and myself—space. She hands me my wineglass and leans back into me. I stiffen a bit, hoping she doesn't notice as we sip what's left of the wine. It tingles my upper lip and seems to pacify my mood.

I cross my left leg over my right knee, and Viv places her palm over it. I can feel the heat of her hand through my jeans and onto my skin. My heartbeat is riotous in my ears, watching her hand inch its way up my thigh. I take another shaky sip of wine, further dulling my awareness.

Viv takes a final sip, cups my glass, and places it, along with hers, on the coffee table. She leans back into my arm and immediately puts her hands on my neck, slides them through my curls, and pulls me toward her lips. The touch is comforting and relaxes all my nerve endings. But then her lips come closer to my face, and I feel her blistering breath on me.

Aside from a friendly peck on the cheeks, we've never been this close. I've made my feelings clear, but as I realize now, she's been trying to coax me into intimacy. The frigid electricity running up my spine is paralyzing.

Tito Horacio's voice is in my head, when he told me, "Un clavo saca otro clavo," after I told him about Viv. It's a Spanish saying and it's all I've been thinking since mentioning it the other day over the phone. But can one nail really drive out another? What if this one doesn't? Will sleeping with Viv drive Isa out of my veins?

Isa is the only one I've ever kissed. How am I supposed to start kissing someone else? But before I can pull away, Viv gently places her lips on mine. Her lips are soft and moist, and I convince myself to go with it.

She opens her mouth for me, and I sink into her, cupping her face in my hands and deepening the kiss. The oakiness of the red wine on Viv's lips seeps into my pores. Her hands are everywhere fast: in my hair, scratching my scalp, my back. They run down the side seams of my shirt, and I barely notice when she tugs at it, pulling it out of my jeans. Isa slips her hands under it and runs her fingers up my back with featherlight pressure, which I do notice because it's too much, it's too quick, too aggressive. I flinch from her touch and my neck stiffens. Isa. For an instant, I was sinking into Isa's arms. It had been Isa's lips on my neck, her tongue at the base of my throat.

Before I regret going further, I pull away and scoot backward on the couch.

"Viv," I say, my throat drier than cracked clay. "I can't do this," I croak, scooting farther away, giving myself a respite. "I'm sorry, but I just can't." I motion with my hands, slapping them on my knees as I stand.

"You can't or you don't want to?" Viv protests from the couch.

I turn to face her. "What's the difference?" After a beat, I continue, "I don't know. Both? I can't because it wouldn't be fair to you. And I don't want to hurt you." I pause because I want to be mindful with what I say next. She doesn't need to know I was thinking of Isa. "Viv, I like you. I really do. You're smart, funny, and I feel great around you." Her hopeful smile sinks into my stomach.

"That's good, right?" she insists. "That you feel great around me."

"Yes, but someone else is still here." I point at my chest. "Whether it's all the time or some of the times, she still fills this space. I thought I made that clear from the beginning."

"I know, and I'm sorry," she replies. "I was just in the moment. Don't tell me you didn't feel it, too?"

"I did," I say. "Of course, I did. But it won't erase the consequences of what might have happened in five minutes." One gaze at her eyes assures me this can go no further. I sit beside Viv and reach for her hand.

"Having sex with you will not cure my sixteen-year relationship heartbreak. I'm still coming to grips with my reality here."

"Right." Viv pulls her hand from my grasp. "Got it. I should have been more careful. I'm sorry."

"Can we be friends. For real, now?" I ask.

"Just friends?" she asks. "You don't want to give sex a little chance? I've never gotten complaints before."

I chuckle. "I'm sure you haven't, but you've said it yourself, indecisive exes have burned you. Isa may not be indecisive, but I still do have feelings for her, and sleeping with you won't erase them."

Viv purses her lips. "Yeah. You're right." She stands. "I'm gonna get going. I'll call you tomorrow and we can make plans if you want." She's walking toward the door.

It takes a bit but I remember I'm phone-banking tomorrow night, after Isa picks up Susana. Standing to walk her out, I tell her, "Listen, how about I call you on Wednesday?" She turns to me. Her doe-eyed gleam makes me feel awful, but the distance will give her some time to cool off.

Viv nods with a touch of her lips on both my cheeks. She pockets her phone, pulls out her keys, and walks out the door.

CHAPTER EIGHTEEN

Isa

"Isabel!" The harsh voice and simultaneous thunderous knock drill through my office door. "Meeting in the conference room in fifteen minutes." Dr. Peterson, whirling around pathology like a hurricane, is summoning all his lead biomedical engineers.

"What's going on with him?" Cami asks, peering through my door. She's juggling two mugs of hot tea and a copy of *Biomedical Today*.

"Not sure yet." I stand and reach for one of the mugs. "Must be another funding announcement. I wonder who's laying down another eleven million today?"

She holds up the magazine. "Well, I hope it doesn't have anything to do with this." The Chief Biomedical Engineer at Broward Medical Research Hospital gleams the cover with another apparent breakthrough. *Mother of fucking pearl!*

"Have you read it?"

"Yes, another breakthrough. But this time in lymphoma using a therapeutic produced using embryonic stem cells."

"Shit, that's huge," I say. "How long did it take them?"

"Four years," Cami answers.

"That's...that's really fast." She nods and drops the magazine on my desk. Snagging the publication up, I lean back in my squeaky chair and skim through the forty-five-page article.

"You know," I say, flipping through to one of many images of Dr. Renée Ezra. I fold back the one that shows her whole team and turn it to show Cami. "She did her doctoral research here." I point at Dr. Ezra. "I was her supervisor seven years ago. When she completed her PhD, Dr. Peterson disregarded my recommendation to offer her a research position here. He didn't think she was the right 'fit' for this research hospital and didn't offer her the position. But I see Broward, apparently, did." I lay the magazine back down on the desk. "I went behind his back and wrote her a recommendation letter."

"He's disgusting, how do you put up with him?" Cami asks. "In fact, how did he even hire you? The man hates women." *Yeah, that's not all he hates.*

I smirk at Cami. "He wasn't the one who hired me. That was my supervisor, Dr. Henry Cohen, who at the time was the Chief Biomedical Engineer."

"What happened to him?" she asks.

"He died of a massive heart attack."

"Oh. Damn. I'm sorry," she says.

"Thanks," I reply, glancing at my watch. I stand, sending my office chair crashing against the wall, select a good pen from a holder of fountain pens Gene has given me through the years, and grab my notebook—also supplied by Gene. "Sorry, I've got to get going to this meeting."

"Good luck," she hollers as I step past her.

I throw her a "Thanks" over my shoulder.

Dr. Peterson stands by the conference room table, speaking in low tones with Dr. Amos, the lead biomedical engineer for the Alzheimer's research group. Dr. Amos is all smiles as Dr. Peterson pats his shoulder. Unable to hear anything they say, I walk past them to grab an empty seat next to Dr. Rams, the team lead in developing therapeutics for respiratory infections.

Dr. Amos takes his seat next to Dr. Peterson's chair and waits for the meeting to begin. I glance at my colleagues around the room, not another female among them. The chatter of opinions and suppositions dies down as Dr. Peterson takes his chair at the head of the table.

"Gentlemen," Peterson announces. He locks eyes with me. "And Isabel, of course." His smirk leaves the tips of my ears boiling as I imagine my hands squeezing his neck. I sit back in my stiff boardroom chair, glowering at him. "Let's get to business, shall we?

"Due to the fact that Broward Medical Research Hospital had a major breakthrough in cancer research with their new lymphoma therapy," Peterson begins with one of his quintessential verbose intros. "The state of Florida has decided to increase the funds they allocate for cancer research statewide. With the shortfall of benefactors this spring, I've decided to focus on one major research avenue. However, the funding won't come in until the state's next fiscal year, so you all have three months to tie up loose ends in your fields and focus on a cancer specific to your fields." His statement is met with a symphony of groans and protests.

"Dr. Peterson, I'm sorry, but many of us are amid consequential breakthroughs in our own research. You can't let the state dictate how we distribute our research grants." That was Dr. Rams. Peterson doesn't flinch.

"Dr. Rams, and the rest of you, listen up. Changes are coming. With the eleven million we're receiving, the hospital has approved a new Alzheimer's research wing." Dr. Amos, the only one applauding, tucks his hands under the table.

"Dr. Peterson." I raise my voice to get his flagging attention. "I agree that cancer research deserves a significant increase in funding—it affects nearly two million people in the United States alone. I'm sure our engineers who are already focusing on cancer would appreciate more funds immensely. However, what the rest of us do is of equal importance in our own fields. For instance, my research, which deals in the development of heart valves using human tissue—as an alternative to animal heart valves—to replace artificial mechanical heart valves that calcify inside the body and lead to premature death, is also pivotal for heart patients. As studies have shown, heart disease is the number one cause of death among women. It's the silent killer. And besides, I thought only a portion of that eleven million was slated for Alzheimer's."

"Isabel, I invite you to make arrangements in order to meet with me at a later time, where we'll be able to talk about your research funding prospects," he says. I lean back in my chair, sliding my notebook with me. Turning the pages until I come to an empty one, I write out the word *ASSHOLE* all caps, in neat block letters.

"As I was saying," Peterson continues. "Many of you know…"

CHAPTER NINETEEN

Gene

Jay, sitting at the end of the long conference table at the Equality Miami headquarters, wraps her knuckles against it. "Folks. Let's get to our seats, we have a great deal to cover tonight." She raises her voice at the end because everyone is still milling around. Located on the third floor of an art deco building, facing Biscayne Bay, what the office lacks in function, the building more than makes up for with its view. Late nights are whimsical, staring past the placid water of the bay toward the dazzling lights of Miami Beach's skyline. It almost makes up for the 1970s donated office furniture, held together by duct tape and staples; the elementary school linoleum floors, peeling off in more than one area; and the musty, retirement home scent.

Swiftly getting to my chair, I remove my notebook and fountain pen from my backpack, ready for board of directors' president, Salo Ibañez, to start the meeting. He waits patiently for everyone else on the eleven-member board to take their seats. It's like herding cats just to get everyone settled.

"Everyone ready?" Salo knocks his fist on the table. "Okay, let's begin. I'm calling the board meeting to order on this first day of June, 2007. Before I begin, does anyone have new business to bring forth?" Salo glances across the table at each of us and waits. When no one replies, he continues.

"I'm going to let Jay take the helm tonight since there are a few developments in the court cases we're following. Jay?" Salo turns his face toward her, points to the chair behind him, and shuffles to the other end of the table.

"Thank you, Salo," she says with a nod. She sits and folds her hands over the table. "Up first is the Gill case. In January, the state rejected Mark Gill and his partner's petition to adopt their two foster boys the state placed in their care three years ago. Last year, the judge terminated parental rights for the boys' biological parents. The case is now in the Eleventh Judicial Circuit Court of Florida, right here in Miami-Dade County." Jay taps the table for effect. "This organization is partnering with the ACLU to gather evidence to support the foster parents' claim that they are model parents. There's no date set for the trial, but we're very close." The applause and table-pounding reverberate around the room as her lips curl and chest puffs.

With my nose tingling, the scent of excitement is in the air. And instead of jotting down notes, I'm nervously strumming the corners of the pages in my notebook with my thumb and index finger. Snapping out of my trance, I write down today's date, so I can keep track of the time this case will take to get resolved. A positive ruling might mean an adoption for my seven-year-old.

"This is amazing!" Salo chimes in, clapping his hands together. He and his partner, Fausto, have been waiting to adopt but haven't begun the process. "What do we do until the court rules on this case?"

Jay stands, leaning her hands over the table. "We must stay the course. Fundraise, fundraise, fundraise. The Gill case is one of a long list of cases to be heard before the Circuit Court." She backs up to the easel and flips the page, revealing the bullet points of the plan. "We'd like to plan some workshops and luncheons to update the community about what we're doing. This is the strategy the fundraising committee developed to get us through to next summer."

After discussing other pressing matters, Salo adjourns the meeting. I busy myself packing up my backpack when I hear Jay calling my name.

"G," Jay says from behind the divider that separates the conference table from her desk. "Can you stay for a few minutes? I'd like to discuss something with you."

I nod and zip up my bag. Jay is standing at her desk, riffling through her mail.

"Jay." I hold out my hand for her to shake.

"Get over here." She wraps her arms around my body. With her warm smile and inviting demeanor, despite her Cuban heritage, she doesn't greet me with a customary air kiss to one cheek that I had grown accustomed to in Miami. Instead, she welcomes me with open arms, enveloping me in a warm embrace that instantly puts me at ease. It's as if she's known me for years, and I'm drawn in by her immense kindness.

"I wanted to chat about…uh, your family," she says. "And I hate to use your situation as a science project of sorts. I know your issue is different from the ones we're presenting, there must be many co-parenting couples in the community like you and your ex."

I nod at her and simply say, "Okay." I trust that she'll have something enlightening to say.

"Do you have time to grab dinner? I want to go over all this with you, and I'm starving. There's a great restaurant on 71st Street I think you'll love."

"Oh, really?"

"Yes, it's a tapas bar." She winks. My growling stomach reminds me that lunch was anything but a forgone conclusion and breakfast might as well have happened yesterday, so I bob my head enthusiastically.

"Do you want to ride with me?" I ask. "I don't mind dropping you back off here later."

"Sure, let me just sort through all this mail over here," she says, stacking the envelopes that had been strewn about her desk into one neat pile. "And there you go." She points at her masterpiece and says, "I'm ready!"

In all the months that I've been coming to headquarters, I've never noticed this restaurant. Although it takes us five minutes to get here, I'm relegated to weaving through the nearby streets in this urban jungle, looking for a good parking spot for the Jeep.

One glance at the building's façade, you'd think it's any American restaurant on the ground floor of a residential building. The interior of El Toro Restaurant, however, is another story. With its rustic cave-like walls—stucco probably—black wrought iron light fixtures and accessories, matador capes and hats hanging on hooks, and two bull's heads with necks and humps still stuck with pikes and pujas hang like trophies on either side of the room, watching over the patrons like gods—it's all a bit over the top, but I'm game. The scent of traditional Spanish tapas lingers as well: patatas bravas, pimientos de Padrón, and croquetas de jamón iberico. The place is brimming with foodies while in the background, Rocío Dúrcal belts out the chorus to her beloved torch song "La Gata Bajo la Lluvia" as they dine.

"Wow, this place is something." I'm astonished as soon as we walk in, my eyes absorbing the scene before me.

Jay winks, trying to cover up her smug I-told-you-so face. "I thought you might like it. But I won't mind if you do all the ordering."

To share, I order a half carafe of Rioja, gambas al ajillo, chorizo al vino, perfectly shaved slices of jamon iberico with artisanal bread, and a thick slice of tortilla española—that's just to start. The fresh aroma of the garlic slowly simmering in olive oil reminds me of a time when I didn't have to worry about parenthood—or heartbreak, for that matter.

Slowly savoring the intoxicating red wine, I refill Jay's glass. "How long has this place been here?" I'm surprised that such a place exists outside of Coral Gables, the home of so many wonderful Spanish restaurants. "I've never heard of it."

Jay glances up at the ceiling. "It's been here for a while, and it's always packed."

"The true testament of a good restaurant." I laugh and pick up my wineglass. "Do you live around here?" It suddenly dawns on me that I barely know anything about Jay.

"Mmm," she hums, popping a gamba in her mouth. "I live a bit north of here. Eastern Shores, to be exact."

"Wow, that's a hundred blocks away from headquarters."

"Yeah, but I'm going against traffic, so the commute is a cinch in the morning. So, as I was saying before," she says, holding her fork, ready to dive into the sausages. "I think you should petition Children and Family Services to adopt your daughter as her second parent."

"You sure do get right down to business." My laugh forces the wine down the wrong way. She wiggles her eyebrows and bites down on the piece of sausage pierced on the end of her fork. I tear off another piece of bread and dip it in the remaining juices of the shrimp and garlic and slip it in my mouth. The garlic-infused olive oil is like an orgasm for my taste buds.

"Oh bread!" I rave with satisfaction. "A day without bread to dip in all this Spanish goodness is like a day without oxygen." What I don't say out loud is that it's more like a day without Isa.

I wipe my garlic-oil-laden lips with my napkin. "Sorry, I got a little carried away. Okay, but wait." I pause, repeating my bread-dipping ritual. "I thought Isa and I had to be married for the second-parent adoption to be approved."

"Every case is different," she replies. All this lawyer-speak is in riddles, or maybe I just don't understand her nuance. Or it could be this wine that's whirling my brain, the hipster atmosphere that makes it hard to hear, or the exquisite food with which I'm stuffing my face that distracts me.

I wait for a beat and take another sip of wine. "What do you mean?"

"I think your best course is to have your lawyer draw up an affidavit stating that your ex gives consent for you to legally adopt Susana as her second parent, with her signature, of course. You'd prove to the state of Florida that married straight couples aren't the only ones who can have children. As it is with straight people, we're not always coupled up when it comes time to parenting children. You have every right to want to be recognized as one of Susana's parents, despite your separation."

"But what about my ex?" I swallow hard.

"Don't worry about…Isa, right?" she asks with a pause.

"Yes, Isa. Susana's biological mother," I reply.

"Well, Isa's parental rights will never be affected. You're only going to petition the court to be Susana's second legal parent. How old is your daughter?"

I mindlessly break off another piece of bread. "Just turned seven. If Isa signs this affidavit, then what?"

"Then your lawyer will file the petition, along with the affidavit, to Family and Child Services, asking to grant you a second-parent adoption. And unless you're declared unfit, you should have the same parental rights as Isa," Jay says.

"If I petition the courts now, what happens if I'm denied? Isa will want all the details before she signs anything."

"Well, in that case, which is the likely scenario," she says, "we will take the state to court. That's the point here, G. The court is where we fight for our rights." Her confidence is dizzying.

"Right," I say, unsure how I'd present this to Isa. "Isa won't want public scrutiny, though. These court cases, they're a matter of public record, aren't they?"

"They are, but what's more important? Having parental rights for your child or saving Isa from possible public embarrassment? She will have to accept that your sixteen-plus-year relationship produced a child—at her behest, I might add. And you have every right to be recognized as that child's parent. Especially since you were pretty much the sole provider for the first two years of Susana's life."

"There's a problem, though," I say with a bit of trepidation. I'd rather not mention this, but it's going to come out.

Jay cuts into the thick Spanish omelet wedge. "What's that?" She pops the morsel in her mouth, and her eyes clench shut. She takes a deep breath, and exhales pure satisfaction. Eggs, onions, and potato—who knew this combination of bland, stand-alone ingredients would turn out so savory?

"Isa is dating someone who, I'm afraid, will hamper my chances of adopting Susana." I say the phrase as quick as possible before it leaves a sour taste in my mouth.

"How's that?" she asks, putting her fork down and wrapping her fingers around her wineglass. "If she didn't marry you because she was afraid of public attention, what's wrong with her dating another woman?"

"That's the thing." I take a sip of my wine. "She's dating a man."

"Oh, I see." With a frown, Jay lets go of her glass and leans in closer to me. "I'm sorry about that." She pauses for a few moments to gather her thoughts, I assume.

"How long have they been dating?"

I swallow the knot in my throat. "I don't know, little less than a year, maybe." It's a lie. I know they've been dating eleven months. But if I say it out loud, then it's real.

"Has Isa given any indication that she wants this man to adopt Susana?" Jay's last words send a shudder through my body, curdling my blood, but I disguise my uneasiness by popping another chorizo in my mouth, almost gagging in the process.

"She hasn't," I admit. "But look, Isa is a catch. Anyone with half a brain will want to marry her. And unfortunately, that's what I've been fearing will happen." Choking on my own words, I stop and gulp down water, lifting my glass slightly, locking eyes with the woman going around the restaurant with the water jug to refill. With an uncontrollable shaky hand, I place the glass back on the table. "As time goes on, the possibility of Isa marrying this guy becomes more of a certainty, and I'm afraid to lose them both."

"Both?" Jay puts her hand over mine and squeezes, her unwavering support uplifting. It's a bit gratifying because I haven't spoken to anyone about this, and it's been consuming me.

"Yes, because if Isa marries a man, I...I'll cease to exist for her, and more worrisome, I'll cease to exist for Susana." My voice shakes just as intensely as my hand.

"Look, I don't know Isa, right, but I don't think you should worry about this for now. Let's take it one step at a time. Talk to her and see if she'll agree to give you permission to adopt Susana. That's the first hurdle, G. This is going to be a long and arduous process, so get the ball rolling with Isa and we'll decide the rest later. You can't beat yourself up without even knowing what she thinks."

"Okay," I say with a sniffle. "I'll ask her. Thanks so much for your advice, Jay."

"You know," Jay says, boring me with her clear eyes. "I really admire you."

"You do?" I ask.

"I could never be a mother."

"Why not?"

"Because you have to have ovaries of steel to take care of another human being. Especially the ones who can't take care of themselves."

"What do you mean?"

"I run," she says. I should have known. "One day, I took my sister's kid—my niece Gabby. I took her to one of my 5K runs. They had like a kid's dash type deal. My sister was with us, I forgot to mention. Anyway, while I zipped through my course, they waited at the finish line for me. When I was done, it was my niece's turn to race. Now, she was only five at the time and my sister left me watching her do the race.

"Kids five and older were supposed to run by themselves, and parents were able to accompany their smaller kids. But the distance wasn't far at all, it was like five cones, and the kids ran around the cones. It was maybe a tenth of a mile long. Well, my sister was off at one of the kiosks getting beer, and I was watching little Gabby getting ready at the start line next to some husky six-year-old kids. Gabby's a wiry kid, medium height, but she's lithe. Then I see her standing across the start line with her big, brilliant grin and brand-new sneakers, with all these bigger kids crowding her and I freaked out. When the start horn sounded for their race, she was off like a little puppy. Then, these bigger kids started to edge her off the path, and I was pulling my hair out of my scalp watching all this unfold. Well, I got pissed at these bigger kids—and the whole organization of this thing. From the minute she started until the minute she crossed the finish line, my eyes were lasered on her with my heart in my throat. I stopped breathing, I was sweating, and my hands were shaking…I was a real mess. And Gabby was running, unaware of her surroundings."

I stare at her with a crooked grin. "Well, that's how I feel every day of my life since Susana was born."

"I know! That shit is stressful. I just don't know how you or anyone else does it. I was afraid these kids were going to kill her."

"So, what happened?"

"Nothing happened. She finished the race as happy as a fly in honey, a sweaty little mess. Meanwhile, those ten minutes added like a thousand gray hairs to my head."

"Ha!"

Jay finishes the last of the chorizo and wipes her lips with her napkin. "But look, about your case, it's more than advice I'm giving you, Gene. Take it as friendly guidance from someone who cares about you." She shines her boisterous smile at me. "Now, let's enjoy what's left of this scrumptious food."

CHAPTER TWENTY

Isa

"¡Isa, cálmate!"

"Mami, that little girl is unbridled. She's attacking Susana out there!" My voice has ticked up a few octaves as I watch someone else's untethered kid take out her aggression on my daughter on the soccer pitch.

"Mi cielo, it's only practice," Mami says, pointing at the field. "The girl covering Susana is supposed to body check her, it's how Susana improves. Look see, now they're moving on to another activity. You were right, this is fun! Thanks for getting me out of the house." Mami claps her hands and cheers anytime Susana is near the soccer ball.

"Yeah, sure thing," I reply. "If I'd have known that Susana's soccer habit would be this violent, I would've never let Gene sign her up for the league. How dare she miss this barbarous event?"

"Well, it's the opening night of the film festival. She's only trying to get out there and meet other, you know…lesbians."

"Yeah, well, I hate it," I reply and nearly slap my mouth shut. "I mean because now she's missing all this." And just as I point toward the field, I stare in utter horror as Susana leaps up for an apparent header. Oof. It's the move she's been practicing since she became interested in soccer. Goddamn Gene and her insistence on watching women's soccer with Susana and that Abby Wambach with her fucking effortless headers. Susana wouldn't want to try any of this if she hadn't seen Abby do it first.

"Susana! Watch the..." I scream. And then my body tenses, like an angry cat ready to pounce. My hackles spike up. "Susana?" She and another player slam heads and fall to the ground. *Fuck!* A blaring whistle goes off. At a breakneck speed, I'm off the bleachers. The coach, Mami, and I run toward the two girls, pushing past the other parents, and I fall on my knees beside Susana.

"Susana? Bebé? Bebé?" She's clutching her head, eyes clenched, feet shaking. "Give her room!" I scream to the gathering crowd. These fucking people!

"Mami, my head," she whimpers.

"Okay, try not to move. Baby, how's your stomach?"

"I feel...I feel..." She groans before rolling to her side and hurling. Knees to her chest, arms at her head, everything that went in her is shooting out onto the grass.

"Mami," I yell, throwing her my car keys. They bounce around a bit over her palms before she grasps a steady hold of them. "Grab my car and get it as close as you can to the field. We've gotta take her to the hospital." Mami is out of my sight before I can attend to Susana's retching body.

"Bebé, I'm going to pick you up, okay?"

"Mami, it hurts."

"Here, let me help you with her." Coach Jorge moves parents out of the way. "Everyone, please give her some space."

In the distance, I hear Mami screeching my tires to a halt just inside the park fence, as far as she dared enter. I watch as she runs toward the back passenger side door and opens it while Jorge swiftly walks toward her with Susana in his arms.

"Coral Gables Medical Center has the best kid's trauma unit," he says. "We've been there a dozen times with Emma."

"Thank you," I say, jumping into the back seat with Susana as Mami speeds off. I reach for my BlackBerry that I shoved just inside the waistband of my tights and immediately dial Gene.

CHAPTER TWENTY-ONE

Gene

"We don't need to hurry," Viv says as she digs into the eggplant parmesan, a new recipe I found online. She snagged us a couple of tickets to the opening-night party of the Gay and Lesbian International Film Festival. So, I thought, what better way to thank her than to try a new recipe on her? "The doors don't open for another two hours."

"I'm a little nervous," I admit.

"Why?" she asks, her fork midway to her mouth.

"I guess because this is a public event, with the media, cameras everywhere, I'm not used to prying eyes. I feel as though what we've been doing all these months has been bar-hopping around town, going from happy hour to happy hour. And it just so happens that lesbians are in attendance."

"You had said that Isa wasn't out, or was it that she didn't identify as a lesbian?"

"Both," I say. I think about it for a second. "But mostly because of Isa's work. It's a bit more problematic than that. Being with Isa for half my life, I learned how to be with her in ways that wouldn't out us—or her, rather. We spent most of our time alone at home. There's a lot of state and local politics at play with her position at the research hospital."

"Oh?"

"Yeah. Her research work is incredibly competitive and securing funding, sometimes from political sources, makes her hyperaware of our surroundings. Plus, the people she works with aren't the most tolerant people. Her boss is a misogynist pig who makes her work life miserable when he's at the office. He doesn't even address her by her title of Doctor."

Still chewing, Viv puts her fork down and takes a sip of her wine. "Why does she put up with all that?"

"Well, because she was offered an internship and then a position with the hospital that was attached to a seven-year contract in exchange for paying out her student loans," I reply. "And since we were paying for the fertility, plus the debt she had accumulated from her master's degree, we thought it was a good way to manage our finances."

She nods as she chews.

"I'm an advocate of the performing arts," Viv says, delightfully shifting gears. "Would you be interested in going to the theater or the symphony with me? Just as friends, of course."

Before I can answer, my BlackBerry starts buzzing. I turn to the last place I remember setting it down and find it sitting on the kitchen peninsula.

"Let me just check that," I say to Viv, catching her eye roll before turning around to get the phone.

Before I can say hello, Isa is screaming in my ear. "Susana and a teammate slammed heads at soccer practice! She has a two-inch contusion on her forehead and has thrown up on the pitch, so she might have a concussion. Mami is driving us to Coral Gables Medical Center right now. Can you please meet us there?"

"I'm on my way." I turn to Viv and press the end button. "I have to go." I stand so quickly, my chair tips back and slams on the floor.

Viv purses her lips. "What is it now? Is the cat throwing up again? Or does she need you to change a light bulb?"

"No, Susana and a teammate apparently slammed into each other, and now she might have a concussion." I stare down at the table; dinner is half-eaten, the dishes need to be washed, the table needs wiping down, and oh my goodness I forgot about the opening-night party. "Jesus, Viv, I'm sorry about this. Can I pay you for my ticket, so at least it's not a total loss?"

"Go! Don't worry about that. I'll clean up. If you want, I can wait here for you," she says, her eyes gleaming.

"I don't know how long I'll be." I rush into the kitchen and remove a spare key from the utility drawer and toss it to her. "Here, make yourself at home, the dessert is in the fridge, but if you gotta go, please lock up and leave the key with the upstairs tenant in 2B."

Grabbing my backpack and car keys, I scramble out of the apartment. Racing to get to the hospital, I do my best to avoid traffic violations. As I drive, the canopy of trees, the streets, and even the traffic signs blur into insignificance. All I can feel is the hurried thumping of my heart, as if it's trying to break free from my chest. My blood courses through my veins with a feverish intensity, as if it, too, is caught up in the moment. It's as if time slows down, and all that matters is this moment: get to the hospital in one piece. Backing the Jeep into a spot I find in the farthest reaches of the parking lot rather than wasting time looking for a closer one, I sprint toward the entrance.

As soon as I cross the automatic sliding doors, I swallow down the memories from the first time we came to this emergency room: me sitting at a corner of the waiting room, pouring my feelings into baby Susana's diaper bag.

Eyes wide open, scanning the entrance, I catch sight of Martha leaning against a cylindrical concrete pillar. Her heavy purse is shouldered over her right side, arms crossed over her chest, and she's fixated on something on the floor. My stomping footsteps must have alerted her because she immediately straightens, opening her arms to take me in.

"She's okay," Martha says, before I have a chance to ask. "She's inside with Isa now. Come on, I'll take you." I nod but remain silent. We walk up to the patient intake desk where Martha proceeds with a seemingly prepared speech.

"This is my other daughter." I crinkle my brow as Martha is gesturing to me. Her words touch my heart, but she puts a viselike grip on my arm and tugs at me until I lean in. Teeth clenched, she whispers to me, "Shut up, and let me handle this." I double down on the silence.

"My daughter is in there with my granddaughter. I was just waiting outside for her. Can we go in?"

The receptionist requests my ID and nothing else, quite a difference from the first time Isa and I were here with Susana. Grasping my ID in her minuscule hands, she swipes it through a pint-size contraption attached to an LCD. As I stand, I hold my breath and hope the magnetic tape on the back of my license does not include evidence of my lesbianism. A silly thought, but you never know. With a few stabs at the keyboard, a label maker spits out a visitor tag.

The receptionist tears the label off the machine and hands it back along with my license. I glance at Martha, wide-eyed, thankful, even in awe of her wily plan to sneak me in to see my daughter.

My eyes drift down to her visitor's tag, haphazardly plastered over the breast pocket of her T-shirt, and mindlessly stick mine somewhere on my polo. I don't even care anymore. I want to see my daughter.

"Do you know where they are?" the receptionist asks Martha.

"Yes, I'm sure I can find my way back there," Martha replies, already halfway to the double doors of freedom.

"Okay." She touches a button under her countertop, and magically the double doors open to another white, antiseptic corridor.

As we walk through the doors, I can't help but ask, "What was that all about, 'My other daughter'?"

"Isa asked me to tell them you're my daughter so there would be no question to let you in. I'm sorry. I know you don't like lying, but it was the only way to make sure they let you in here with me."

Martha escorts me around a maze of stark white walls, the smell of bandages, dried blood, and other body fluids linger in the air. And then, I spot Isa. Sunkissed Isa, whose hair is a tousled mess in a loose ponytail. Dressed in a T-shirt, black tights, and her trainers, she's holding her BlackBerry to her ear, pacing about in an area separated by a drawn curtain. No sign of El Argentino.

I don't even have to call out her name. She just somehow turns to face me, knowing I'm here, disconnects with whomever had been on the phone, and locks her chocolate gaze on me. In my mind, it's as though I'm running to her, but we must have met somewhere in the middle. Her arms feel as though I'm climbing up my favorite Banyan tree in the backyard, strong and steady, inhaling me with her gravitational force. As she envelops me with her corded arms, I nuzzle into her neck. Her familiar vanilla fragrance is in my nose, my mouth, my tongue. I'd eat it for dinner if I could, use it as a sauce over a thick, medium-rare solomillo. Reaching around her waist, my arms instinctively press tighter.

Isa loosens her grip after a few moments, and I'm left bereft from the sudden chill.

"Where is she?" I ask, snapping out of her Svengali clutches.

"Don't worry," Isa says—not the picture of calamity I'd thought I'd find, since I was the one pushing for soccer. She wraps her hand around my wrist. "They took her for a CT scan. I just got off the phone with the doctor and Susana is already in radiology."

"A what?" Now I'm the calamitous one. *Don't worry*, she says! "That sounds serious."

"It's standard procedure to have a CT scan with her symptoms, especially because she briefly lost consciousness right after throwing up," she replies, somehow serene. "We wait for her here. This is her little room of sorts." Isa snakes her hand through a sliver of space between the curtain panels and pulls one side across its ceiling track. The space is barren, except for the one plastic chair and several cubby holes stuffed with purple rubber gloves.

"Oh. I see." I shift my eyes to Martha and tell her, "You should sit."

"No. I'm fine," she replies. "But I'll put my purse down."

When Martha steps into the space, I gently pull Isa aside by the elbow and whisper, "Please, tell me what happened."

"Well, the kids were on the soccer field, lined up and ready to receive an incoming corner kick. Susana had her eyes on the ball—you know how she has always wanted to send a header shot into the goal. Well, Becky jumped up just as Susana was about to hit the ball. Her head was pointing toward the goal, and that's when Becky slammed into Susana's forehead with the crown of her own head. They both fell to the ground. Becky was able to sit upright immediately. She was holding the top of her head but otherwise seemed fine.

"Then, I noticed Susana was not getting up. She was twitching in pain but couldn't even sit up. The coach blew the whistle to check on her, and I flew from the bleachers. I got there just in time for her to open her eyes, turn her head, and throw up. When she tried to push herself away from the ground, she said she felt dizzy. Jorge helped me put her in the truck. While Mami drove, I called my friend, Zania, ahead of time—she's a neurologist here in the hospital. And thank goodness she was on call because she immediately got Susanita into the CT scanner."

I look at my Swatch. I left the apartment no more than ten minutes ago. This doctor really did get Susana in there fast!

"When did you call me?" I ask. My brain always wants to build a timeline of events, just to see how everything fits together. Also, I'm making sure where I place on the totem pole. Vis-à-vis Roberto, that is.

"You're the first person I called," she says, without hesitation. "I wasn't going to exclude you."

"Okay."

My face is numb, drained of blood, and cracked, I'm sure. A tinge of a headache starts to spread from the top of my head down to my temples. With my thumb on one side and my middle finger on the other, I dig into my temples to alleviate some of pressure that's flaring up.

Barely ninety minutes elapse when I spot a woman in navy blue scrubs and running shoes, absorbed in whatever's on her phone, walking next to the stretcher carrying Susana.

Zania. Her bowed head forces her silky, short brown hair to hang, covering her face. Around her neck, her stethoscope and lanyard hang, and her badge says that Dr. Zania Olan is Chief of Neurology.

I sprint to Susana's bed mid-transport. Her eyes are open, and seemingly responsive when she sees me.

"Hola, cariño. How're you feeling?" I ask, grasping the bed's side railing. With some twisted footwork, making all kinds of skid noises with my sneakers on the glimmering linoleum floor, I reverse my direction and return with them to her area behind the curtain. I don't trip over my Reeboks, so kudos for me. Susana doesn't vocalize her answer, instead her face has all the makings of feeling ill. Ashen skin, disheveled hair, dried lips, sulky eyes, she looks worse for wear, and there are three butterfly sutures on her forehead, holding closed her two-inch gash.

The last thing a parent wants to see is their child hurting. At least for me, just the sight of Susana's tears, her quivering lips, and her silent pleas for comfort shatter me. It's as if the world has suddenly lost its color and all that's left is a bleak, damp, dark thunderstorm. I'm trying to find the strength to accept that she's in good hands here in the hospital and that I can't do anything other than give her my warmth so that she may know we love her. And I hold her hand as a silent assurance that I'm here for her.

Dr. Olan opens the curtain and greets Isa, who's standing, one hand tucked in the fold of her elbow, while the other hand is busy scrolling through her phone. Martha, sitting in the plastic chair, shoots up as we come in and moves aside to let the hospital techs situate Susana's bed in place. When they leave, Isa walks stolidly up to the foot of Susana's bed and caresses her exposed toes, taking care to cover them with the starched hospital blanket. Around her bed, we're a triangle of women linked to each other by more than love and devotion to this little girl. We're her family, here to comfort her. Susana smiles at each of us, knowing that we're not going anywhere.

Isa places her hand in the small of my back. "G, this is Dr. Zania Olan. She's the friend I told you about." She turns to Zania and gestures to me. "Zania, this is Gene López-Pérez, Susana's other mother." Isa says it so matter-of-factly that a sudden gloss of moisture gleams over my eyes. It's this moment, this modicum of time, that gives me a pang of regret—buyer's remorse, or in my case seller's remorse for ever leaving the house. I push it all aside and extend a brittle, feeble hand toward Zania.

"Doctor," I say, voice a bit unsteady. "Boy, am I glad Isa has friends like you."

"Susana's CT scans are normal," Zania says, brushing off any salutatory etiquette. Meanwhile, I emit an audible sigh of relief that she gets down to business with swift efficiency. "We cleaned up the laceration on her forehead, and she'll be ready to go home in about an hour. But she has a minor concussion." Zania faces Susana and says directly to her, "No school for two days, and no sports for at least a week." She pats Susana's little thigh and gestures for Isa and me to follow her out through the curtains.

"She needs to be monitored closely for the next twenty-four to forty-eight hours," Zania says once we get out of Susana's hearing range. "I suggest you both take turns looking in on her every two, two and a half hours or so," she says, staring at the clock on the wall by the nurse's station. "Today is Thursday, so I'd like for you to follow up with her pediatrician on Monday to make sure she's okay to go back to school. She needs at least eight hours of sleep every night. No TV, no computer, and no reading for the next forty-eight hours. Give her an over-the-counter children's acetaminophen if her headache worsens."

"That's it?" I ask, her instructions seemingly rudimentary.

"That's it. The concussion will heal on its own if she can rest without stimulation of any kind. That will help her recover faster. So as soon as you get home, put her to bed and check in on her."

"You got it," Isa replies as if replying to one of her old volleyball coaches. "Zania, thank you so much for personally taking care of this. I know how busy you are. I really appreciate it." Isa lightly touches the doctor's forearm.

They hug a few seconds longer than I think appropriate, but whatever. And with an extended hand in my direction, she says,

"A pleasure to finally meet you." She wraps her cold, thin doctor fingers around my palm with a firm grip, gives it a quick shake before letting go, and disappears into the elevators.

"'A pleasure to finally meet you?'" I ask, turning my head toward Isa. "You've been talking about me to other people?"

"She's not other people, G. She's a trusted friend. Besides, I don't work in this hospital."

"Well, what a relief."

Isa turns away from me and saunters back through Susana's curtain. With a shrug, I pull out my BlackBerry and call Susana's pediatrician to make an appointment for Monday.

CHAPTER TWENTY-TWO

Isa

"Do you mind staying the night?" I ask, with a furtive hand supporting the center of Gene's back as she hefts Susana up the stairs. She's an octopus, limbs suctioned around Gene's torso. She's too heavy for me to carry her upstairs, but Gene has always been stronger than me.

Susana hasn't uttered a single word since we put her in my truck. This from someone who doesn't wait to spill her thoughts, ideas, and off-the-cuff comments once she sees someone who's worth telling them to, of course. It's usually Gene, Martha, or me, the kids at school, too. Oh, and the kids she sees at the pediatrician, and the park, and yeah, I think that's it. But now, her little lips are dry, even cracked. Her knuckles have gone white from grasping her wrist, holding onto Gene so tightly. Eyes closed, her brows crunch up, as if the music in her head is too loud to bear. I brush the back of my fingers on her forehead, and she loosens the clench on her face.

Gene's husky whisper is so delayed I almost forgot what I asked her. "No, not at all." Her breath drifts into my ear, tingling my spine as I glance at the back of her long, elegant neck, wanting to trace my thumb over her reddish birthmark that her freshly shaven undercut scarcely covers. But I don't. I keep my hand at the small of her back instead. "Just let me run to the apartment to get a few things. You don't have plans with Roberto tonight?"

The mere mention of his name dampens the flames in my imagination, the image of Gene putting Susana to bed, gently sliding the quilt over her little body, dashed. My stomach contorts into an untangleable knot.

"I don't see him when I have Susana." This is true, of course. I have no business with anyone else when I have my daughter with me, and I'm not about to have him visit me in this house.

"Oh," is all she utters.

Between Gene and me, we carefully undress Susana and bathe her in my bathtub. With Gene's secure hand at the back of her neck, I gently pat Susana's forehead clean with a damp hand towel. Mine is a free-standing tub with no glass doors, and unlike Susana's, there's room for both Gene and me to sit on the ledge and maneuver around her.

In her room, after helping her get into a pair of plaid pajamas, she sits up on her bed while I remove a butterfly strip from the box Zania gave me and hand it to Gene. As I dress her wound with the ointment Zania also gave us, Gene unwraps the first Steri-Strip and smooths it evenly over the cut on her forehead. Meanwhile, I unwrap another and hand it to her. We repeat the same steps until Gene places enough bandages to cover the wound.

Working like this, I realize, *this is us.* A symbiotic partnership of two people devoted to their child. Gene, with her sheer determination to make things fit, make our situation work, seemingly morphs herself and her life to prioritize our co-parenting relationship. Meanwhile I don't bend, I don't morph, I don't prioritize them. Not really when you look at it. Despite her own hectic schedule, Gene takes Susana to school every day and picks her up whether it's her week to be with our daughter or not. She's the catalyst that makes this family function.

As Gene gently places the last Steri-Strip on Susana's forehead, she lovingly kisses the taped-up wound and draws Susana to her chest. I shudder as the dressing wrinkles on her forehead with every furrow of Susana's brow, causing her to wince and sigh. She unhinges herself from Gene and lies on her back.

"How are you feeling, baby?" I ask. The twinge in my heart deepens as Gene stands and motions for us to switch places so I can get a turn to be at her side. She sits at the foot of her bed and kneads Susana's stiffened calf.

Susana gazes at me, her eyes sullen and wide. "I feel better, but my head still hurts."

"I'll run down and get you some Tylenol." Gene stands. "Be right back." And she leaves the door cracked open on her way out.

I gently push the bangs away from Susana's forehead. "You gave Mamá and me quite a scare."

"I'm sorry, I was just practicing."

"I know, Bebé," I say with an extended sigh that Gene can probably hear all the way downstairs in the kitchen. Waiting for her to come back up, I nestle my fingers at the back of Susana's neck, stroking her baby hairs. I think about our first trip to the emergency room, and how much easier it would have been had I just told the idiot receptionist that Gene was my sister. It's not as though she would have asked for proof. But I guess that's not really the point. A gay couple, a lesbian couple, a straight couple, an unmarried couple—family is a family, regardless of biology and ideology.

My thoughts disappear into the abyss the minute Gene walks in. She places a napkin down on Susana's nightstand, situates a glass of water on it, and lays the pill next to it on the napkin. I glance up at her, my eyes dry, and the stinging behind them is begging for respite. Even with my weary eyes, I still catch a gleam in Gene's when she looks at me. Her tawny curls fall over her forehead. It took me a while to get used to her shorter and shorter hair as we got older. The first cut of her golden mane came up just below her shoulders. That was the year she joined me in Ithaca. By the time we moved back to Miami, she'd been getting an undercut and having the rest haphazardly styled. Had we chosen to go to LA, she'd have looked the part of a surfer. We didn't have the ocean in Ithaca.

"I'm going to run home and pack a few things, then get my car from the hospital," Gene whispers in my ear. She'd driven us all back home in the Land Cruiser and dropped Mami off at her house. Before she slips away, she caresses my cheek with the back of her hand, meticulously running her knuckles along my jaw. It's brief, but my peach fur stands on end, and the touch is like a diaspora of sensation spread throughout my body. Her hands are smooth and exquisite, but when they're on me—when they *were* on me—they're like two determined beavers digging a burrow. Her delicate touch frazzles my skin and everything it covers.

With a heavy breath, I clear my throat. "Do you mind bringing enough clothes for the whole weekend?" My eyes are closed, still feeling her warm, silken caress.

"Sure. I'll do that."

CHAPTER TWENTY-THREE

Gene

It's nearing eleven, but the evening has only just begun for me. Walking back to the apartment, I think about the constant worry that goes into child rearing. The first three years of Susana's life, I had been in a ceaseless state of alarm and fatigued by the rhythmic changes in her routine. Her first three months were plagued with rigidly timed feedings; while Isa breast-fed Susana throughout the day, I chipped in with the bottled breast milk for the one and five a.m. slots. When she graduated to mush at five months, the schedule changed to every six hours, but she still needed that breast milk at five a.m. That's how it was until we couldn't remember a time when it wasn't like that.

Viv's cream Outlander is still parked in my second space, but the apartment is silent when I walk through the doorway. The dining room table has been cleaned off and arranged with my live orchid centerpiece sitting atop the six stacked cloth place mats. In the kitchen, the dishes have been washed, the countertops and cooktop cleaned, and the garbage taken out.

Putting my keys down on the peninsula, I turn to find Viv asleep on the couch. She's lovely. Her friendship has meant so much to me. Viv is warm, and kind, and honest. I don't have the heart to wake her and tell her to leave. But with no other choice, I walk over to her and sit on the edge, beside her. She opens her dark lidded eyes and fixes them on me for a few seconds.

"How is Susana?" she asks with a yawn, my hand still on her shoulder.

"She got hit pretty hard and has a minor concussion, but she'll be fine."

"Oh, thank goodness," she says with her hand drawn up to her heart. "I was worried. I'm glad it wasn't anything more serious. But why didn't you call me sooner?"

"I didn't have a moment, and I didn't think to use my cell phone in the emergency room. I was nervous enough without wondering if I'd be disrupting the radio waves of an important piece of hospital equipment."

She brushes my hair off my forehead with a warm hand. "I was worried." She reaches her arms up to pull me to her, and I sink down into her embrace. As she holds me, my lower back pinches with the strain of her pull, and I imagine how long is long enough until I can sit up again. In my head, I count to three and pull away, splintering the contact.

"I came back to pick up a few things," I admit. "The doctor said we should watch over her, so Isa and I agreed to do it in shifts. She's taking the first one now while I pack a bag."

"Oh." She shifts on the couch.

I get up and stretch the knots out of my back and shoulders for a second before ambling to my bedroom. My overnight bag is in the closet on the top shelf, so I get on my tippy toes and manage to reach the bag with my fingertips and nudge it to the edge of the shelf. It falls perfectly into my hands. Viv's voice hangs behind me and turn to face her, bag in hand.

"I'll get going, then. I don't want to be in the way. Besides, I need to get home. I was only waiting to see how Susana was doing, but I *was* hoping for a phone call." Her words slap me in bursts of passive-aggressive wallops. I ignore the snap and focus on getting back to the house. Joder. I still need to get the Jeep from the hospital.

I catch Viv as she turns to leave my bedroom. "Wait." I wince just thinking to ask her for a favor, but here goes nothing. "Do you mind dropping me off at the hospital? In the rush to get Susana back to the house, I drove them all back in Isa's car."

"Sure," she says and disappears into the hallway.

Back at the house, I drop my black duffel bag on the shiny floor inside Susana's bathroom. Eventually, I'll set up the trundle bed that's currently tucked under Susana's daybed, but for now, I just want to wash away this hospital scent and all the stress of the evening that now feels more like grime.

It's a strange sensation, returning to this house, using my old bathroom, and sleeping in my old bedroom. Everything feels the same, despite the renovations we made to the upstairs before Susana was born. The wood flooring is the same, the walls are the same walls, the ceiling is the same high ceiling that keeps the upstairs cool in the summer. The essence of my childhood is still up here. If I close my eyes, I can hear Lui on the phone with his girlfriend, now his wife. I can hear my parents planning out our winters and summers in Spain. If I reach out, I can almost touch my younger self, bashful but joyful. Lucky. That's what I was. It's what I am, for I have my memories. I still have this house, my kid, my life.

Leaning against the doorjamb, I watch as Isa, still with her arms around Susana, comforts her, and a painful stab of envy hits my gut. But this time, I'm envious of Susana. What I wouldn't give to have my parents' warm embrace.

This room—where I spent many brooding hours, raking my feelings for Isa over imaginary coals—holds many poignant memories of my childhood. It's where I kissed Isa for the first time. On top of that daybed. At first, it was a hesitant peck on the lips. Bumping noses even—we hadn't a clue what we were doing. It was a disaster, at first, even with my meticulous planning on how it would be, what I would say, how she would react. But nothing has ever come close to giving me that delicious tingle from my toes to the tops of my ears as that first kiss Isa and I shared. When our lips met for the first time, it was like watching my room burst with fireworks. The walls reverberated with Yanni's instrumental music. My heart throbbed in my ears. *Boom! Boom! Boom!* The magic of us was sensational, but at thirteen, it couldn't be anything less.

My bedroom is also where I cried myself to sleep during the two years Isa was away at Cornell without me. Faced with the insurmountable task of getting through my junior and senior years of high school without hearing her cheesy love songs playing on her candy-red boom box, her math tutoring, her braces-clad smile, and deep dimples. Without her. Of course, eventually, I got through them.

Now, I'm back in this house, and we both want to care for and comfort our daughter. I can either push my feelings aside and prioritize Susana, or I can drown in my own wistful despair to have Isa back in my arms. I choose the former.

Quietly getting in the shower, I scrub at my regrets: leaving this house, Susana, Isa. Despite forging a new life, my activism, and my fight, there's a hole in my soul made the minute I stepped away from this house.

After toweling off, I rummage through my toiletries, finding everything except my body spray that I spritz on after showering. *Joder, if only I hadn't been in such a hurry to get back here.* On the vanity, I spot Susana's Agua de Colonia de Agustin Reyes perfume that smells of lavender and violets, and without a second thought, I reach for the glass bottle, dab a few drops in my hand, and indulge in its nostalgic scent as I splash it all over. At this hour, it's nothing short of revitalizing, taking me back to when Susana was a baby. She'd explode with laughter during the after-bath routine when I'd run my hands over her cherubic body, covering her in violetas. She had been a jolly baby—when she wasn't screaming bloody murder, of course.

Untangling my unmanageable curls away from my face with a comb, I wait for them to spring back to life. Just as I open the bathroom door, Isa is across the landing, gently closing Susana's bedroom door. She motions for me to follow her downstairs. In my bare feet, I pad down behind her.

"Do you want some tea?" she whispers as we descend.

"Yeah. That'd be nice."

We…*she* keeps an assortment of teas in a jar next to the teakettle. While I fill the electric kettle with water, she removes the cover from the jar.

"What flavor do you want? I just got some tasty herbal teas with fruit flavors if you want to try one." She pulls out three pouches filled with loose-leaf tea.

I glance over at her. "Whatever you're having is fine with me." Isa knows I'm not a big tea fan, but when we lived together, I drank it when she offered. Aside from the grassy, dirty taste that lingers on the tongue, staining your teeth, drinking tea conjures pleasant, homey vibes for me—but I still prefer coffee.

A few years ago, when I renovated the apartment building my parents left me, I copied the design of this U-shape kitchen for the apartment in which I live now. The floor plan of a large peninsula and the appliance triangle (fridge, sink, and cooktop) is the same. Of course, the one in the apartment is half the size. I didn't know I was going to move into the apartment when I renovated it, but the kitchen at least feels more like home because it reminds me of this one.

Sitting at the granite-covered peninsula, waiting for the teakettle's piercing whistle, Isa busies herself affixing the tea steeper in the kettle. I delight in watching, and when the water begins to boil and swirls the liquid into a brownish color, before the kettle has the chance to unleash its formidable shriek, Isa flips its power switch. She lets the tea leaves simmer as they brew for a few minutes before pouring the steamy, tea-stained water. She grabs both teacups by their accompanying saucers and turns to set them down in front of me.

"Let's go to the family room." I nod and follow her, keeping the teacup from slipping off its saucer with my other hand as I walk. "I set up Susana's old baby monitor in her room. That way we can hear her down here without bothering her when we switch shifts." She removes the receiver from the back of her black Lululemons, places it on the coffee table, and sits on her side of the sofa. I mirror her on the opposite end.

We're sitting with enough space between us that we can move our limbs without touching. Mamá had this couch specially made to fit perfectly in this space, so it's not as long as a standard-size couch, but it's slightly longer than a love seat. Isa sits sideways, facing me as she leans on the back of the couch. She pulls up her right knee and tucks her foot under the fold of her left knee. Her teacup is in her left hand as she rests it on the bend of her knee and props her head up with her right fist.

Her intense stare slices my insides like one of those hard-boiled egg slicers, leaving all my pieces vulnerable, yet strangely exhilarated at the same time. My heart accelerates as the seconds of quiet linger. Sitting here with her overwhelming gaze on me, I realize how completely under her spell I am, I've been. I'd do anything to keep her eyes fixed on me.

"Good idea," I force myself to say, trying to keep the tingles off my body. "I was planning on sleeping in her bedroom."

"Oh, I don't think that's a good idea," she says.

"Really. Why not?"

"Gene," she whispers. "Because you snore like a truck driver."

"I do not!"

"Honey, I slept with you for nearly seventeen years. I should know."

"Well, this is news to me."

"But not to me," she deadpans and pins me down with her smoldering chocolate eyes. I clear my throat, shoving down the lust, the desire, the heartache.

"Fine," I say like a petulant child, waving a surrendering hand. Because she'd never once mentioned it when we were together, her words don't choke me. I take her exaggeration as a quip but wonder why she made the insinuation anyway.

"Where would you like me to sleep?"

She pats on the cushion spaced between us and smirks. I smirk, too, and we're suddenly Isa and Gene again.

"I don't fit on this couch," I say, half smiling.

She clicks her tongue. "It's only for the weekend, it's not forever."

This familiar banter between us feels half-comforting, half-dangerous. I sink deeper into the plush couch, taking my teacup with me. Its warmth against my chest alleviates some of the daunting tension.

"You know, it's funny," I murmur, needing to kill the silence between us. "I never thought I'd ever get used to seeing you without your braces, but I guess, given enough time, we can get used to anything." That last part is a lie. I take a sip of the scalding tea, not because I want to enjoy the liquid, but because I want to stop my mouth from moving. It burns going down my throat, spilling over the barbed wire that's wound up in a knot deep in my belly. I swallow hard but only manage to down a sizable air bubble that doesn't quite fit, scraping the insides of my throat.

She chuckles. "I never thought I would get used to your hair so short." She says it as if it's been on her tongue, waiting for the right moment to deliver. She slowly reaches over the space between us, grazing her fingertips across my forehead, brushing my sandy curls away and tucking them behind my ear. The electricity between us prickles my nipples. But her efforts fail as my curls spring back onto my forehead.

I imagine suppressing a blush and hope she doesn't notice my tingling flesh, the goose bumps forming on my arms, or my reddened ears, forever burning when I'm around her. She hasn't touched me this way in more time than I care to remember.

"You were my dirty-blond Julia," she says suddenly.

"Your who?"

"Julia Roberts," she replies. "Because, when we met, your hair was exactly like hers was in *Mystic Pizza*. You were my preppy Julia Roberts but with blue-rimmed glasses and dirty-blond hair, of course." She smiles that smile that deepens her chin dimples. They're pools of joy in which I would gladly spend the rest of my life treading, and I clench my thighs together to prevent myself from jumping up and taking her on this couch. As if suddenly realizing the mayhem she's causing my insides, Isa retracts her fingers.

"Now, you're more like Meg Ryan in that movie about angels."

"*City of Angels*?" I ask. We've seen that movie a dozen times. And the only reason I remember it, apart from its shocking ending—well, not so much shocking because I saw it coming, literally, a mile away—is because Sarah McLachlan sang the breakout song of its soundtrack, "Angel." For a long time, it was one of our sexy-time songs. Hearing the silk of McLachlan's voice coupled with the melody of the lyrics and the somber music behind her vocals put me in the mood to snuggle against Isa.

A hesitant laugh escapes my mouth when she nods her assent while I'm over here trying keep from drowning in this cup of tea. I want to kiss her. It's an urge I've been hiding since we got back to the house tonight with Susana. I've always had the urge to kiss her. Throughout our separation it's always been there, dancing in the background. All I can do is ignore it; all I *should* do is ignore it. Yet, it's not just the want to kiss Isa. How can it be? I've been pining for her way too long to trivialize my feelings to merely a kiss. I've loved her more than half my life. Not before, and never since this wretched separation, have I ever felt more love for any other person. It's difficult not to with her magnetic eyes. But I've learned to love her from afar, keeping my distance—otherwise, I'd go insane. I can only sit here quietly and smile like a bumbling idiot at her while she pierces through me with her gossamer gaze.

My breath deepens and I switch gears. "Thanks for earlier… when you sent Martha to make sure they let me be with Susana, I mean."

"She's your daughter, Gene." Her tone is so confident, it makes me want to believe her. "Your place is with us." It's the way she says it that shifts my gaze away from her.

"Yeah. But I mean because you remembered that they wouldn't have let me in the room."

She stretches to put her teacup on the coffee table and shifts to face me. "How could I forget? Fuck, Gene!" Isa slaps her thigh, and it startles me. "I don't ever want that to happen again." Her sorrowful eyes are empathetic. "That bitch at the reception desk was wrong to make you sit and wait. I'm sorry for being a zombie that night, for not fighting harder so you could join me."

I shrug. What's done is done.

There's a bit of a bridge between us, and I gather my nerve to cross it. "I've been thinking that there might be a way around that." The words shoot out of me. "I've been wanting to ask you for a while, but tonight, with the incident, I just back-burnered it."

"What is it, ho..." she whispers, stopping short of saying something more. The thickness of her voice sends delightful shivers through me.

"I want to adopt Susana..."

CHAPTER TWENTY-FOUR

Isa

"I mean as her second parent," Gene clarifies. As I stare at her for a moment. My neck is stiff and my shoulders blades press together. My breath quickens at the word *adopt*.

I adjust my position so that I'm facing Gene on the couch. "Wait. I thought that adoptions by gays and lesbians were banned." She's confusing me and honestly, I'm a little taken aback.

"It is, but when they reject my petition, I would sue the state and go through the court system to prove they're violating my equal rights protection under the Constitution. Down the line, if the court rules the ban to be unconstitutional, then every couple who have children, regardless of their sexual orientation will, hopefully, be recognized as legal parents whatever their circumstances," she explains.

"I see."

She's quiet for a few moments, seemingly to take the time to plan out her words. "It will take time, but I'm willing to wait. The courts are hearing similar cases, but because we're not married…err…*were* never married, my situation is different. And that's why Jay, the Executive Director of Equality Miami, suggested it."

"So, you've been planning and discussing this with Jay, a stranger?" I fold my arms across my chest. A blaze is smoldering inside my head. It's as if they've been plotting behind my back.

"She's not a stranger, Isa. She's my friend. She's also an attorney," she says. "And she understands the nuances of my situation. During our last board meeting, she approached me about it."

"Should you go through with this…this petition, will it become public record once it goes to the courts?" The fire, flickering.

"Technically, yes," she replies, darting her eyes all over the room, strategically evading mine.

"With whom else have you been strategizing this plan of yours?" My tone topples the flameless red coals, simmering in my head.

"Sergio."

"When?" I ask.

"When what?"

I clench my teeth. "When did you start plotting all this?" My inclination is to storm out, but I live here, so I stay put.

"Isa, there's no plotting. Jay and I first spoke about it at last month's board meeting. I consulted with Sergio, and he said he'd produce an affidavit for you to sign, if you're willing, of course."

I shoot up off the couch and pace the width of the family room. Once, twice, three times I walk from the cloister-style arches that separate the great room from the family room, across to the concrete exterior wall, digging a trench in front of the couch.

I stop my pacing and face Gene. "That's pretty methodical of you. After you spoke about this to Jay, you didn't think to come to me before going to Sergio?" Glaring at her, hands on hips and hackles raised, I feel as though horns are about to pop out of my head and black wings spread from my back. *How could she do this to me?*

"I went to Sergio to gather more information, that's all."

"You mean, you went to him to see what *your* options were."

Gene rises as well. Her voice shakes, but she's surprisingly calm. "Isa. Can you please try to understand my side of all this? Just for once, get your head out of your ass and put yourself in my shoes." Gene and her histrionics. She motions to her bare feet with her index finger, and I can't help but look down. The action distracts me into looking at her toes. I'd almost forgotten she, like her father, loves to be barefoot.

"I'm just having a hard time understanding why you didn't discuss it with me first. When I was thinking about having a family with you, I told you. Remember?" I reply, blinking a few times to stop the angry tears itching to be released.

She clears her throat. Her eyes, nostrils, and everything else on her face seem to widen. Her jawbone tightens. "Yes! You did, *didn't* you? You told me *when* you were going to get inseminated. You told me *where* the procedure would be done. You even told me *who* the donor was going to be. What you *didn't* do was share any of the info-gathering process with me. So, no te hagas la inocente. ¡Joder!"

My jaw slackens, but before I can retort, she has more to say. "And yet, it was one of the most poignant moments of my life with you." She suddenly steps closer to me and takes my hand. I almost flinch but let the sudden touch soothe me instead. "I never meant to leave you out of any of my fact-finding, but I needed to gather all the information before I came to you. I've been freaking out about my parental rights since I was banned from the emergency room that first time with Susana." She pauses, her eyes as sullen as an abused dog's.

"I freak out every time you go off for a few days on one of your medical conferences. That's when I hope to God nothing happens to Susana because you're not here to sign the paperwork or accompany her into the emergency room.

"Isa, I believe the only way to do this—to get the adoption ban off the books once and for all so the state recognizes me as one of Susana's legal parents—is through the courts. You can understand that, can't you?"

My face feels feverish, and sudden tears stream down my cheeks. Gene rushes to take me in her arms, and I instinctively wrap my arms tightly around her. Her embrace is comforting and familiar, and I don't want to let go.

Abruptly, Gene pulls away from me, but her hands...her hands slide up my back until they grasp the dome of my head. I pull her to me, and I have no idea what's happening when I feather a kiss over her lips. Surprised by my own actions, I stiffen. My body is tingling, my skin is agog to do it again.

"I'm sorry," she says with a gasp, as if appalled at what we'd done, loosening her grip on me. "I shouldn't ha—" she starts to say, but I won't let go. My hands cup her cheeks, my lips are on hers, my tongue is in her mouth.

CHAPTER TWENTY-FIVE

Gene

Oh, God. Isa's tongue! Her magnificent thick and hot tongue—it's everywhere. When I open my mouth wider, it's as if I've unlocked the door to paradise. This kiss is nothing like we've ever experienced with each other before. Yes, we had plenty of passion before, but this is a longing for who we once were to each other. She's missed me, too. And as we tug at each other, trying to subdue the other, we're rewriting our story. Because we share Susana, our story has no end. But this bit, this is us: Isa and Gene unbridled.

I reach for her waist and get a handful of her top instead. My hands reach inside her T-shirt. With widely splayed fingers, I'm trying to feel every bit of her skin. Her skin. The feel of it is what I miss the most. The smooth expanse of her back, the tight, muscular curves of her scapula, the velvety dip of her lumbar. My fingertips run up and down her spine as if reading the words her goose bumps leave behind.

Her shirt is off in a snap, and I toss it somewhere behind me. Now she's trying to unbutton my jeans, then changes her mind, hoisting up my shirt off my torso instead. My heart thrashes a warning: stop, pause, take a breath, slow down? It's impossible.

Decided, I step away and extend my hand to her. It's now or never, but more likely now, and never again. Isa pants as she examines my hand before she makes her decision. There's no denying the yearning. I've felt it since I left this house more than two years ago. Isa takes my hand, inhales deeply, and leads me upstairs.

The silent climb calms me, though not enough to change my intention. But it's not until I follow her through the door to the bedroom we once shared that a twinge of reality twists into my throat. I cringe from the thought.

I don't want to ask, but I need to know. "Has he been in here?" My voice is husky, and I'm frightened, no…petrified of the answer. And no doubt I want to slap myself for asking, but I must know.

"He's never been in this house," she assures. Her sharp tone comes without malice. I do my best to wipe the thought of her doing with him what we're about to do somewhere else.

The mattress is different. The bed, taller now with an extra top layer, is softer but firmer at the same time. Nothing else is different about the bedroom. The dark oakwood bed frame we brought from Ithaca still has Floyd's scratch markings. The Islamic rug we got in Andalusia is still spread out on the floor at the foot of the bed. And the ornate full-length mirror, that miraculously matches the bed frame, is still affixed to the floor with its swiveled mirror tilted up ever so slightly. Isa sits and slides back on the bed, her abs deliciously engaged, extending her arms to me, wanting me on top of her. Sliding over the bed, I follow suit to feel the heat emanating from her sultry body.

Relieved that no one else has been on this bed with her, I take my time kissing the areas on Isa's skin that have driven me crazy, that drive me crazy. She grazes her fingertips along my lower back to my shoulder blades, leaving tight gooseflesh all the way to my toenails. I shudder with her familiar caresses.

Once again, she takes me to another era, as I remember the nuances of her hands on my skin, how she loved to touch my peach fur. A moan escapes my lips from the titillation. We're situated with our hips and legs laced together. Still in my jeans, she in her Lulus, I slip my hand under the elastic waistband and slide down her abs. Her lacy underwear is rough on my fingertips, but it does nothing to deter me. I slip underneath the fabric to continue my quest toward her center. Finding her warm lips, I'm pulled in farther. And as I slide inside her, she exhales another groan. Or was that me?

"Oh, God," I whisper. "You're so wet." I can't help myself, but the hot moisture draws me deeper. The way I'm lying on top of her with my hand contorted inside her tights, my lips on hers, and my quivering elbow bearing my weight is uncomfortable. Reassessing my position, I retreat my hand from Isa's pants. She takes the hint and quickly wriggles out of them. Her bra comes off, too.

Everything else I'm wearing gets stripped off, landing in a pile in the corner. The navy blue bed sheets look as inviting as the deep blue of the Mediterranean Sea, and all I want to do is dive into the warm water, lift my head back, and bask in the sun's nurturing rays. The luxurious mattress cradles my body like the sand on the beaches of Barcelona as I dig myself a niche to keep my body still. I gesture for Isa to come to me; I'm done with foreplay. Her naked body on mine heightens my anticipation. It's as though I'm coming home from vacation. For two years, I've been in limbo, waiting in the customs area in that dreaded line that zigzags until forever. Waiting for the customs officer to clear me and stamp my passport so that I may rejoin Isa, waiting outside. Waiting. She always seems to be waiting.

We don't have all the time in the world, and I keep thinking this will end tomorrow. Isa pays no mind to that as she grasps my butt with both hands and grinds her hips into me. My heart is sucked up into my esophagus as she rolls us over so she's on top. Isa's dark chocolate stare is pinned on me, heating me, devouring me. The impulse to hold her face and pull her down so I can devour her lips takes over me. Those lips that always, always ignite a fire in my gut taste of lemon and verbena, from the herbal tea neither of us finished. We move rhythmically, but I need more. I need to be inside her, and I need her inside me.

I trace the line of her spine down to her round, heart-shaped ass that has always managed to roil my insides and give it a squeeze before lowering my hand to adjust her leg across my hip. Languidly caressing the back of her thigh, I inch closer to the opening I just created. We're kissing and moving in tandem, my heels digging into the bed. When I run my finger along the surface of her tight sphincter, it's wetter than I had anticipated, and a groan catches in my throat.

Isa's hands are on my breasts, her thumbs circling my rigid nipples. She squeezes them as I begin to rub her. Slipping her hand between us, Isa slides through my lips. She gasps as she feels my own arousal, digging her forehead into my chest. She rounds one of my nipples with her scotching tongue, then bites into it. I'm on the fringes, desperate to hold on.

I circle her tight hole, knowing I'm giving her pleasure, as I drown in my own desire for her. My climax is right there, on the cusp. When she removes her mouth from my breast, holding herself up by her free hand, she sears her gaze down on me. Her fingers find their way inside me, and I pant with agonizing delight. While I'm stimulating her with my right hand, she strokes me with her left. It's utter madness. She's thrusting inside me, and I do my best to restrain myself from getting louder, for Susana's sake, sleeping right next door.

"Oh, fuck," we both murmur, because, goodness, this is getting intense. Isa slips what feels to be three fingers into me, and I'm about to come all over them. As her sex throbs on my pelvis, she pauses her grinding. Unable to hold it any longer, we reach our orgasms together, surrendering all emotion. Pain, jubilation, anguish, nostalgia, all vanish into nothing.

Isa drapes her body over mine, muscles relaxing, chest expanding and contracting, appetite sated. She nuzzles her lips in the crook of my neck. My arms are slackening around her, and I run a lazy finger up and down her back, needing a few seconds to catch my breath, but I want more. I need her in my mouth.

CHAPTER TWENTY-SIX

Isa

Luxuriating in the plush satin of the duvet, the crisp, downy sheets, and last night's orgasms, I exhale a hefty, exquisite breath. That was necessary. The release, the familiar naked body on mine, Gene inside me—all over me—me inside her, Gene quivering in my mouth. Stretching my achy limbs, I reach over to wrap my own body around hers. Nothing. I reach farther across the bed, only to tap the cold emptiness of her side. Sitting upright, my eyes dart around the yellow hues of our sunlit room, expecting to find a regretful Gene tiptoeing away. I see nothing. With a sting, Gene is gone. It's not until I smell the hazelnut wafting through the air vents that I realize she hasn't left the house. No. She's made coffee.

Her clothes, lying in a pile on the chair in the corner of the room, are a sign that Gene wasn't so much in a hurry to leave. She'd have plucked each one of her garments clear off the chair, gotten dressed, and left. But she didn't. That, however, doesn't mean she's not somewhere downstairs brooding about what happened last night. With a sigh of regret that I'm forced to get out of this bed, I scoot off and shove my feet in my fluffy sherpa mules because, like it or not, it's time to face the music. I walk into the dressing room, grab my robe from the hook on the bathroom door, and step into the foyer.

The silence on the second floor is almost resonant as I plod across the landing to check in on Susana. She's quietly sleeping, strewn on her back across the bed. Waiting a few seconds until I catch her chest moving methodically, I ease the door shut, careful not to make a sound, and head downstairs.

The shirts we stripped off each other and scattered on the family room floor, the half-emptied teacups, and the baby monitor are all picked up and cleared away. Gene and her obsessive compulsion for tidy spaces has apparently remained unchanged since our separation. Meanwhile, my OCD has all but dissolved into the wind since Susana's birth. Children tend to keep the need to constantly clean at bay, at least until they learn the proper way to clean up after themselves.

In the kitchen, the coffee maker is still dripping its mahogany elixir into the glass carafe. Gene is on the other side of the sliding glass door, swiveling left and right in her patio chair under the covered deck, probably waiting for the coffee to brew. I'm sure she has a timer set for it on her phone. Mussing her unruly sandy curls even more, she runs her fingers through them from the back of her head to the front. A heavy sigh escapes my nostrils as I twist my torso to check on the coffee, halfway done.

Why can't she be content with what we once had? Why must she always overanalyze, scrutinize, and pick apart every nuance of our parenting journey? I'll bet she's sifting through everything we did last night and shaming herself for giving in to our desires. Our needs. *Damn it, Gene, why do you have to be so fucking complicated?*

DNA. Sigh.

Susana's sleeping position when I checked in on her, the chin dimples Gene loves so much, her long wavy brown hair, thick fringes of eyelashes surrounding dark broody eyes, even her extroversion—no one can question that she's mine, that her DNA runs through me.

The coffeepot chimes as I stare through the sliding glass door, waking me from my own convoluted ruminations. I head over and remove two mugs from the cupboard above, noticing my BlackBerry on its charger. I type out a quick email to Cami, letting her know I won't be in the office today and not until Monday, after Susana's follow-up with the pediatrician.

With a steaming mug of coffee in each hand, I slide open the patio door with my elbow and find Gene looking as guilty and shameful as I'd thought she would. I place the mugs down on the glass table between the two swivel chairs and gaze out into the yard. The pool glistens under the fresh morning rays. The vine growing on the side of the back building is blooming, specks of purple and blue sprinkle up the stone wall. The two potted bougainvillea we'd planned two years ago, flanking the ground-floor studio entrance, are nearly an inch from forming the perfect arch we wanted above the door. Out here, the atmosphere is as steamy as it was upstairs, last night, with summer's lingering effects. The dense humidity, even in September, has always been Miami's calling card—it's what keeps the garden in bloom year-round. It's a new day, but we still have our old problems.

I sit down with my foot tucked under my butt. We sit quietly a few moments while I take my first few sips of coffee. Dread builds in my stomach; the silence is the worst. No, her words to me the night she left me were the worst. *"I need to make my own way."*

"I didn't have an ulterior motive when I asked you to stay the weekend, you know," I admit. She remains silent. "I know you were as worried as I was about Susana's incident."

"I am," she says. "But it doesn't change what happened between us."

I glare down at my coffee, holding less important words at bay. "No, it doesn't."

"What do you want to do?" she asks, as if it were a transaction. "Should we forget it ever happened?"

"I don't think I could ever forget it ever happened." Last night was enchanting, thrilling, and heart-wrenching. I put my mug back on the table and swivel toward Gene. "Nothing has changed between us, has it?" I ask with a millimeter of hope that she'll admit the contrary. She stays quiet.

Relenting to her silence, I charge ahead. "We still have this animalistic magnetism for each other. But also, nothing has changed *with* us. We can't get married here, and you don't wanna be with me unless we get married and live wherever it's legal."

"You know why that's important for me," Gene says.

"And you know why I can't leave Miami." The impasse between us is a vast desert. She nods, her eyes losing their brilliance. I don't know what I expected, or what I hoped she'd say. Maybe that she could somehow resume her life with me, quietly making strides for her LGBTQ community. That makes the same sense as a police officer living with a jewel thief.

Fuck. She's right. Gene will never feel safe unless she adopts Susana. Or, at least, tries to. Maybe things will change and maybe they won't, but I can at least give her this. I can at least give her the opportunity to fight—for herself and other nonbiological parents.

I swallow my fear and face her. "Okay. Let me know when you want to sign the consent to adopt affidavit, or whatever you call it." I stand and pick up the empty mugs. "You're right to fight for your parental recognition of Susana. It's the least I can give you."

CHAPTER TWENTY-SEVEN

Gene

It's as though there's a flu outbreak at the pediatrician's office. Sniffling children crawling about the place like fire ants, parents trying to pacify them, and Isa and I sitting still, hoping the germs don't penetrate our pores. Despite the chaotic waiting area, we're ushered into an examination room quickly, but I'd give up the house and the Jeep not to be in this tiny box of a room right now.

Susana sits on the flimsy paper draped over the royal-blue padded exam bench, and it crunches under her butt. She swings her legs as Viv administers the preliminary physical exam. Isa stands to Susana's right, analyzing Viv's every move—with daggers.

"Open up," she says. Susana stops her legs, and Viv places a wooden tongue depressor on her tongue, slipping it just far enough to shine the penlight down her throat and see her tonsils. "Looks good."

Then, she removes the otoscope from its wall mount, places the conical side in Susana's ear, and looks through it, one eye clenched tightly while she gets close enough to the loupe to see clearly, humming during the whole process.

"Looks good there, too." Viv straightens, replacing the tool on its mount. "Next up, I'm going to take a look at your eyes." Viv grabs the ophthalmoscope and stretches its coiled cable to face Susana. "There's a bright light, but don't look at it, okay?" At Susana's nod, she continues, "Look at the top of my ear."

Isa, eyes wide open, fingers deepening their indentation into the padded table, holds her breath as the bone in her jaw stiffens. Although there's no romantic connection between Viv and me, having both in the same room eerily feels as though I'm Hester Prynne wearing a giant, iridescent letter A on my chest, standing on the scaffolding, accepting my due punishment.

I watch Viv's meticulous examination of Susana's left eye, and when she switches to the right, she asks, "Any headaches?"

"No, just in the weekend," Susana replies, with her little hand grasping the table, squirming against the bright light.

Viv returns the ophthalmoscope to the wall and turns to face me. I've been leaning up against the door, watching it all play out. "Everything seems to be fine. I'll wait until the pediatrician confirms it, but I don't see any side effects from the minor concussion she had on Thursday. And the cut on her forehead is healing nicely. You guys did a good job." My eyes drift behind her to where Isa is burning a hole in Viv's head. "I'm going to write up my notes, and the doctor should be in shortly." Viv turns her head for a quick glance at Isa, then returns her gaze to me. In a whisper she says, "Can we talk outside?" I nod and follow behind.

"I'll be right back," I say to Isa.

We get up to the counter where the receptionist sits, and Viv turns to face me, eyes wide, but seemingly happy. "Susana is going to be fine. You shouldn't worry."

"Oh, thank goodness." My relief is palpable as I run my fingers through my frazzled hair.

"How about I come over and bring some dinner, later? We can watch one of the movies we missed over the weekend."

I stare at her for a bit. "Sure." I let the word stretch over my tongue, and she seems to push her smile past her lips.

I catch the doctor entering Susana's exam room and hurry after her. "I'll see you later," I say over my shoulder.

Later, picking Susana up from school, I barely put the Jeep in neutral, with the emergency brake pulled, when I see Susana, all smiles, sprinting her way toward me. If ever there were an indication that she's all better, I'm staring right at it. Her teacher waits on the sidewalk with the other kids, dispatching a child at each approaching parent. I curl my lips and wave goodbye.

Walking to the passenger side, I open the door and slide the bucket seat forward for Susana to hop up and into the back seat. Why she always seems to be in a hurry, I don't know, but that's part of her personality that I love the most: her eagerness. Susana's little friends wave a final goodbye as I shut my door, and they disappear from my rearview mirror.

As soon as I merge into traffic, Susana pounces.

"I heard you and Mami fighting."

I glance at her through the rearview mirror. "When?"

"When I got hurt."

"Bebé, we weren't fighting." But her question makes me wonder what else she might have heard, or saw, for that matter.

"Yes, you were. You were in the family room, and I heard everything." Oh, brother.

Trying to figure out exactly what she may have heard is futile.

"Susana, I promise you," I say. "Mami and I were not fighting. We were disagreeing and then we came to a harmonious conclusion." Okay, maybe not harmonious. A flashback thumps my forehead of us glued to each other on Isa's bed.

"You said you have to adopt me," she says. Her glaring eyes drill on me through the rearview mirror. I can't concentrate on my words and the road at the same time, so I pull into a gas station and park next to the air pressure and vacuum machine. My seat belt gets stuck in its latch as I contort myself to face Susana in the back seat.

"What exactly did you hear?" I ask, finally dislodging the seat belt out of its death grip.

"You said that you have to adopt me and that you need Mami to sign some papers."

I steady my voice. "Okay, you're taking some of what you heard out of context." She's still only seven, so I'm treading carefully because at her age, she hates it when I talk down to her. She may be a smart cookie, but if she overheard Thursday's conversation, she might be as confused as I am.

"No, I didn't. How could I hear something out of context?"

"Well, because you may have started hearing us in the middle of our conversation," I respond. "Why don't you ask me what you want to know?"

"Why do you have to adopt me?" A chill creeps up my spine.

"What do you mean?" I ask.

"You're already my mother, aren't you? Why do you have to adopt me if you're already my mother?" I release a heavy sigh and get a little more comfortable.

"Cariño." I reach out and put my hand on her knee. "With people like us, it's a little more complicated."

"What does that meeeeen?" she whines. "Mami is always telling me that, but she never says why everything is always so complicated." She throws up her hands and then folds her spindly arms across her chest. A mini giggle escapes my lips. And I can't help it, but the scene is adorable.

"Okay," I say. "In your second-grade class, how many of your friends have parents like yours?"

"Mamá, like half the class!" she replies. The singsong way she says it is exactly how Isa used to speak to Martha when we were kids. It's starting to grate at me.

"Okay, you have friends in your class with two mothers?" I ask.

"No. But half the kids in the class live in more than one house, like me." She says it with a toothy smile.

"So, some of your friends' parents live in separate houses?"

"Yes. Like us."

"Okay, but none of them have two moms or two dads?"

"No. But Karyn has two dads. They all live in one house, though. She doesn't have two houses like me."

I don't want to get caught up in semantics with her because I don't want to confuse her further. And I realize I might be stalling for time, but it's so I can figure out how I'm going to explain our situation.

"Do you understand what it means to be a biological parent and an adoptive parent?" I ask.

"Yes, Benny is adopted, but he isn't in my class. He's in Mrs. Rodriguez's class. But I *don't want* to be adopted!"

"And why not?"

"Because then, I won't know who my parents are," she says and is just about to add a "duh" at the end, but my wide-eye mother's glare prevents her from uttering another word.

"Why do you say that?"

"Because Benny doesn't know his real parents."

"But you do, don't you? Who are your real parents, Susana?"

"Mamá! Pa-leeze! Can you just answer me?" she says, and I try to stifle another laugh but fail. "You and Mami are my real parents, who else?" This kid really knows how to push my buttons.

"Okay. I'm really happy that you said that, but answer this: Do you know who carried you in her belly?"

"That's easy! It was Mami. There are pictures with me inside her big belly."

"And what about me?"

"You're…" She pauses to think. "You're like the daddy." She chuckles. "But you're a mommy too 'cause you're a girl? You pay for everything!" she concludes, aglow with pride over her summation.

"Ha!" A guffaw escapes my lips with a little projectile spit. "But that's only because Mami and I share a bank account, and I pay everything that has to do with you." I stop laughing long enough to clear my throat. "So, you understand that I didn't give birth to you, meaning that I'm not related to you biologically, right?"

She nods. "Is that why it's so complicated? Because there aren't too many of you in my school?"

"Sort of," I reply. "Mami is your biological parent, but because we were never married, there's no record of me being involved when you were born, although I was right there next to Mami, holding her hand. Do you understand?"

Although skeptical, Susana nods, so I continue.

"When parents like us—two moms or two dads—have children, the parent who isn't biologically related to the baby would apply for a second-parent adoption. That's how it is now in cities such as Madrid. Here, Florida doesn't allow me to be your other mommy the way Mami is. And because she is, she signs your field trip forms, she can take you to the emergency room by herself like she did the other day, or when you're not feeling well. And she can make decisions for you that you can't make yet."

She pouts, kicking up her leg. "Because I'm too little."

"Right. So, that's why I'm trying to adopt you. Tomorrow, Mami and I will see the lawyer who will make it all possible. You see?" I ask. "It's important to me to be allowed to be your other mother. But only I would adopt you. Mami will always be your mom, too. Do you understand that?" I sit and wait for the information to filter through her. It's a lot for a seven-year-old to understand, but she's a smart kid.

"So, you want to adopt me, that's a good thing?" Her deep dark eyes, still so innocent, I can't help but hope they stay like that forever. But behind those innocent eyes is a critical thinker.

"It's a very good thing."

When I pull up to the apartment, I inhale deeply, close my eyes, and let it all go. That conversation with Susana could have gone in an entirely different direction if she weren't so bright. I get out of the Jeep and flip the passenger seat to let her out. Not paying attention to what she's doing, I fiddle with the passenger seat lever, making sure it stays forward. As I straighten, she pops out of the Jeep and throws herself onto me, wrapping her arms around my neck and her legs around my waist. Tentatively stunned, I gather myself to hold her with the same fervor as her squeezing arms. Her sweet gesture knocks me out of my head and fills me with tiny bursts of happiness fireworks.

"Come on, cariño," I say in her ear. My voice has all but vanished. "Let's get dinner started." But before she jumps down, she places a honeyed kiss on each of my cheeks.

"I love you," she says, melting away some of the calluses this process has developed over my heart. "You're my Mamá."

Hugging her tight, I swing her left and right, the way she's always loved. She lets her legs hang loose and squeals. "I love you, I love you, I love you," I say with about a thousand kisses to her neck, check, and nose.

While Susana is in her bedroom finishing her homework, I get a handle on dinner. She's only in second grade—far from curing cancer—but I love that her teacher makes the students read much more than I ever had to at her age. Since Isa had to work late, I've packed their dinner, so she won't have to worry about that.

Stopping at her open doorway, I tap on Susana's jamb to catch her attention. She's nose-deep in her reading book.

I lean up against the doorframe. "Dinner is almost ready, and Mami is on her way to come get you."

"Can we eat together?" she asks, doe-eyed, tearing at my heart. I look at my Swatch.

"Cariño, I think Mami would rather relax, take off her work clothes, and have a quiet dinner with you at the house." I wipe the image of a naked Isa from my mind. "Besides, I already packed your dinner." She gets up from the floor—her favorite place to do all her reading—looking as if she's just lost her puppy. I do hate to say no to her. My heart can't decide whether to break apart or crack up at this subtle manipulation tactic. I internalize the latter as I turn around and head into the living room, hiding a smirk.

I hear a quiet tapping on the front door, which is odd because Isa will normally ring the bell. Glancing through the window, I see Viv on the other side, and I tamp down the instinct to check my Swatch. Still in her green scrubs, she's holding a brown paper bag in her hand. Jesus, what has she brought now?

"I got takeout," she says when I open the door for her.

"Hi," I say, perplexed. I don't move to let her in the apartment. "I'm sorry, I haven't seen my phone in a while, did you message me?"

"No," she says, perhaps rethinking her idea. "I thought I'd pick up dinner. I'm sorry, I just got out, did I interrupt something?"

"No. Not really." I step outside with her and close the door behind me. "Susana hasn't left yet. The schedule got a bit out of whack today. And I've already made dinner."

"Oh. I can leave if you want, but I thought we were hanging out tonight."

"Yeees," I reply, tentatively. "But I thought you were getting here closer to eight." I'm hoping she won't realize I'd forgotten all about our plans tonight. There's a bit of a lull between us, but I relent and open the door for her. "I'm sorry, come on in." She follows and places the paper bag on the counter, next to the sink.

Susana runs into the living room thinking, as I had, that Isa is waiting for her. She pulls on the brakes when she sees someone else in the room. The inertia of her backpack slaps Susana in the back as she stops.

"Cariño," I say as I approach her. Standing behind her, I run my fingers around her shoulders. "You remember Viv from the doctor's office, don't you? Remember, she's also Christian's aunt and the one who brought you those cute pajamas you like so much."

"Hi," she says curtly. "Did you bring him?"

Viv smiles and steps closer to Susana. Bending to her eye level, she says, "No, honey, I didn't bring him today. But if you want, the four of us can do something fun together soon. Would you like that?"

Susana shifts her gaze up to me for approval. Fighting the urge to grimace, I nod in agreement to something that probably won't ever happen. Just when I think it can't get worse, from the corner of my eye I see Isa through the window, pulling the door open. Isa—in the same fitted pinstripe pantsuit as this morning—unwittingly, is walking into my worst nightmare. Well, my second worst, anyway.

"Hi," she says, clearing the step up to enter my apartment. She shuts the door behind her, cutting off all the oxygen in the room. As sweat gathers on the crown of my head and trickles down the sides of my face, my back muscles tense. My forehead, upper lip, and neck are also developing beads of perspiration.

"Well, it looks like the family's all here." Viv clasps her hands together. She lets them drop to her pelvis and remains speechless.

Isa turns to face Viv. It's a purposeful, slow-motion twist. "Oh. Hi. I didn't see you there. I'll get out of your way in a second." She turns around to Susana and says, "Bebé, are you ready to go?"

"Yes, Mami."

Isa turns to me. "I guess I'll see you tomorrow? Do you just want to meet there?"

"Yes, let's do that." I give her their dinner container.

"I'll text you when I'm leaving the hospital," she says, delivering a kiss to both my cheeks, then turns to face Viv. "It was nice seeing you again, Viv. Thanks for today."

Viv folds her arms over her chest. "Yeah. You too. Thanks."

Bending so Susana can wrap her arms around me, I kiss her goodbye. They disappear through the front door just as casually as Isa appeared.

After the door closes, Viv fixes her gaze through the window, watching Isa and Susana walk away. She turns to me. "Wow. That was…awkward."

I inwardly groan. All I want to do is melt in a puddle and sink underneath the floorboards. "How about we eat?" I take a deep breath and saunter back into the kitchen. "I can just put what I cooked away, and we can have the takeout you brought. Thanks, by the way." I lift the brown paper bag.

"Okay," she says, following behind me. "Here, let me get the plates."

"How was the rest of your day?" I ask mindlessly once we've served ourselves from the massive amount of fried rice Viv brought.

"Busy." She digs into her rice, moving bits of vegetables around. "Susana will be fine, you know. Kids take a tumble, but they always get back up." She sings it as if it were a jingle, but it feels as though she's mocking me.

The churn in my stomach is more of a gurgle than a rumbling of stomach acid aggravated by bad, greasy takeout.

"Yes, I know." I put my fork down and peer up at her. "But Isa said that she had thrown up and then passed out, so she rushed her to the hospital. Had it been just a simple bang, the way it had been for the other girl, I'm sure Isa would have applied an ice pack and called it a day."

"Oh. Right, there was nausea."

"Yes, *and* loss of consciousness."

"Right. But only for a few seconds."

This conversation is giving me the kind of headache that can only be subdued by something sharp. I suppose she'd sing a different tune if she had a child of her own. Doesn't she worry for her nephew's safety if he plays a sport as physical as soccer? I certainly do with my nieces. They are prone to roughhousing when they visit. And when Flor visits, my nerves are on the fringes with her boys practically throwing themselves off the roof.

"The neurologist saw fit to order a CT scan. I don't think she'd do that if she didn't think it was necessary," I say.

"Right. The neurologist." Viv also puts her fork down. "Didn't you tell me she was friends with your ex?"

"That's beside the point. I hardly think the head of neurology would order a CT scan for a child on the whim of the mother."

"No," she says. "But maybe for a special friend."

"Are you seriously telling me that we've exaggerated Susana's concussion?"

Viv taps her fingertips together above her plate. "Not exaggerated. But you must admit that your ex's professional reputation is intimidating, even to the director of neurology at Coral Gables Medical Center, who, I'm sure, would do anything to please the woman in charge of distributing therapeutical protocols to regional hospitals."

"Viv," I say. "This isn't like you. Why are you on offense?"

She ignores my question. "And how many times a month does she call you to come to her rescue when she can take care of matters herself? Because it's been at least four or five since we met." She pauses for a second because, apparently, she's not finished interrogating me.

"I called you *three* times on Thursday and sent *three* text messages, to which you've yet to reply," she says. "What were you getting up to with your ex that you couldn't at least reply to one of my messages?" The question grabs me unawares, and I'm speechless.

"While you spent the last four days, jugando mamá y papá, I was pulling double shifts at the hospital and worrying about your daughter—with whom you never let me spend any time—when maybe I shouldn't have," she says before I'm even able to answer her question about the messages. Or was that rhetorical? Admittedly, we were playing house over the weekend.

"Viv, what are you getting at?"

"What am I getting at?" She gets up from the table with her plate in hand and scrapes what's left of her fried rice into the trash can. Taking the empty plate to the sink, she throws it in with a crash, followed by her cutlery, its cacophony reverberating in my shoulders. She takes a deep breath and exhales it all out, as if giving her renewed life.

"I wanted to give you the benefit of the doubt. I really did. Even going so far as getting us dinner to spend a nice quiet evening together. *But I knew!* Something was niggling at me not to come tonight. And that you had probably spent the last four days in your ex's arms." She pauses for a moment. I guess she's trying to gauge my reaction, but I'm too stunned from her outburst to say anything at all. The disgusting food in front of me is making my stomach turn as I listen to her rant. And I deserve it. Has she said anything that isn't true? I mean, apart from our hyper-focused parenting, which I know isn't far-fetched. But I'm behind Isa in this case, as I am in most cases. Our seven-year-old daughter had a concussion. That is enough to scare the bejesus out of any parent.

"I saw you! I saw how you looked at each other. The energy between you and her was all over this room." Viv glares back at me, her hands glued to her hips, waiting for me to say something. But I have nothing to say. What can I say that won't sound super condescending?

"Did you sleep with her?" she asks.

"Viv," I say, getting a bit exhausted by her reprimands. I clear my throat. "I'm sorry, but I don't think that's any of your business."

"No. You know what?" she says with a grimace. "You're absolutely right. It *is* none of my goddamn business. But let me say this: she's never going to marry you, Gene. And *I'm* sorry, but Isa will never ever be the out lesbian you need in your life. You'll be miserable, pining for her the rest of your life."

She grabs her bag and throws it over her shoulder. Before she reaches for the door handle, she turns around with what are the closest I've ever seen to a demon's eyes and says, "A friendly tip, Gene. You should face the fact that she's going to marry Roberto. Because, you know…he's a man. And with him, she can have the family she's always wanted." She turns back around and slams the front door. I shove my own plate away from me and sink my face into my hands.

CHAPTER TWENTY-EIGHT

Isa ·

"Dr. Acosta." Cami calls out my name as I walk by her desk. I stop to glance at my watch, making sure I'm still okay for time.

"Yes, Cami?"

"Roberto asked me to give you this message." She hands me a pink slip of paper. I grab it and shove it in my pocket and enter my office. It's not until I'm at my desk that I remember I had stashed it in my lab coat.

Meet me in the atrium at 11:30 a.m.

I glance at my watch again, it's five till. Ugh, I hate kinks like this in my schedule. I became a scientist because I love the austere precision of the work. I meticulously plan every detail, down to the time of day an experiment starts. These types of unscheduled meetings Roberto loves—his work thrives on chaos, emergencies, and irregularities. They irritate me.

I'm meeting Gene at the lawyer's office in an hour and a half, and I don't have time for detours, especially not with the traffic I'm going to hit getting into Coral Gables. Pressing the speakerphone button and her saved number code, Gene's mobile rings once before she picks up.

"Hey," I say before she has a chance to answer. "I'm leaving the hospital in twenty minutes, so I'll be at Sergio's office in an hour and ten minutes. Can you have lunch afterward?" I can't continue to pretend that what happened on Thursday was meaningless, and I can't just put it behind us and move on. It won't stop replaying it in my head.

Gene agrees, and after we hang up I glance at my watch, pack up my computer, and change out of my lab coat and slip into my blazer. No one stops me as I enter the elevator. Burning a hole in my blazer pocket, I feel Roberto's note and sigh hard before slapping the L button instead of the parking garage.

As soon as the doors open, I'm out of the elevator, speeding toward the sunny atrium behind the lobby reception area. No one comes here in the middle of the day. The midday sun hits the glass ceiling and turns the atrium into a sauna. It's too hot for me, but he seems to take pleasure in sitting here alone. Opening the heavy glass door, I see him sitting by himself in his everyday green scrubs.

When he hears my heels clatter on the limestone garden tiles, he looks up from his phone. He's always on that damn thing. Not like Gene, who always keeps her BlackBerry on silent and in her shorts pocket or thrown somewhere around the apartment. I laugh to myself, thinking of Gene in her Bermudas, her basketball player's legs, muscular calves...

He gets up as I approach. "Hi. Thanks for meeting me."

"Hey." I lift my watch at him. "I have less than ten minutes." He gestures for me to sit, and when I do, he sits in the seat adjacent, not the one he'd been sitting in.

"I think we should formalize this relationship," he says abruptly. My ass hasn't even hit the fucking plastic chair.

"Isabel," he says, and the sound of my name on his lips feels like multiple stabs on my scapula. "We've been dating for fourteen months now, and I know it's been difficult to see each other on an ongoing basis, with our schedules not coinciding. But I think if we get married, we'll have the time we need to give this relationship wings."

"What?" I reply. And has it been that long? "Roberto, where is this coming from?" I ask, trying to remember the last time we even saw each other. He puts his hand in his scrub shirt pocket and pulls out a little red box with a goldleaf outline embellishment on its cover. *Mother of fucking pearl!* My eyes widen as he flips the Cartier box open, and sitting in the center is a rather garish solitaire engagement ring with a brilliant white diamond the size of a fucking garbanzo bean. Roberto plucks the ring out and, when he notices my wide-eyed reaction, grasps hold of my hand. I almost wince and pull it back but remind myself that he still thinks we're an item. Why can't men take a cold shoulder to mean it's over?

"Put it on. Wear it for a while and let me know what you think. You don't have to answer me now but wear it so you can get a feel for it." What the fuck? I'm in a bizarre dream as he slides the ring on, forcing it past my knuckle, until it sits at the base of my finger. I stare at this thing, and it looks to be cutting off my circulation.

"How did you know what size to get?" I ask.

"The last time you spent the night," he says. "You left your graduation ring on my dresser while you were showering. I outlined the size on a notepad."

Mother of fucking pearl! He fucking touched my graduation ring? That's my high school ring! The one that Gene locked into place when she was the last person to turn it. I try not to seethe in front of him or roll my eyes because my class ring goes on my smaller right hand.

"Roberto, I don't know what to say," I say, feigning a smile. I don't even know what that looks like. What I really want to do is tear the ring off my finger and throw it at him, but when I discreetly try turning it to slip it off, it doesn't budge over my knuckle. Damn my bony fingers.

"Don't say anything now. Wear it and give me an answer a month from now."

"A *month* from now?"

"Yes. Remember I'm leaving in the morning for the medical conference in Houston. I'll be gone for the week, and then I'm going to see my mother in Argentina for three weeks."

"Fine," I say as I stand. "I'm sorry, I really have to go."

"I'll call you tonight," he hollers at my back. Without turning, I wave at him with the back of my hand. A month? What the fuck?

CHAPTER TWENTY-NINE

Gene

Preoccupied over this petition, it's difficult to concentrate on my drawings. Knowing Children and Family Services is going to reject it, it's the lawsuit that really worries me. Jay seems to think that the uptick in positive public opinion toward the LGBTQ community gives us an edge in the courts, an edge that should compel judges to look beyond religion and rule that our rights are being violated. Contrary to what the opposition says about children reared by LGBTQ parents, studies have shown them to thrive.

It's almost eleven thirty, and as I gather my things to get out of the apartment, my phone starts buzzing on my drafting table. I grab it, knowing it's going to be Isa.

"Hey," she says, her voice smooth, almost sweet. "I'm leaving the hospital in twenty minutes, so I'll be at Sergio's office in an hour and ten minutes. Can you have lunch afterward?" she asks. And since it's impossible for me to say no to her, I agree and end the call.

Sergio Rodriguez was my parents' lawyer. Hailing from a long line of Basque Country fishermen, Sergio fled Spain, escaping Francisco Franco's authoritative, anti-gay regime. He was also Tito Horacio's onetime lover when they were students at the University of Miami. My parents immigrated to the US with Tito, also for fear that Franco's henchmen would arrest my uncle and institutionalize him for his homosexuality.

After my parents' death, Sergio had all the answers when we didn't even know what questions to ask. Together, they had set up the trust that left both Lui and me financially stable after their horrible wreck. Sergio also set up a revocable trust for Susana that includes all my assets.

Because Isa and I had agreed to meet at Sergio's office at one in the afternoon today, Martha will pick up Susana from school and bring her to the apartment to start on her homework.

I'm at his office building early. It's barely twelve thirty, so I'm waiting for Isa in the lobby, facing the bank of elevators she'll use to enter the building from the parking garage. Although I live nearby, I like to give myself enough time to sit and collect my thoughts so I'm not jumpy in his office. If Isa is punctual, I'm habitually early. But sitting here, I can't help the tinge of anxiety bubbling over the surface. This great plan of mine might blow up in my face. I smooth out my slacks as if smoothing out my tense muscles. Not used to wearing dress pants, they feel alien and stifling on me, and impossibly, my knees are sweating. The long-sleeve button-down shirt doesn't make me feel more confident, either. I wish I could do this in a pair of khaki shorts and Birkenstocks.

The elevator doors slide open and Isa pops out in a white button-down blouse and a solid navy blazer. Her fancy pants have a gray pinstripe so fine, you can barely tell it's there, but I can. She's commanding in her needle-like heels, her medical ID badge clipped to her lapel, laptop bag strapped to her left shoulder. Isa strides into the lobby like a rooster roaming through the henhouse, her left hand loose in her pocket as she holds the strap of her bag in place with her right.

Trying not to fall over my tongue, I right myself to greet her as she approaches. Isa delivers a light kiss on both my cheeks and says, "Ready?" as she glances at her own watch. She still wears the stainless-steel Mont Blanc Star Legacy Automatic that I bought her when she finished her PhD. The way she wears it loosely on her wrist catches my eye every time. Since she's a lefty, she wears her watch on her right wrist.

"Yep, let's go." We walk toward the bank of elevators for his floor and wait for the doors to open. "You want to go to Sergio's after?"

She furrows her brow, and I realize her confusion. "The restaurant on the corner, I mean." I hold the elevator doors open for her to step inside and hit the number fifteen button for Sergio's floor.

Isa emits a light chuckle and shakes her head. "That place is too loud, and I don't want to smell like a deep fryer when I return to the lab. Why don't we go to the house? I have plenty of leftovers I can heat up."

"Oh. Eh, sure," I say as cold sweats trickle down my spine. "Sergio should have the paperwork done, we're just signing it today, I think."

"Yeah, that's fine," she says indifferently, hitting the fifteen button twice more. As we wait for the doors to open, I catch Isa rapidly tapping the right toes of her alluring leather pumps. Finally, the elevator drops us off, and we amble the few steps it takes to get to the double doors of Sergio's office suite. Tamping down the nostalgia that first brought us to this office ten years ago, I take a few deep breaths and open the door for Isa.

We're instantly greeted by a cheery Andrea from behind her bulky wood desk as I close the door behind me. She gets up and rounds the massive piece of furniture to place a kiss on each of Isa's cheeks and follows suit with me. Not until I became an adult and moved back to Miami did I encounter so many Spaniards. I guess my parents had their own network to which I was not privy.

"He's ready to see you." Andrea sweeps her right arm toward Sergio's closed door. "Please go ahead." She picks up her extension to let him know we're coming through.

Sergio is gathering paperwork at his conference table just as we walk into his office.

"Ladies, it's nice to see you again." He gets up from his luxurious office chair and walks over to greet us. "¿Que tal está Susanita?" The first time we were here, Sergio was a bit dry with us. After years of doing business with him, he and his staff have become like an extended family—great-aunts and uncles you'd rarely see if it weren't for the family gatherings during the holidays.

"Well, she had a minor incident on Thursday, but nothing serious," Isa replies and briefly glosses over what happened.

"My nephews get into all kinds of mischief playing sports. But now they're into American football and my sister has gnawed off all her fingernails." His arms are outstretched, leading us toward the conference table. "That's what she gets for marrying un gringo. Let's have a seat, shall we?"

Isa turns and reaches for the chair right in front of her and sits resting her hands in her lap. I walk around the table and sit on the opposite side, facing her. Sergio sits in his spot at the head.

"Gene, thank you so much for including me in your family and estate planning." Sergio pans his gaze from me to Isa. "It's been a pleasure witnessing how well our meticulous planning has functioned."

Yeah, I'll bet, I think, hearing the cha-ching of a cash register. But I shouldn't be annoyed with him. It's not his fault we're lesbians having to file extra paperwork so the government doesn't screw us over.

"What you're doing with this petition is leading the way for others to freely participate in their children's upbringing. And I commend you for that. You're as tenacious as your uncle, and I see so much of him in you." I smile and nod because it's all I can do to hold down the waterworks. That's honestly the kindest thing he's ever said to me.

"Isa," he says, placing a document in front of her. "This is the document stating you consent to Gene's petition to adopt Susana as her second parent. Please take your time reviewing it and sign this page, and initial here." After pointing to the areas she's to initial and sign, he places a heavy black pen on top of the document.

While Isa reads every page he placed in front of her, I busy myself picking at a thread in the outer seam of my slacks. My thumping heart forces the blood through my veins with so much pressure that I'm surprised no one hears it splashing through the walls of my arteries. Meanwhile, it's as though an hour goes by when I hear the rubbing of the fountain pen nib as Isa runs her signature along the bottom of the last two pages. Staring at my hands, I'm willing them to stop jittering because I just can't bring myself to watch Isa sign the papers, in case she decides she doesn't want to sign anything and scratches out her name.

"Perfect," Sergio says, taking the pages and setting them aside. He takes the other set of pages and puts them in front of me. "Read this through. I've already included the pertinent information, and as you can see, I've checked off that we have a signed affidavit giving you consent." The pen thumps audibly as he sets it down on the document, almost like a gavel striking its sound block. I swiftly pluck the pen up and rest it between my index and middle fingers. Lifting the pages, the first thing I see in bold caps is the title.

JOINT PETITION FOR ADOPTION BY SECOND PARENT

It feels official. I skim through its contents, making sure my legal name is spelled correctly and all the right boxes are ticked. On the last page, my heart lodges in my throat when I read the oath.

I understand that I am swearing or affirming under oath to the truthfulness of the claims made in this petition and that the punishment for knowingly making a false statement includes fines and/or imprisonment.

With a hard gulp, I sign my name under the printed version Sergio typed out beforehand and slide the pages back to him. I think I need a minute to collect myself. While Isa is busy reading, I close my eyes, and try to relax the muscles bunched up at the base of my neck and shoulders.

"Here you go," Isa says to Sergio. I open my eyes and lock onto her gleamy gaze for a moment. I think I see hope in her eyes.

When she slides the pages back for Sergio to notarize, the relief on my shoulders is immediate. A weight as burdensome as this conference table was bearing down on me, and today, for the first time, the pressure seems to ease off. The light, however dim, is there at the end of the tunnel.

"Okay, well," Sergio says as he evens out the pages and stacks them neatly next to the consent form. "I'll file these with the court first thing tomorrow morning. They will contact me once a decision has been made. But you know what that will most likely be." Almost as if on cue, my stomach yelps a growling protest.

Isa walks through the double doors, and as I turn to follow, my heart pounding with a mix of emotions, I instinctively reach out to shake Sergio's hand. But then, something strange urges me, beyond my control, I find myself tugging on his pudgy hand and pulling him into an embrace. Smelling of musk and heavy aftershave, Sergio wraps his arm around my shoulder, and a rush like electric currents run through my body. My heart shakes up a heady cocktail of feelings, using gratitude, admiration, and a sense of camaraderie as ingredients. Seemingly taken aback by my sudden display of affection at first, Sergio relaxes into the embrace, and we stand together, lost in our own thoughts.

Finally, as we pull away from each other, Sergio's lips have curled into a faint smile. It's a tiny gesture, speaking volumes about the bond we've forged over the years. In this instant, I know, regardless of what the future holds, I have a friend and ally in him.

"Thank you so much for everything you've done for me and my family," I say, eyes stinging with hot tears.

Following Isa to the house, my hands stick to the steering wheel like humid suction cups. The knot in my throat lingers. Parking behind Isa's SUV, I sit for a moment planning out my next move. *What does Isa want to talk about?* Suddenly, I'm walking to the gallows as I make my way to the side door behind her. Entering the house, immediately the stagnant air chokes me. Isa must have the air conditioner set at eighty degrees. September in Miami is still stuffy, and as I think about today's date, I can't help but notice it's been two years and two months since I left. The stiff realization makes breathing arduous, and my neck itches with the sudden need to flee. All is quiet as we approach the kitchen archway. I can't help remembering what happened on Thursday as I glance to my right, past the cloistered arches leading into the family room, and why it happened.

Isa peers inside the refrigerator. "Okay. We can have the boliche I made over the weekend, or we can have the arroz negro you gave us yesterday."

"I'll have the boliche. It was delicious on Saturday, it'll be even better today," I say of her Cuban roast, marinating in its sauce. I'd rather not subject her to my squid ink rice—it would be like eating mounds of tiny toothpicks. I threw mine out the minute I tasted it.

Isa fixes two plates to heat up as I watch in silence. There's a cozy air about the scene before me. I sit back in my chair at the corner of the kitchen table. This is where I've always sat, where I'll always sit, I'm sure of it. But I can't help but suspect that the only reason she wanted to have lunch with me is to drop some horrible news. And the anticipation is nauseating.

"What do you want to drink?" she asks as she sets the plates on the table.

"Uh, water is fine with me."

She makes her way back to the cupboard beside the refrigerator and grabs two water glasses. When we moved back, we hadn't changed the essence of the house. I remodeled the kitchen but left the footprint intact. Everything here is as familiar as the picture before me. The woman, whom I once considered my wife, moving about the kitchen is as beautiful as ever, and that's when I notice it. I can't believe I hadn't seen it before. Running through everything like an instant replay, I only saw Isa's right hand. Her watch hand. Her left hand had been in her pocket the whole damn time. Was she hiding it from me?

The ring, a solitaire with an enormous, shiny diamond on a simple gold band, sits tightly around her left ring finger. A subtle piece of jewelry, a simple white gold or platinum band with a delicate, meaningful engraving inside would have been better than this gaudy status symbol. It would have matched Isa's taste for classic elegance. Ugh. I stop the fairy tale in my head, the romance that sent us astray on Thursday, the memories this house invokes. Everything.

As the rug is yanked from under me, I begin to feel the same falling sensation from my nightmares. Viv was right.

Sitting down, I don't have a perch under my feet, but Isa casually brings the items we'll use for our cordial lunch together, and I can't stand it. Should I say something or wait for her to bring it up? Because that's what I'm here for, right? I really am in the gallows. She's going to tell me that Roberto has proposed to her, and she's accepted. A tiny hand wraps around my heart, clutching at it, draining it of life, and is now serving me my own clotted blood's morcilla with my lunch. And the funny thing is, I knew this would happen. It was only a matter of time, and when I met him, with his cocky smile, his sophisticated yet cavalier air, his menacing eyes, I just knew it.

Isa finally sits in her chair next to mine, and all I can do is stare at this dead slab of beef as my eyes bleed salted tears. I'm frozen with my hand hovering over my cutlery-laden napkin, trying to keep my composure. Talking myself off the ledge, I can't quite get a grip on my emotions. Enfoca! But I can't focus.

"What is it? You're not eating," Isa says, oblivious to my silent soliloquy.

I edge up on her, and by now my tears are just surfing down my cheeks.

"That's some piece of jewelry," I say with a voice so broken I can't put it back together again with the strongest of the superglues. I gesture at her ring with my index finger. It turns out, I couldn't wait. Isa bites her lips as she stares down at the ring. That ring, tacky, garish, and so unbelievably pretentious. How can anyone with an iota of taste purchase such a thing?

With her knife still in her hand, it would be easier if she'd just throw it at my heart. "You…didn't have that on…over the weekend," I say slowly as if she wouldn't understand my words otherwise. But she does.

"It just happened…this morning, Roberto and I…in the hospital atrium." *How romantic, a hot Miami atrium.*

"You said yes," I say, because it's more of an expectation.

"He asked me to wear the ring while I made up my mind. But, look, I can't take it off." She grasps the ring with her fingers and seemingly tries to pull it off.

"Yeah…no…right," I babble nonsensically. "Of course." I rise from my chair. It doesn't matter, none of it matters. Glancing at my Swatch, the band is millimeters from breaking off, I tear out of my chair.

"I'm sorry, I didn't realize how late it was. I actually have a meeting at three and…I gotta go." Leaving the food untouched, I sprint out the side door, jump in my Jeep, and take off to the apartment.

Martha's minivan is in the driveway, jarring my memory that she picked up Susana from school today—a lifetime ago. I've got to calm down before walking into the apartment. One glance at myself in the rearview mirror and I'm a hot mess. Maudlin eyes, blotchy ruddy cheeks, and a frown so barren, the best I can do is wipe my face with my sleeve. I get out of the Jeep and amble up to the front door. *Just breathe.*

The apartment is silent, so I put my backpack down on the couch and search for warm bodies. Opening Susana's door, I get a glimpse of Martha sitting on the floor with her granddaughter. Susana, lying on her tummy, writing in her math workbook. Using her forearms, she holds her torso up like a cobra. Her legs are bent and the bottoms of her shoes point toward the ceiling, one foot then the other, swing toward her butt.

"Hi," I say, catching them off guard. Susana pushes herself upright and greets me with an impenetrable hug and a kiss on each cheek. Martha is slower to get up and her knees crack, but she greets me just as warmly.

"How did it go?" she asks as Susana settles herself back on the floor. I hitch my thumb toward the hall, and she follows me back out to the living room and sits on one of the club chairs.

"It was easier than I thought," I say truthfully about the first part of my afternoon. I sit on the arm of the couch. "Did you want something to drink or eat?" I ask, minding my manners. When Martha shakes her head, I continue recounting the meaningful hour we spent at Sergio's office, my sweaty palms glued to my knees.

"What else did you do?" she asks, turning her wrist to check her watch. "It's almost three."

I hesitate for a second, searching for the words. Does she know? If she doesn't know, how am I going to tell her? But it all tumbles down over my face like a sudden avalanche of sorrow. I slide down the arm and thump into the couch cushion, my cheeks rigid from dried tears. A sob breaks free, and I dig my face into my palms.

"Pero ¿qué te pasó?" Martha asks, rushing beside me on the couch. She wedges her hands between my head and my palms to pull my face toward her. "What is it?" I don't want to open my eyes, but when I do, all I see are images of the Argentine and Isa tangoing toward the altar. I inhale so deeply not even a Hoover could manage the suction and launch into what happened.

"Isa wanted to have lunch."

"Okay?"

"He's asked her to marry him," I spit out as if it were a mouthful of sour milk. I hadn't meant to blurt it out, especially because I don't know whether Isa has told Martha.

"No!" she says, surprised by my news. "She hasn't told me anything. When did this happen?"

"This morning, apparently," I reply, standing up. I wander into the kitchen, spaced out, and rip off a paper towel to wipe my face. "The proof is right there on her finger." I'm unable to keep the sarcasm from my tone.

"What?" she asks.

"She's wearing his ring."

CHAPTER THIRTY

Isa

The lab is somberly quiet when I get off the elevator and head toward my office. Camila sees me, and automatically she's on her feet with a pile of messages in hand.

She keeps pace with me. "The mayor-elect wants to speak to you." The clacking of our heels can surely be heard clear across the lab.

"Which one?"

"Coral Gables."

"Oh. So, not the county mayor?"

"He's not the mayor-elect, now, is he?"

"No, guess you're right. Who else?"

"Richter Pharmaceuticals called you back," she answers, not even panting. "A Mr. Brooke, from their cardiac department is what he said."

I nod, recognizing the name. "Who else?"

"Dr. Peterson wants to see you in his office at four today." I roll my eyes and check my watch. Three thirty. I want to deal with Peterson about as much as I want to spray myself with pollen to attract honeybees. In fact, I can call everyone else tomorrow, but Dr. Peterson... I just can't bring myself to meet with him.

"Okay," I say, unlocking my office door. "Anything else?"

"Your mom. She wants to talk to you as soon as you get back."

"Of course she does."

"What?"

"Nothing." Reminding myself that Cami is Roberto's cousin, I zip my lip. I don't even know if he's said anything to her.

"Thanks, Camila, I'll just take these," I say, extending my hand to receive my messages.

"What do you want me to do about Dr. Peterson?" Her eyebrows arch, and she adjusts her cardigan so it wraps tighter around her torso.

"Tell him I'll be there at four." Walking into my office, I slam the door behind me.

At my desk, I drop my head into my palms, drill my fingers through my temples. With a puff of *how can this get any worse*, I press the speakerphone button on my extension and tap the button for Mami's house.

"Isabel Susana Acosta!" she yells, surely after checking the caller ID. "What the hell happened?"

Should I play dumb? Probably best to get on with it.

"Gene told you."

"How could she not? She's devastated, poor thing. What's going on?" Mami was never the disciplinarian. That was my father's job, and he did it well. But since Gene left the house, she's been at her defense, wagging her finger in my face for every hurt feeling I've caused her.

"Mami, I love you. I really do. But my relationship with Gene has nothing to do with you. ¡Caballero! You can't be on her side all the time. *I'm* your daughter." As I begin to feel the sting of tears, I take a moment and count to ten.

"Yes, Roberto asked me to marry him. It happened this morning. That's when he put that god-awful ring on my finger. I tried to take it off, but I'd have had to go back up to the lab to get it off with soapy water, and I just didn't have time if I wanted to meet Gene on time. I was in a rush to get to Sergio's office. I wanted to talk to Gene about something else, but when she saw the ring, she bolted. I didn't even get a chance to explain—to tell her how I feel."

"Well? How do you feel?" When I don't immediately respond, she continues, "Amor, be honest with yourself, not just with Gene. You're unhappy. You both are. Admit it. Están miserable."

I clear my throat, preventing my voice from falling apart. "Mami, it's not that simple. Gene needs to find herself. That's what she told me. And whether it's with this woman she's been seeing or with her organization or whatever it is, she told me she needs to find her own way. And I need to stand down to give her the space to figure it out for herself."

"What about Roberto?"

"He's kind. A respected surgeon. With Roberto I can have a normal life."

"Normal, ha!" She exhales. "You know what's normal? Love is normal. You spending your time with a man you don't love is not normal."

"Mami, te tengo que dejar. I have to get back to work." I slam the phone down.

Sitting back in my unreliable, piece-of-shit chair, I hate the way I ended my call with Mami. It irks me to talk to her like that, but I need time to think. I need to think about my own life—what do I want to do? I mean, I know what everyone wants me to do. And I know very well what I want to do. But is getting back together with Gene the right thing *to do*—for all of us?

CHAPTER THIRTY-ONE

Gene

The clacking of my BlackBerry against my nightstand wakes me out of the repulsive nightmare where Isa tells me she's marrying Roberto, again. I reach to silence the phone, but in my haze I press the wrong button and the call is now on speaker. *Goddamn this BlackBerry!*

"Get up," she says. "Let's go to Apple."

"What?" I look at the screen. "Martha, it's five thirty in the morning."

"I want an Apple Phone thingy, and I know you want one, too." Her tone is as unrelenting as a weed.

"Wait, you mean you'll wait in line with me?" I shuffle upright in bed.

"Well, I will now."

"Okay." I peer at my Swatch. "Give me thirty minutes to get ready, and I'll pick you up."

"¡Perfecto! I'll have café con leche and tostadas waiting."

I arrive at Martha's house twenty-nine minutes later. The gate is already open for me, and I slip the Jeep through. She's kept the Mediterranean-style exterior of this house the same for decades. A majestically gabled, single-story stucco house with a dark-brown barrel-tile roof and a light cream base color, the house is quintessential 1920s Coral Gables architecture. The windows and trim match the dark-brown roof. Every few years, a crew comes out to touch up the paint and replace fixtures, ensuring it's as pristine as it was when Martha and Carlos bought it nearly forty years ago. The house stands thirty feet behind a dark brown wrought iron gate flanked by cement posts, painted the same cream color as the house. It's one of my favorite architectural homes in the Gables.

Martha answers the door immediately after I ring the bell, as if she's been waiting for me in the foyer. The smell in here always reminds me of my parents. It echoes the early nineties, when we all gathered here for special occasions. It's a homecoming, much like the first time my family and I set foot in this house.

Even with Isa's loud family members—everyone talking over each other, salsa music blaring on the stereo, couples finding small spaces for dancing, Isa's grandmother in the kitchen making a raucous with pots and pans, las comelatas—this house has always been a source of serenity for me.

Since Carlos's death, Martha has updated the bathrooms and the kitchen, and had the sunken floor in the family room leveled off for better flow. Her stylish taste shows up in every detail she puts in her home. All the changes make me wonder if she's planning to sell it. It would be the end of an era if she does.

I make my way to the kitchen, and she's already served me a plate with the tostadas right next to my mug of café con leche. I don't drink cow's milk anymore, so this is a real treat.

Martha saunters behind the bar and wipes down the countertop. "If the line at the Apple Store in Dadeland is too long, can we go to the one on the beach?"

"Martha, the iPhone has been out for a few months now, so I don't think the lines are going to be as bad as that." I glance at my BlackBerry to be sure and realize that we're already in October.

"And why, if you were so excited to get an iPhone, did you wait so long to get it? I mean if it's been out for months."

I look at her, nearly drop my tostadas. "Well, let's just say I've been preoccupied with life."

Martha wipes down my area of the countertop, again. "You mean you've been eating your feelings. Bueno, espabílate. You have to get out of the house and get your new phone."

I move past her quip and perk up about the new iPhone. "I've actually been excited for this phone to come out. It's the first phone to have multi-touch technology."

"Oh, that's great, wonderful. What's that again?"

"It means that the phone recognizes multiple points-of-contact on the screen. In other words, it's a touch-screen computer."

"Oh. And that's good?" she asks.

"Very good." I hold up my phone. "Better than this BlackBerry, anyway. The new phone will give me better functionality than any other mobile device, especially with my firm's MacOS-based network. It's like having a computer in my pocket."

"Bueno, what are we waiting for? Let's go!"

Although the iPhone has been available since June, the lines are still annoying. We're at the Dadeland store, and after waiting an hour, we're finally fourth in line.

"Isa hasn't made a decision yet," Martha says.

Somehow, I knew Martha had an ulterior motive to wait in this long line with me.

"Well, what is she waiting for? He asked her a month ago," I say with a brusque undertone. I hadn't intended it to come out that way, not with Martha.

Martha glares at me from the top rim of her readers. "She might be waiting for a reaction from you. You can't just ignore what's happening."

"Well, what else am I supposed to do? Someone else wants to marry her. Someone, I might add, who has every right to marry her. He put a ring on her finger! There's nothing for me to do, Martha." I cross my arms over my chest. The next person in line gets called to enter the store and the rest of us move one step closer.

"She doesn't love him," Martha says.

"What do you mean she doesn't love him? They've been together for longer than a year."

"Oh, he doesn't matter to her. They barely even see one another. As far as I know he's been out with her and Susana twice, and I was with them for half those outings. He talked so much about absolutely nothing. Isa thinks I didn't notice, but she spent the entire lunch rolling her eyes at him. You know very well if she were serious about him, she'd invest in developing a relationship between him and Susana."

"Really?" I ask. "What did he talk about that she rolled her eyes?"

"Nonsense about how he inserted an I-don't-know-what in the heart of a newborn. I mean, it's not nonsense, of course, but I don't know anything about that. He could have talked about something interesting. Maybe talked about his life in Buenos Aires. But no, incessant talk about his job that I don't care about. Ay, es un pedante."

I let out a minor chuckle at her last comment. "Even so, it's up to Isa to decide if she wants to marry him."

"Hmm," she hums.

"Hmm, what?"

"How's Viv?" she asks suddenly. I drop my chin to my chest.

"For your information, Viv and I were never dating. But, since you're so curious, I haven't heard from her in a while," I say with a heavy sigh.

"And what happened there?"

"I happened," I admit. But Martha is undeterred. She rolls her index finger forward, motioning for me to go enlighten her.

"I think I forced myself to create a friendship with her when I knew she wanted more. I was clear with her from the start that I wanted to be friends and that I wasn't looking for anything more than that. She must have misinterpreted that into thinking she could change my mind. And she went along with our friendship, waiting until I ended up falling in love with her. But now I think I...unintentionally...deliberately... sought out her company, partly because Isa had moved on with someone else. I don't know. I didn't want to be lonely, but I didn't really want to be with her either." The enormity of the revelation weighs on my shoulders.

"And what was the final straw?"

"Last month when I spent the weekend at the house, taking care of Susana was what blew up in my face," I reply. "I'm not good at hiding my feelings. And I suppose when Isa walked in to pick up Susana that Monday, everything became clear to Viv as to why I haven't advanced our relationship."

The Apple Store rep interrupts, motioning for us to come inside. Martha and I walk into the minimalist store, and instantly my architect's eye roams around the interior, focusing on every sharp angle, every light wood-toned table, marveling at the high ceiling. This structure could easily be a three-story building, but these ceilings make this space feel airy.

An energetic woman with braces on her teeth greets us. "Hi. How may I help you today?" She looks to be in her early twenties. Her dark eyes and broody features triggers memories of Isa at that age.

After a few quiet moments, Martha interjects. "We want Apple Phones, of course!"

At lunch, over a plate of southwestern-style appetizers, Martha and I run through a quick but informative tutorial and compare the insane features the other has discovered. The new phone is intuitive, and I've already added some of the apps Lui and Flor keep raving about, one of them is a handy texting app that will let us text with our cousins in Spain for free. They've already got a family group going, which I haven't used because the app is not compatible with my BlackBerry model. I send Lui a message asking him to invite me to the chat group so I can see what the heck I've been missing.

Suddenly, my iPhone comes to life in my hand with an odious default robotic ring tone. I'll have to change that after I get off the call. Flor's name appears on the screen with the slider on the bottom to answer the call. Lui must have told her about my new purchase.

I turn the phone so Martha can see. "It's Flor." I wouldn't answer the call in the middle of our lunch otherwise.

I greet her with an, "¡Hola guapa!" But before I can say anything else, she exhales a deep sigh. Or was that a sob?

"Gene! It's Don Rigoberto. He fell off the grape truck during the harvest, hit his head on the way down, and hasn't regained consciousness."

I don't think I heard her right. "What? Can you say that again? What happened?"

"On Monday," she replies. "He was with his workers, harvesting the grapes. He was standing in the back of the truck bed. The workers threw the grapes over while he sorted them. Well, apparently, during one of those throws, he tried to catch a batch that was too far for his reach, and it propelled him back and over the side of the truck. He hit his head on the way down. He's in a coma in the hospital now."

"¡Joder! But why did you wait until now to tell me?"

"Gene," she says, trying to hold her frustration. "Honestly, I didn't want to worry you in case it was just a bump on the head. You know how he is with his vertigo. But now it's Thursday and he's still lying in a hospital bed in Cadiz, ¡coño!"

"Okay. I'm coming over there!" I say, determined not to freak out.

"¿Qué pasó?" Martha asks as soon as I end the call.

"It's Don Rigoberto," I say and give her a synopsis of his condition as I wave down the waitress for the check. Martha places a comforting hand over mine as I share the news.

"I need to go to Jerez."

I haven't seen my grandfather in more than a year. Despite the distance between us, we've managed to keep in touch through letters. When my parents were killed, he was instrumental in maintaining our relationship, sending me the sweetest letters. At first, they were informational letters about the land and the vineyard. Recently, though, they've been more sentimental, writing about how he and Abuela met and fell in love. Lui receives his fair share of correspondence from our grandfather as well. And when our grandmother died, the letters seemed to increase. In fact, I just got one last month that, because of Susana's incident, I haven't finished reading.

Once I pay the bill, Martha and I rush back to the Jeep. My heart speeds faster than I do in the Jeep, and we arrive in our neighborhood without me knowing exactly how we got there. Martha puts her hand on my forearm and says in the most serene voice, "Take me to the apartment. I'm going to help you get your things together and arrange your transportation. Everything is going to be okay." She leaves her hand where it is. As I park in my spot, my heart slows to a normal rhythm.

"I have to call Isa," I tell Martha as I retrieve my suitcase from the top shelf in my closet. Unzipping the bag and tossing it on my bed, I look at her in what I'm sure is bewilderment because it's how I feel. "She has a medical conference in a few days, and Susana is supposed to stay with me for the week." Still at a loss, I want to be in Spain with my family, but the older I get, the harder it is for me to leave Susana.

"Don't worry, I'll get her on the phone," Martha says, disappearing toward the hallway. I'm relieved she's here. Swiping through the phone's weather app, I search for Andalusia to pack the right clothes. It's October, but the south of Spain can still be quite temperate this time of year. I'm only planning on taking a carry-on to make it easier to haul on the train, but if I end up staying longer, I can always do laundry at Don Rigoberto's house. His house might look like an ancient Mediterranean farmhouse, but he has all the modern amenities for this gringa. Or his gringuita, as he'd call me.

It's certainly not a Spanish tradition to call my grandfather Don Rigoberto—Mamá and Tito Rigo called him that all their lives. The López side of my family are rather formal people, so we spoke to my grandparents using the Spanish formal you, usted, rather than the informal tú.

"Hi, Mami," Isa says through the iPhone's speaker. "Did you get your precious iPhones yet?" She must still be ticked off because I asked her to take Susana to school today.

"Hola, mi amor," Martha replies in a somber tone. "I'm here with Gene, you're on the speaker thing."

"What's going on?" Isa asks.

"Isa," I say raising my voice. "Don Rigoberto is in the hospital."

"Oh my God, what happened?"

I reiterate the events for her. "He's been the in the Hospital General de Cadiz since Monday. I'm packing a bag so I can get there in the morning and see him."

"Gene, I'm so sorry," she says. "What can I do? When are you leaving?"

When my grandmother died suddenly, scarcely a year after my parents, we were able to make it to Jerez the following day. I'm hoping to do the same now.

"I'm leaving on the first flight I can find."

"Let me book it for you while you're packing. Should I just get you a one-way ticket?"

"I'm not sure," I say and stop what I'm doing to think for a moment. "Yeah, better leave it as a one-way ticket, and when I get a handle of the situation, I can book my flight home."

"I'm on it," she says, and the call ends. Martha places the phone in her back pocket and folds the clothes that I'm throwing on the bed into neat stacks that I can shove in my packing cubes. Making sure everything in my toiletry bag is topped off, I toss it in Martha's direction on the bed. I always make lists of things to pack on trips, but I don't have time to be fussy.

As I'm looking at the clothes Martha has already folded and the items left to pack on my bed, my iPhone buzzes in my pocket. *Shit. What if Isa couldn't find a flight?*

"Hey," I say, disillusioned about making it to Spain by tomorrow.

"Okay. I booked you on the next flight. It leaves at eleven tonight, so you have plenty of time to get to the airport, so breathe."

And I do. I exhale a heavy sigh of relief. "Thank you so much. I thought for sure I was gonna have to wait a few days to leave."

"Well…" she says, hesitantly. "Thank me after you see the account balance."

"What do you mean?"

"The flight is full, so I got you on the last seat available…
in first class."

"Oh. Wow. I'd better transfer some money into that
account."

"Don't worry, I took care of it."

I close my eyes tightly. "Thank you, Isa."

"Consider it an early Christmas gift."

CHAPTER THIRTY-TWO

Isa

Hanging up with Gene, my belly surges with urgency in an otherwise bleak set of circumstances. The clock on my computer screen reads 2:10. Decision made, I shut down my laptop, shove it in my bag, and lock up my office. On my way out, I hear my name bellowed behind me and avoid stopping, but Dr. Peterson is persistent.

"Isabel!" he calls out again. "Where are you rushing to now?" He suddenly catches up to me, and I can tell he doesn't care about the answer, whatever it may be.

"I'm sorry, Dr. Peterson," I say, mentally zoning out his likely derogatory comment. "I'm on my way to pick up my daughter at school."

"Oh. All this time I thought you had a nanny service to pick her up."

"I don't know why. I've never said anything remotely similar regarding her. In fact, I've never mentioned how I manage my life outside of these walls." I wave my free hand toward the dank laboratory, teeming with eager interns.

He's silent for an instant, crossing his arms over his chest as if measuring his words. He staples his filmy eyes on mine. Moving closer to the elevator, I take my eyes off him and push the down button.

"Have you secured the funding for your human tissue heart valve yet?"

"Not completely, Dr. Peterson, but I'm on top of it. I should know what's coming down the pipeline by the end of the week." He knows better than to ask. These things, especially funding for scientific research of this magnitude, take time.

He makes a show at peering at his watch, his balding scalp oily—a definite consequence of too much product to paste down whatever flecks of hair he has left. "Tomorrow is Friday, Isabel. To me, this *is* the end of the week."

"Yes, I realize that. I meant the end of next week. If you don't mind, I've got to go," I say as the elevator doors open with a most welcoming ding. As the doors slide closed, I shut my eyes, squeezing the railing that lines the back wall. The elevator makes its descent toward the lobby and freedom.

"Mami?" Susana says, puzzled at seeing me at her school pickup line. "Where's Mamá?" She jumps in the Land Cruiser and buckles herself into the back seat.

I stare at her through the rearview mirror. "There's an emergency with Don Rigoberto."

"Where?"

"In Spain. He had a little accident on the vineyard in Jerez. You remember when we'd visit him, the three of us together, don't you?" I ask, although it's been a while since she's been there.

"I sort of do."

"It was where your grandmother lived when she was your age."

"I know that. But I don't know if I remember it."

"Well, that's where Mamá is going," I say, looking through the rearview mirror.

"Where are we going now? Aren't you supposed to be at work?"

"Don't worry about all that." I get out of the school's pickup roundabout and maneuver the truck onto the street. She's quiet the rest of the way, a short drive to the apartment.

"What are we doing here?" she asks, trying to hide her exuberance. I park perpendicularly behind Mami's van and the Jeep, hoping the passenger side isn't sticking too far out onto the street.

"Wait a second," I say before cutting off the engine. "Slide out this way, I don't know if there's enough space to get out on that side." Susana huffs a little before she removes her hand from the door handle and slides my way. I open the door for her, and she pops out of the truck only to race to the front door. Carefully, I step in front of the truck and check my parking. All good.

When Gene and I lock eyes through the window, the world stops on its axis. She can't hide those felicitous hazel eyes. It's hard for her, I know. Feeling happy we're here to see her off—maybe take her to the airport—while her only living grandparent is somewhere stuck between limbo and purgatory. I don't know how long she'll be gone, but surely she and Susana will miss each other.

Gene pushes the door open, and Susana climbs up her body and attaches herself to her chest as if she were a squid.

"I'm sorry Don Rigo isn't doing good," she says. Her compassionate words sting my eyes as she clings to Gene. I should videotape this poignant scene for those government baboons who only think of gays and lesbians as lecherous pedophiles. Gene is probably a better parent than I am.

"What are you guys doing here?" Gene asks, still glued to Susana. Her eyes, greenish with a speck of yellow now and slightly glossed over, are a bit doe-y, and all I want to do is curl up inside them. She stretches out her hand to me, and I take it greedily.

"Yes, what are you doing here?" Mami asks. Her knowing grin sends heat to the souls of my feet.

Gene puts Susana down with a thud. "Gosh, soccer is putting some dense muscles on you! I can barely carry you for long before I have to set you down."

Mami and Gene are still waiting for a response from me. I wrap my hands over Susana's shoulders and say to both, "We wanted to see you before you left and maybe give you a ride to the airport." I glance down at Susana for moral support, but she's just as flabbergasted as they are.

CHAPTER THIRTY-THREE

Gene

On the plane, I go through my backpack in a pointless attempt to make sure I have everything I need for my laptop. If I don't, I'll just have to deal with it, as I can't do much about it from the air. Tucked away in one of the long-forgotten interior pockets, I find a hard leather flip case for photos. When I open it up, I find a photo of Isa holding up a baby Susana in the air, both soaked with chlorinated water and giggling crazy mother-daughter nonsense at each other, neither aware I'd taken it. Their goofy grins remind me that I took the image right after we finished building the pool—Flor and her brood had been visiting that summer to help us inaugurate it.

I remember putting this photo in here years ago to keep my family with me when I was traveling often for work. Those days are gone now. Without another thought, I lightly brush Isa's wet cheek with my thumb. The clear plastic cover feels far from wet, but the image sends an electric current through my fingertips that I feel through my whole body. I shut the flap of the case and stash it back in my bag and zip it up.

This tiny cubicle-like cocoon Isa booked for me makes me feel like a kid again. The paper menu is full of tempting treats that I can order anytime I want, as much as I want. In front of me, the entertainment screen is stocked full of all sorts of movies, TV shows, and news. I could watch at least four movies if I want on the eight-hour flight to Madrid. But I won't, though. Ready with my elastic waistband joggers, I'm planning to recline this puppy all the way flat, curl up like a Tasmanian devil in its mother's pouch, and sleep till we're over Portugal, having breakfast.

The wheels on my carry-on lead me through Madrid's massive airport down to the train station for the long haul to Jerez de la Frontera. Once on board the high-speed train, I lug my carry-on into the overhead storage, sans the little essentials bag I snagged in the first-class cocoon (the cream, lip balm, and eye mask will come in handy), and drop like a zombie in my seat. Let's hope I get some rest on this three-and-a-half-hour train journey.

Exhausted and waiting for the train to depart, I call Flor to let her know I'm on the way to the vineyard. It's only eight minutes from the Jerez train station to Mamá's childhood bed (if I can survive the ride) where I can sleep off this brain-fogging jet lag.

Once the train is out of the city and zooming south through rural Spain, we pass several connecting villages. With my eye mask strategically placed on my forehead, I zone in on the hypnotic malaise before me. The Spanish countryside is picturesque in the fall. The only way to see this spectacle is along the tracks of the high-speed train: rows and rows of neatly planted vines, almost welcoming you with their gnarly cordons full of bunches of swollen grapes, ready to burst, and leaves colored in quintessential Andalusian hues of yellows, oranges, reds, and greens; the romantic fog that hovers just below the branches on the orange trees in the citrus groves, skimming the surface of the ground; and the earthy stone houses scattered throughout the farmland that send you their delightful ¡buenos dias! You'll think you're in Tuscany, but no. Andalusia's landscape rivals anything you'll see in Italy and all of it worth the trek. I watch the drama unfold before my drowsy eyes until I slowly descend into the realm of the REM sleep I've been missing for months.

Only the sudden shriek of the halting train after pulling into the station wakes me from my dreamless slumber. As I open my eyes, the intricacies of the ornamented Jerez de la Frontera train station come into focus. Architecturally, it's Islamic style—as are most of the buildings in southern Spain—leaving no surface of the station's main building untouched by local artisans paying homage to Andalusian lore.

Off the train, I lose myself in the detail of this magnificent building—the wrought iron and wood benches, the curled-tipped cornices, wood doors with arched windows in the upper third, and the mosaic tile work of its interiors—when a familiar voice in the distance calls my name out in Spanish. "Heneh, Heneh." That's phonetically what my name sounds like in Spanish, and now, I feel at home. My birth name is Eugenia. But after the disastrous visit to the ER when Susana was a baby and I wanted to slap the receptionist silly for several reasons—the least of which was mispronouncing my name—I've been seriously considering legally changing it to Gene. No one in the States says it right, and I hate the way it sounds in English—one day, I'll do it.

The sight of my cousin sends a burst of exhilaration that explodes in my chest. I haven't seen her in at least two years, and I nearly forget the solemn reason I'm here in the first place. Flor, arms spread wide, rushes toward me like a raging bull and pulls me in tight to her lanky frame. Taking after her father, Mamá's twin brother, she's nearly two inches taller than I am. I sink into her and coil my tired limbs around her waist. We squeeze each other momentarily and forgo the double-cheek kiss.

"Papá is waiting in the car for us," she says, and for a nanosecond I think she's talking about my own Papá. "Let's get out of here."

"Vale," I agree, and wipe the moisture from my ruddy cheek.

The drive along the winding country road to Don Rigoberto's villa opens my eyes wide and bright; this is like another homecoming. And, to prove it, when we pull up on the long gravel driveway to the main house, Tita Carmen awaits us, wrapped in one of her many colorful pashminas.

Two inches shorter, she's as fresh as autumn's midday sun here in Jerez, but warm and inviting at the same time. I want to stay in her arms and revel in her love, if only because she reminds me of my own mother.

"¡Hola, mi niña!" my aunt says, greeting me with the same enthusiasm as Flor. "Qué tal? How are Martha, Isa, and Susanita?"

Tita, originally Mamá's best friend in university, never forgets to ask about my family. When Isa and I were teenagers, our families, including Tito Rigo's, traveled together throughout Europe during our winter breaks from school. Tita Carmen, Mamá, and Martha became inseparable. Carlos and Papá had a special relationship, too. Spanish by birth, they became boon companions almost as soon as they met.

When my cousins were on their summer holiday, they'd all come visit us in Miami or sometimes we'd meet somewhere in the Caribbean. My teenage years of carefree bliss, when we were all together, were the best of my life.

"We can wait until David Luis comes in tomorrow to go see Don Rigoberto," Tito Rigo says, getting to business. He's delicately mixing his dish of huevos a la flamenca Carmen has graciously prepared for my arrival. If Mamá had been an amazing cook, Tita Carmen is admittedly a notch above. As soon as I finish unpacking, placing the last of my toiletries in the bathroom, Tita calls me down for lunch. Granted, in the countryside we eat late, but it's nearly three in the afternoon. It's a real treat for them to hold lunch until I got here, though.

"He might arrive the day after tomorrow because he said he wanted to meet with the head of training for Real Madrid tomorrow," I say of Lui's "now that I'm here" plans in Madrid.

"Is he planning to play for them?" Flor asks, purposely reaching over me to grab the bread. Plowing my shoulder into her, I push back, grabbing the basket to keep it away from her, and hand it to Tita Carmen at the other end of the table.

"He wasn't specific," I say after swallowing a forkful of the savory egg and tomato dish. "But I doubt it would be for him to play for Real Madrid." By athletic standards, Lui, being thirty-eight, is winding down his soccer career. He has a doctorate in physical therapy, so once he retires from the sport, he'll probably start a new career as a physical therapist with the franchise. When he studied to be a physical therapist, Major League Soccer didn't exist in the United States. But when their inaugural season was announced, Lui was recruited to play for Chivas USA in LA. He's played for them ever since.

"He's likely looking for advice about how to set up a team of physical therapists to keep on staff full time. Lui and the lead therapist at Real Madrid played soccer in college together."

"And you? How are you holding up?" Tita asks with a sympathetic stare. They've been asking me this question since Isa and I separated. Spanish tradition insists on the elders being busybodies.

"Tita," I say, placing my fork down on my plate. Interlacing my fingers together over it, I take a second to think over my reply. "We've been apart for more than two years. I've been holding up just fine." And just as the lie crosses my lips, a pang of guilt jabs at my side.

Tita Carmen busies herself scraping the sides of her dish to get the delectable burned edges of tomato sauce. "Did Isa accept? Roberto's proposal, I mean." I snap my head to glare at my cousin, who apparently can't keep her mouth shut.

"What?" Flor asks defensively. "She was going to find out soon enough."

Tito Rigo clears his throat in a forced, guttural grunt. "Flor, that's not for you to decide."

"Thank you, Tito." I turn my head away from him and stick my tongue out at Flor. "Honestly, I'm not sure. Like I told Flor, I didn't really give Isa a chance to tell me one way or another. And over the last few weeks, I've been trying to avoid any conversation with Isa that have nothing to do with Susana."

"Amor," Tita Carmen chimes in, glancing my way, her meadow-green eyes consoling. "You will need to come to terms with her getting married one way or another—if she gets married, of course."

"I know, Tita," I reply, stomach acid bubbling toward my throat. "But I'm terrified he's going to want to make Susana his daughter and ruin any chance I'll have to sue the state of Florida for second-parent adoption," I admit.

"What do you mean?" Tito stops eating and focuses on me.

"Because we were never married, it's hard to prove that I was ever involved in the process of having my daughter. That's why I petitioned to adopt Susana as a second parent. And since it's not legal yet in Florida for LGBTQ people to adopt in general, I need to wait until it's formally denied, which hasn't happened yet."

"Well, that's promising, isn't it?" Flor says.

"Not really," I say, disenchanted by the whole process. "I'm afraid that once we take the state to court, Isa will back out because she can't afford the media scrutiny at work. And this will be all over the news. Her work involves securing funding from the state or private sector but mostly from the state, so that's why she's worried about looking like she's…you know, anything but a model citizen."

"Ohs" and "Ahs" accompany cocked brows and pitying glances at me—I'm getting sick of it.

"Can we please talk about something other than my problems?" I plead, hands on the side of my face.

"Eugenia," Tito Rigo says. And it never fails to make me cringe to hear him say my name so sternly. "You didn't answer me. Do you want to wait until your brother gets here to go see Don Rigoberto?"

"No, we can go tomorrow," I answer. "I really need to settle in and sleep off this jet lag."

"We heard you were in a first-class capullito," he says of my spacious cocoon. "Shouldn't you be rested already?"

"That was definitely not my choice, Rigo, it was the only seat available," I explain. Damn, Flor really does have a big mouth.

"All that luxury didn't prevent the turbulence, so I had a hard time falling asleep." I neglected to mention that the turbulence was coming from me.

CHAPTER THIRTY-FOUR

Isa

"There's not much for us to do now but wait," Gene says on the other end of the phone. Her voice is hoarse, as if she'd just woken up. She's been in Jerez for two weeks, and Don Rigoberto's condition has worsened. "His brain activity is slowly deteriorating instead of showing signs of recovery."

"Ay, G. I'm so sorry. Is he on a respirator? If he is, does the family have the right to decide about keeping him on life support? Did he have a plan?" I've no idea what happens in Spain when a loved one falls ill the way Don Rigoberto has.

"He's in a coma, but believe it or not, he's breathing on his own. So, there's no choice but to wait it out."

I nod although I know she can't see me. "And you said Lui already left?"

"Yes, he left yesterday. The MLS Cup finals are in a couple of weeks, and since his team is in the playoffs, he's gotta be back in time for training. It might be his last season as a player, you know? But the coach still has him starting at midfield."

"Who else is there with you?" I ask, hoping she has more than just her aunt and uncle there for moral support.

"Tito Rigo and Tita Carmen are still here. They're not going back to Madrid for now, and Tita's hovering over me," she says. I glance at the time to make sure I have a few minutes until my meeting with Dr. Peterson but time is evaporating.

"I'd better let you go, G. I'll try to call you when I leave the hospital. Love you." I slam my office phone on its cradle, frozen with the words I just uttered. *Mother of fucking pearl!* Was that a knee-jerk reaction? I haven't said that to Gene in god-only-knows how long.

I pull my wild mane back tight, twisting my hair behind my head, then let go. Repeating it twice, I massage my temples and finally muss my hair with both hands to shake off all this built-up tension. Standing, I walk out of my office and into the lab. There are a few notes I must dictate before we proceed with the tissue growth.

"Enrique," I say to my doctoral candidate. He turns from his microscope slides, observing the growth and jotting down each measurement. "How's it going?" I peer at his scribbles on the note pad next to the microscope.

"They're growing," he says with a hesitant pause.

"But?"

"But not at the rate we had anticipated, Dr. Acosta."

"Okay, I'll be back to go over the progress. I have a meeting with Dr. Peterson." And just as I finish uttering the last syllable of his name, I catch Enrique in an eye roll.

"I'll be here," is all he replies.

Every time I have a meeting with this prick, he makes me wait more than an hour. "He'll see you now, Dr. Acosta," his assistant says with a cunning smile.

"Thank you, Eric." I get up and rap my knuckles on the door twice before letting myself in.

"Isabel," he says, sitting at his desk, his smile guileful and his small eyes aiming at my chest. He smooths back his three whisps of hair as he stands and juts his greasy paw for me to take. Admonishing myself for not wearing gloves, I manage not to recoil as I connect with his reptilian hand. "How's the research going?" he asks.

"We're making some progress," I reply.

"Interesting," he says, elbows poised on his leather desk blotter, hands forming a pinnacle in front of his face. "And what about the funding. Is that in place yet? The new fiscal year is upon us, Isabelita." With his I-only-speak-English accent, it sounds as though he'd said *Isabel-litter* instead.

I remove my notebook from my lab coat pocket, open it to the bookmarked page, and begin to inform him. "Well, Dr. Peterson. We have three new legacy donors, one in the platinum tier. This one will fund my team's research until the end of the next fiscal year."

"Fantastic. I do love it when a plan comes together, don't you, Isabel?" His tiny teeth salivate and I'm barely able to stop my body from recoiling.

Unconsciously smoothing out the rough cuticle on my left thumb, I dig into the edge of my nail bed as though I were digging for gold. That's when Peterson's gaze darts to my hands.

"You're not wearing your engagement ring?"

I press my eyebrows together. "Who told you anything about an engagement ring?"

"I saw it on your finger the other day," he replies. "I imagine it's new since I've never seen you wear one. Well, since I've never seen you wear any kind of jewelry on that hand at all."

To silence the sudden buzzing of my BlackBerry, I plunge my left hand into my lab coat pocket—God I hope it's nothing to do with Susana.

"I'm not engaged," I say, defiant and sick of his pedantic face.

"I thought you and Dr. Ruiz were an item?"

"That is none of your business."

"It seems to me that since you've been, or rather, since he's been sniffing around here, I assume that he's been helping you with your important funding. And perhaps even your research?"

"Dr. Peterson." I raise my voice three octaves. "Frankly, I'm sick of you treating me as though I'm merely a wall hanging in this department. My research is important to this hospital. Or at least it was when your predecessor was the chief of pathology." I stand, my head about to burst.

I lean down, resting my weight on my hands at the edge of his grubby desk. "If you want to know about my life so badly, fine! You should know that until two years ago, my daughter's *other* mother and I were happily living together. That is until I let my position in this pathetic department dictate my personal life. Well, that's not happening anymore."

Straightening up, I pocket my notebook and scramble out of Peterson's office, nearly toppling the guest chair in which I sat. Just as I reach for the door, Peterson's baritone voice reverberates against my back.

"Where the hell do you think you're going? We're not done here."

I turn on my heel. "Yes, *Tucker*, I believe we are. Fuck this place, and fuck you. I'm going where I'm wanted." I remove the badge lanyard hanging around my neck, throw it so it lands on his desk, and slam the door behind me.

CHAPTER THIRTY-FIVE

Gene

Love you. I haven't heard Isa utter those words since before I moved out of the house, worrying me more. Could she have been saying it to me from muscle memory, or worse, a slip of the tongue because she says it to What's-his-face? He proposed to Isa more than a month ago, and I've heard nothing on the subject. Not even Martha knows. The waiting is the worst, of course, because the longer time goes on, the more convoluted the fable in my head becomes.

Staring up at the ceiling, I'm lying on Mamá's old twin-size bed in the room she grew up in. It's tiny compared to American standard-size bedrooms. But even as a child, Mamá had decorated her room with a Gothic feel, much like some of the scenes in her novels. Her published works line the shelf opposite the bed, an addition Abuela must have made. Sixties- and seventies-era posters of her favorite musicians cover the walls. They're mostly Spanish artists, but there is an ABBA poster right above the headboard.

It's a museum of memories here in this room, and somehow, I feel close to her. Staying here isn't wistful for me. On the contrary, sleeping in her room reminds me of happier times when our parents would cram Flor and me in here during our childhood when the entire family stayed at the vineyard together. It had been in this room where I told Flor how I felt about Isa and that she reciprocated those feelings.

Until she met Isa, of course, I had been Flor's confidant. I guess because they were the same age, they created this beautiful, secret-society-like friendship, which sometimes (most times) excluded me.

"Amor," Tita Carmen calls from the doorway, nearly startling me off the bed. "I'm sorry, I didn't mean to startle you."

"No, it's okay," I say, holding my hand to my chest. I tap the mattress to make sure my phone is still where I left it. It has a glass front, and the last thing I want is to drop it on this cold, cement-tile flooring.

"Rigo and I are serving cordials of Pedro Ximénez. Have one with us."

Oh, she knows how to entice me for sure. My grandfather has been selling his grapes to Jerez vintners for decades. The Pedro Ximénez grape is one of them, prized by vintners for the sweet, syrupy wines they can create from it. There will be many questions about this vineyard if my grandfather dies. Would Rigo take it over? He would own half of the vineyard. Mamá, his twin sister, left her stake to my brother and me. In the business himself, Rigo sells Jerez or sherry wines and brandies made with Don Rigoberto's harvest to the top wine shops and bodegas throughout Western Europe. My only interest is to keep the vineyard and the house in the family. I would love to create a winery here. Winemaking is the backbone of Andalucía, so a boutique winery would fit perfectly in Villa Guadalcacín.

The main house, whitewashed in a high gloss paint to reflect the sun back onto its gardens, stands tall in the center of the vineyard. Laden with bougainvillea-covered lattices that stretch up to the sky, its Mediterranean-style garden blooms year-round. It makes a beautiful backdrop for a wedding, if we decided to open the garden for events. That would also be a good way to funnel cash into the local economy. I nod in Tita Carmen's direction and promise to join them downstairs in a few minutes.

Running my fingers through my rebellious curls, I meander down the stairs and toward the great room to Don Rigoberto's bar. Compared with the rest of the room, the bar takes up a mere slice in the corner, off the main foyer by the stairs. Festooned with rustic cedar wood planks covering the wall horizontally, the shelves display every single brand of the fortified wine that contains any amount of my grandfather's crop.

As Carmen pours the sherry into my cordial glass, the scent of the sweet Pedro Ximénez grape fills my nose with its mouthwatering essence. Its viscousness might purse your lips at first, but it slides down the throat with a warming wallop.

"Give them the best cultivated grape," Rigo says, lifting his glass filled with the amber liquid for a toast. "And they will deliver a wine that will survive world wars." My grandfather always said this to his vintners.

As I empty the last drop of sherry in my glass, Rigo turns toward the foyer with interest. The buzzing is coming from Rigo's phone, charging on the round table at the base of the stairs. As he excuses himself to get it, Tita offers me another pour, which I greedily accept.

"Bueno," my uncle says, greeting whomever on the other end of the line. I watch as his face turns from celebratory to ghostly in seconds. Tita Carmen and I rush to his side as he nods and holds back a thicket of tears. "Yes…yes…I understand. No, he had a plan. I'll call you with the information as soon as I notify the funeral home. Thank you for calling. Good night."

He ends the call and puts the phone back on the little table. And instinctively, as my uncle covers his eyes and opens his mouth in anguish, Tita grabs hold of his torso, and he sinks in her arms. Devastated, my heart breaks for him, and I'm compelled to cover my family with my own arms, hoping to emit the support I came here to give.

"My twin sister, my mother, and now my father," he whimpers. "The family I had as a boy is no longer." Tears roll down our cheeks as the impact of his words shatters us. Rigo, on autopilot now, lets his arms fall and ambles to the writing desk in the sitting room on the other side of the stairs to make his calls.

Wanting to feel useful, I slide my phone from my pocket and leave messages for Isa, Martha, and Lui. Flor immediately answers my call.

"Thank you, prima," Flor replies after I've relayed the news. "We'll be on the first train we can get tomorrow," she says and ends the call.

Being back in Jerez, surrounded by family, organizing the logistics of my grandfather's death—the people we must inform and the preparations to see to for his service—makes me realize how tight my Spanish family is. We're a team. I miss belonging to my family—my parents. Since their death, my traditional cultural celebrations don't seem hold the same meaning. Many of my family members celebrate Christian holidays because they are steeped in Spain's cultural tradition. My parents, although secular, decorated the house with flourishes of Christmas and Los Reyes Magos.

Losing my parents, I also lost a certain part of my heritage, my culture, my traditions, my sense of belonging. When Isa was inseminated, I longed to reconnect with my culture, which has always stemmed from my family—my parents. And when Susana was born, we instilled in her the same culture and traditions with which I was raised. My link to Susana kept alive my link to my traditions, my heritage, my parents. Susana gave me a sense of belonging because I stopped feeling like an orphan. With her, I'm home. Suddenly, my heritage, my traditions, and even the religious celebrations I grew up with make sense again. Because without a family with whom to share them, how does your culture flourish, especially when those who come before you are gone? Susana is now part of my lineage—someone to inherit my traditions and my culture.

Knowing Don Rigoberto's death was inevitable makes his loss slightly easier to bear. But it doesn't make it less shocking. He was the patriarch. The one who handed down the family traditions, the celebrations, our culture, our heritage. With his death, someone else will pick up the gauntlet—certainly my uncle. But I, too, want the pass down our heritage so that Susana may one day understand where I come from—where the people she's never met set their roots.

I know in my heart I will be allowed to adopt her. But the journey has been taxing, and I don't know how much more heartbreak I can handle.

CHAPTER THIRTY-SIX

Isa

Back at my desk, I happily pack up all my personal stuff and slip the engagement ring, hiding in my desk drawer, into my pocket. Enrique, looking every bit flabbergasted, pops his head through my door.

"What's happening?"

I lug my bag over my shoulder and glance at him as I move around my desk. "Enrique, I just resigned."

"You what?" he asks, mouth agape, eyes bulging from his skull. "When?"

"Effective immediately. I'm sorry, you'll have another advisor assigned to you, I'm sure. Good luck, Enrique, you're a promising scientist, we need more like you. Keep in touch." I leave my office keys on Cami's desk—she's probably still out to lunch. A sense of freedom washes over me as I push the down arrow on the elevator. I pull my phone from my lab coat and notice I have three messages. The first is oddly from Sergio, the second is from Flor, and the last one is from Gene. They'll have to wait.

The elevator doors slide open. I walk in, surprised at my own tranquility, and press the button marked four. The pediatric wing.

CHAPTER THIRTY-SEVEN

Gene

Flor's train arrives at ten this morning. Last night, I told Rigo that I'd make the quick drive to the station to pick her up. I need something to do that's not sitting around waiting for... waiting for everyone else to make decisions. Flor's whole family is on that train too, including her husband, Paco, so I grab the keys to Don Rigoberto's passenger van and zoom over there.

The Jerez train station, seemingly grandiose here, is quite small by Spanish standards, with one set of high-speed tracks and two sets of cargo train tracks. Security here is a low priority, so I'm sitting on a bench next to the platform where the trains roll in.

Scrolling through the Internet on my phone, I skim the news while I wait for the train. There's already a short, heartwarming obituary for Don Rigoberto. It mentions all his survivors, and it melts my heart that it includes Susana as one of his five great-grandchildren. Of course, this is probably information Flor gave the news agency. Even so.

The faint train whistle in the distance catches my attention, and as I glance toward the north side of the station, the voice on the loudspeaker announces the arrival of the ten o'clock train from Madrid. I glimpse my Swatch as the train speeds by me. It surges through the station with such force, it blows my hair out of whack—not that it is in any sort of order. The train stops at the other side of the station, and I scurry closer to the center, to catch Flor and her family as they exit.

It takes a few minutes for the doors to slide open. As they do, a horde of passengers burst through them in the daily hustle and bustle to get to work. I'm looking for Flor's signature lanky frame, but I spot Paco first. He's walking out the penultimate car. Speeding up, I spot Flor, sandwiched between her two sons as they step off the train. I blink once, twice, but I'm sure my eyes are playing tricks on me as I see what must be Isa's doppelgänger hop off the train behind one of Flor's sons. But it's not until Susana steps off, close behind Isa, that I sprint to greet them.

When our gazes meet, a thousand butterflies flutter throughout my body. It's as though all movement at the station stops. The click of a record inserted into the player starts off Robert Smith's intro guitar riff to "Just Like Heaven." The people coming off the train clear the path for me, and Isa and Susana are the only ones in my sightline.

Images dance before my eyes—Isa, on the school bus a million years ago. Sweaty armpits, clammy hands, heart thumps against my sternum, my eyes focus on her through my thirteen-year-old self, wearing eyeglasses. Susana, just as the nurse places her wrinkled body in my waiting arms. A visceral tingling rumbles in my belly. I run toward them, bypassing Flor and her family, and directly into *my* family's waiting arms.

The embrace is tight, but my arms refuse to ease—my left hooks over Isa's shoulder, pressing her to me, my right hand fixes at Susana's back, her little arms snake around my waist. We stay like this as train passengers rush around us—our bond unbreakable. I let go of Isa long enough to heave Susana in my arms. My cheeks are cold with moisture, but I don't care. I reach for Isa again, and again, I feel whole in a way I've never felt before. My family is here.

"What are you doing here?" I whisper. No longer breathing, I take a colossal gulp. "What about Susana's school?"

"I figured you needed your own family here," she says, wiping an errant tear off her flushed cheek. Her gleaming, red eyes make my lips curl. "Susanita is in second grade, she's not going to miss out on learning how to break covalent bonds. Besides, I can teach her a lot more while we're here."

"¡Sorpresa, prima!" Flor sings and opens her arms. Putting Susana down, I greet her and her clan properly with tight hugs and double kisses.

"What do you mean, 'surprise'?" I ask, mid-cousin squeeze. I'm almost too enchanted to care.

"When I got your messages, I called Flor," Isa says. "To coordinate our travel plans."

"And you!" I squat to Susana's height. "You must be exhausted." I envelop my arms around her again. "Two weeks without seeing my little Tasmanian devil is just too long. I missed you so much!"

"Me too, Mamá!" Susana says.

"What did you do with Floyd?" I ask, turning in Isa's direction.

"Mami. She's staying at the house for as long as we're here."

When we all enter the station, I realize Isa and I are holding hands, and I can't tell if it's an instinct, or if it's merely because brain fog from the jet lag. Isa doesn't flinch, protest, or miss a step. No. In fact, she intertwines our fingers and with a clamp on my upper arm, she leans into me as I lead everyone to the van. I let go of Isa's hand and run mine up the indentation her spine makes along her back and pull her nearer. She snakes her arm around my waist, and I'm baffled, astonished, and lovesick, but I'm not about to remind her we're in public.

"The van only holds six, so you'll have to hold Susana," I say to Isa as I slide open the passenger door.

Isa winks as she helps Susana in the van. "She'll be fine in the back with her cousins. I'm riding up there with you."

Rebellious Isa is back.

We say nothing on the drive back to the villa, but Isa and I steal fervent glances at each other along the way. Right now, there's nothing else on my mind. The short road ahead of me seems easier to traverse now that I have my family with me. As I pull into the gravel driveway, Isa absorbs the countryside view from her window. We haven't been here together since before Susana turned five. Our daughter can't possibly remember this place, but Isa does, I'm sure of it. We know this place and all its crevices.

The main house towers over the rest of the buildings. We've all stayed here together on many occasions but not since Isa and I separated. My aunt and uncle have been staying in my grandparents' bedroom suite since they arrived, so that leaves the rest of us to divide the other four bedrooms. Tito Horacio is coming from Barcelona with his husband, Edu, and Tito Rigo has invited them to stay in the small guest house behind the garage.

Flor, Paco, and the boys take Tito's childhood bedroom and one of the guestrooms. This arrangement leaves the two bedrooms across the hall that Isa and I have used in the past: Mamá's bedroom and the adjacent second guestroom.

After putting Susana in Mamá's bed for a nap, I situate Isa's luggage in the guestroom she and I have shared before. A crisp autumn breeze rolls in through the open window, and it's calling my name. It's a balmy seventy-five degrees here, but the wind rustling through the endless rows of grapevines keeps the house cool. The temperature tonight is supposed to drop to the midsixties, and I can just smell the chiminea Tito Rigo will most assuredly fire up in the garden.

"I've missed this place," Isa says. About a foot behind me, she startles me out of my fog. "It's always been one of my favorite places in the world." The heat coming off her body corners me. Her hands make their way to my shoulders, forcing a shiver along my arms. She squeezes just tight enough to make me flinch. Turning to face her, I'm baffled by her affection.

"What are you doing here, Isa? Really."

"Sergio called," she replies. Her chocolate-brown eyes gleam with sympathy. I turn back to face the open window, huff out a breath, and lean my hands on the windowsill. The stone walls are stiff and cold, but they're familiar.

"Yes, I heard his message this morning," I say, prepared to hear that she's changed her mind about my lawsuit. "While I was at the hospital two days ago, Sergio left me a voice message. He wants to talk about next steps, but I haven't had the time to call him."

Isa gets closer to me. Her hand between my shoulder blades massages the tension knot away. "I just thought…I just thought that maybe you need some reassurance."

I grasp her hand from my shoulder and notice something is different. Something is missing. I swing her arm over my head and have a look.

"Your ring. Did you lose it?"

She shakes her head. "I gave it back."

"Why?" I ask, still with the stupid questions, but I need her to say it. My eyebrows stretch straight up my forehead. Her hand is still in mine.

"How am I supposed to marry him when I'm in love with you?" Her lips curl, and I touch my thumb to her dimples. Heavy-lidded, and with dark, puffy shadows below them, her eyes reflect the sun's gleam. They're brilliant.

"You are…still?" I croak, throat sore. My grip on her hand tightens. At her nod, I place her hand on my heart.

"I never stopped," she says.

Isa moves in closer to me and places a delicate kiss on my lips. Caressing her face, I wipe away her tears. Or they might be my tears that have slipped onto her face. I don't know, but I can't stop running my hands over her. All over her.

I pull back a bit, gazing into her dark, hooded eyes. Those eyes that can light up the world have managed to brighten up my life.

"You must be exhausted," I say, brushing my knuckles along her jaw. My thumb is glued to her chin, and as her smile deepens, so too do the dimples. "Let's rest for a little bit."

She nods, and I take her by the hand and lead her to her side of the bed. After she sits, I drop one knee to the floor. Gently, grasping her leg by a booted calf, I pull her foot toward my thigh and unzip her black leather boot, loosen it off her foot, dig my fingers into the bottom of her heel, remove her sock, and repeat the process on her other foot. Wordlessly, she leans back and lays her head on the pillow as she languidly lifts both legs onto the bed.

Upright, I amble to the other side of the bed and lie down behind her. As I tuck my left arm under her neck, she scoots toward me, curling herself into body. My other hand glides over her side, stopping on her hip. Intertwining our fingers, she drags my hand to her chest. Behind her, nuzzling her, I breathe in her familiar vanilla fragrance and kiss the back of her neck.

She leaves a soft, wet kiss on my hand before rolling toward me. "I know we should probably talk, but I just need you," she says. A spark in her eyes heats my center, and I nod my assent.

Reaching in for a brief kiss, I undo the tasseled cord tied at the neck of her flowing, red-patterned peasant blouse and lift it over her head, and she discards her black lacy bra. My clothes come off in a rush, and I shimmy her black tights and thong over her hips, easing them off her legs. Everything gets thrown on the floor, and I don't even flinch.

The breeze coming in from the window caresses Isa's skin with tiny love hills. Pulling the quilt from underneath, I cover us, keeping the crisp wind away. Isa slides her right leg under me and scoops me up on top of her. Her pert nipples tickle my chest and beg for my attention.

Scooting down her body, leaving wet kisses on her skin, I lick a ring around an aroused nipple and repeat on the other one. Isa exhales a husky moan when I drive my knee between her thighs to make room for myself. Her legs that can wrap a dozen times round my hips, inviting me to sink into her. I take her breast into my mouth again as she threads her fingers in my hair, holding me in place, assuring me she wants more. I gently suck her nipple, letting go just as a groan escapes Isa's lips. With her hips tucked, she jockeys for friction, and I follow her rhythm.

Continuing my exploration of her body and supporting myself on my left hand, I arch my back, digging my center deeper into hers. We snap together like magnets, and with a quick motion, I reverse our positions until she's straddling my hips. With no misstep, Isa grinds her pelvic bone on me, stimulating me in the process. I press into her center with my thumb, holding her still. I love this push and pull—this give-and-take of pleasure stirs my insides and drives me crazy.

Salivating with the thought of tasting her again, I hold her in place and shimmy below her until my face is just inches under her folds. They're as plump as a tulip bulb on the cusp of blooming. I kiss my way through her outer lips, holding them open with my index and middle fingers.

"Ah," Isa gasps, reaching forward, placing her palms on the bed, crumpling the bedsheets in her fist, knees digging into the mattress. My blood vessels throb in my ears as she begins to thrust on my face. I caress her back, earning another moan as I lap at her sweet muskiness. Feeling devilish, I run a hand down her back and over the opening of her ass. I reach under and slip my thumb inside her.

"Oh. Fuck, that feels good," Isa whispers as I plunge my finger deeper inside her. She adjusts herself over me, stretching her legs down my torso, holding herself up in a semi-plank position. I wrap my arms around her hips, pulling her closer to my lips as another groan slips out of her mouth. She jerks on top of me and pulsates in my mouth. She falls on the bed, a languorous torso draping over me, limbs too weak to hold herself up.

Sweat trickles down her belly and onto my face as she slides down my body and curls herself on top of me. Our bodies are riddled with bubbles of perspiration and other bodily elixirs. We're positioned halfway down the bed, and my legs are bent over the edge. The quilt is lost somewhere on the floor, the pillows probably thrown out the window. I'm breathless but satiated, and Isa hasn't touched me yet.

She was right when she said we were like animals. Our magnetic connection is too strong to pull apart. I can't stay away from her. And Isa…well, she's never been able to stay away from me for too long.

As if startled, Isa perks her head up and slides completely on top of me, placing her thigh between mine and saying huskily, "Move up the bed." I do as she commands. She doesn't move, though. No. She waits until I'm closer to the headboard to dig into me. Splaying her hand on my wet abs, she marks her territory with kisses all the way down my waiting mound.

I lean back on my elbows, watching her head bob as she licks and licks. With her thumb, Isa tugs at my skin, revealing my eagerness. She gives it a cursory flick of her tongue, teasing me before she indulges herself.

No one else in the world can do this to me. Love me. Taste me. Enter me. I lean my head back and stretch my legs, quietly expelling a whimper. But I'm not in pain. I'm overwhelmed. And when I release, I let go of everything, collapsing on the bed with a thud, and I sob. Isa quickly crawls up my body and scoops me in her arms.

"It's okay," she says, running her fingers on the back of my head. My arms are wrapped tightly around her waist, jerking in her arms. For so long, the warmth of her embrace is what I missed. Her touch is what keeps me whole. She is my home.

The autumn breeze trickling in through the window rouses me from a deep sleep. For a second, I forget where I am until I feel the subtle touch of fingers caressing my face. Turning my head to face her, I open my eyes. Isa places a gentle kiss on my nose, my eyes, and my lips.

"You didn't jump out of bed," she says with a smile. I wrap my fingers around her hand and draw it to my lips, kissing each delicate digit. Dawn's fresh morning filtering through the sheer white curtain panels bathes the room in a crisp sheen of yellow and orange hues. The thick quilt wrapped over us protects us from the brisk air.

"I don't want to be anywhere else," I reply. "In fact, I wouldn't mind staying here, in your arms, forever."

"That doesn't sound half bad."

"It doesn't?"

"I feel good here with you. Susana says all this is familiar to her," Isa says, drawing a titillating line down the center of my chest to my belly button with the tips of her index and middle fingers.

"You do, do you?" I say, covering our heads with the quilt. I sink lower on the bed and pull Isa's feet closer with mine. Our thighs interlock and I wrap my arms around her shoulders. "I've always wanted to be with you, you know that, right?"

"I do," she replies as she brings the quilt under her arm. "I..."

"Isa," I interrupt, clearing my throat and tracing my knuckles along the edge of her jaw. "I want this moment to last a bit longer. I'm glad you're here. It means everything to me. But let's just enjoy the now...for now."

Isa nods and moves in to nuzzle her face at my neck.

CHAPTER THIRTY-EIGHT

Isa

Although Don Rigoberto had been a self-proclaimed atheist, he was also a traditionalist. He attended Catholic Mass every Sunday morning in the village center. He claimed it was a way to network and keep his finger on the pulse of his community, even if that meant going to confession and receiving communion. As of the day before yesterday, he had completed all seven Catholic holy sacraments. Steeped in Catholic tradition as Andalusia is, the church rarely makes exceptions for burying the dead. In Don Rigoberto's case, because so many of his loved ones live outside Jerez, instead of burying him the day after his death—as tradition dictates burial within twenty-four hours—they let us postpone his services for two days to give everyone a chance to arrive. An extra zero on the donation check was also welcomed.

I packed a lovely black dress for Susana to wear to the service, and Gene is doing her best to get it on her. Because she's more of a rugged girl, there are limits to what she will wear—namely dresses, but bows, lacy tops, or anything to hold her hair that's not a plain black elastic band are also on the list. We let her wear what she wants under normal circumstances. But because Don Rigoberto had been such a stickler for propriety during his life, out of respect to him we're practically shoving Susana into her dress. She hates it, and so do we. Ah, parenthood.

As I fasten one of my earrings, I open the bathroom door with my elbow to check on their progress. "G? Are you guys ready yet? Your uncle says the car is downstairs waiting to take us to the church." Gene sits on the toilet lid, brushing Susana's hair as she secures her tightly between her thighs.

"Almost there." Gene sighs. What feels strange is how easily we've fallen back into our old routine. Since Gene's departure, I've been dressing Susana and making her presentable for school when she stays with me. At least I had been until this past summer when Susana turned seven and promptly notified us that she was old enough to dress herself. She's taken a very creative approach to that, wearing all kinds of patterns and styles together, mixing and matching colors as if she were decorating a birthday cake.

"There," Gene utters, holding on to Susana's hips. "Now give me a kiss and tell me you love me." I can't help but let a giggle escape my lips.

"Te quiero, Mamá!" Susana says, turning around to thread her arms around Gene's neck. She places the sweetest kisses on her cheeks. "Bye."

I step back to clear the doorway and let her escape, probably in search of her cousins. Hopefully by now, Flor's boys have dressed as smartly and won't let their cousin muss them up too badly. I leave it in her hands.

"That's your daughter," I say, gazing in Gene's direction.

"No, honey," she corrects. "That's definitely *our* daughter."

Rigo insists on having an intimate reception at the villa after the long funeral services. So, while we are crossing our foreheads and sit-stand-kneeling our way through the Catholic Mass, the caterers are like Christmas elves, feverishly setting up in the garden.

"It's a miracle I didn't spontaneously combust in there, with so much talk about morals after what we did to each other yesterday," I whisper in Gene's ear and watch as the peach fuzz at the back of her neck stands on end, her ears slowly turning crimson.

"Ha!" She muffles a laugh with her hand covering her mouth, but it still jiggles her shoulders. "The priest laid it on thick in there, talking about Don Rigoberto's righteousness, huh? He might be angling for a legacy donation."

After the Mass, the long procession of mourners walk behind us to the cemetery which, thankfully in this village, is a short three-blocks away. My black patent leather heels pinch my toes the entire way there, the balls of my feet discern every teeny pebble.

The village came to pay its respects to Gene's grandfather. Everyone from vineyard workers to bodega owners is present. Horacio and Edu took a quick flight here but are returning to Barcelona in the morning. And because she's still a bit jet-lagged, Susana sat calmly by Gene's side the entire service. I've cemented myself to Gene's right arm since we got in the car this morning. Aside from the ten chairs for family members at the gravesite, everyone gathered is standing around with long faces and chins glued to their chests behind us.

After the coffin is manually lowered and the crowd dismissed to the reception, Gene remains seated. Around us, the mourners are part of Don Rigoberto's community. It's a community comprised of generations of people who revered him. It makes me wonder how my end will affect the people around me. Will they forget me along with countless others? Or will my work and family be my legacy and carry on to the next generation? Regardless of what my professional future holds, I have my family with me, and with their support, my legacy will live on for years after me.

The caterers have subtly but elegantly decorated the garden to go with the mood of this somber occasion. Don Rigoberto may have been traditional, but he was also festive. His funeral, although solemn, also coincides with the harvest festival he's hosted every season. Rigo has pulled out all the stops to ensure the villagers celebrate the grape harvest and Don Rigoberto's life. He loved this vineyard, and he died doing what he loved the most: harvesting the grapes alongside the workers. I love that.

Gene is elegant in her funeral garb of slick black slacks, buttoned-up black shirt, and black fitted blazer. I know she's dying to get out of these clothes, but for the sake of decorum, she'll trudge through the rest of the night in them. But there's more gravel than my feet can handle in my black pumps, so I'm in our room switching my heels for a pair of manageable flats that go nicely with my black tank dress and blazer combo.

As I shut the door, I catch Flor doing the same thing across the hall. She waits at her door to go downstairs together.

"How are you holding up?" I ask. Since they live in Spain, Flor and her family saw their grandfather frequently. Living so far away, we've missed out on annual celebrations, and since Susana has no break in school during October, we haven't been able to travel here for the harvest.

"Life goes on," she says as we descend the stairs. "Fortunately, he's survived by enough of us that we can help each other keep this place going."

Hmm, enough of us.

Horacio is at the bottom of the stairs with a cordial in his hand. He and Rigo are talking to a lady I saw at the funeral but whom I don't know.

"Who's that?" I discreetly ask Flor. "Talking to Horacio and your dad?"

"Amelia Agüero. She's the new sales manager," Flor replies. "She keeps track of every grape that leaves this vineyard. She was here when Don Rigoberto took his tumble." Don Rigoberto's fall resulted in an acute subdural hematoma. When he landed, his head hit the gravel, tearing a blood vessel and causing blood to collect between the dura and the surface of his brain.

Not wanting to interrupt their conversation just to greet Horacio, I send him a short nod of the head as we make our way toward the garden where Gene is talking with Edu.

"Hi," I say as we stop next to them.

"Hi," Gene echoes, curling her lip.

"Wanna go for a walk?" I ask.

There are no hiding places on this vineyard we haven't already discovered. We've visited the villa together so many times, it feels as though I grew up here, too. We head out toward the edge of the garden. There's a gravel path that goes around the perimeter of the garden and leads to the grape processing building. That's where the grapes get weighed and packed in crates to be delivered to their destination.

I thread my arm around Gene's and squeeze tightly. She notices I'm cold and offers me her blazer. Funnily, they call them Americana here in Spain—the blazer, I mean. She takes hers off and drapes it over my shoulders.

"I want you to know that I've done plenty of thinking over the past two years," I say after we've been walking in silence a while. "I've gone over our life together—the good and the bad. The special moments, and the not-so-special ones."

Gene's gaze is glued to the ground just ahead of her shiny loafers. "And what have you concluded?"

"That I'm an idiot." I stop midsentence. She shifts her gaze to me. A sudden blur washes over my eyes, and I'm sure she can see them shimmering under the garden lamplight. "I was such an idiot to think that my work was more important than us, than our life together, than our daughter."

She listens to my words intently. My smile must be infectious because hers beams back at me.

"And?" she asks, refusing to make this any easier for me. She wants me to spell it out for her—of course she does.

I stop walking and hammer my eyes into her. "And you're the one I want to marry, Gene López-Pérez!"

"You want to marry me?" she asks, her voice catching a bit in her throat.

"I do," I reply. "I'm sorry I waited this long. I'm sorry I was so stupid. And I'm so sorry I hurt you, and by extension, everyone else, because of my reluctance to give you what you wanted in the first place."

"Wait," she says dubiously. "You really want to get married?"

"*Yes!*" My face is sore from smiling.

She stares at me, brow cocked. "But we can't. Not in Florida."

"There's a courthouse here, isn't there?"

She nods.

"Then let's get married. I want to spend the rest of my life with you, and I want the rest of my life to start now."

"That sounds like a plan," she says.

"It was your plan from the start."

She shakes her head and smiles. "My best plan."

EPILOGUE

Gene

Isa and I were married in Jerez de la Frontera two days after we buried my grandfather. I filed the necessary paperwork to legally adopt Susana in the Spanish courts. The second-parent adoption was finalized two months later. While we waited, we enrolled Susana in the Jerez village school for three months so she wouldn't fail the second grade when we returned to the US. That was eight years ago.

After we returned to Florida, the state took two more years to give up their fight against LGBTQ families, and stopped defending the ban on adoptions of children by LGBTQ people. But the Florida State Legislature didn't take up comprehensive adoption reform for another five years after that to finally repeal the ban on adoptions. The new bill was signed into law on June 11, 2015.

Marriage equality came to the US seven full years after Isa and I said our "I dos" in el Ayuntamiento de Jerez. For her fifteenth birthday, Susana got a legally recognized family in the United States. I wasn't about to throw caution to the wind in this country, so a month after the Supreme Court ruled that the right to marry is guaranteed to same-sex couples under the Due Process Clause and the Equal Protection Clause of the Fourteenth Amendment to the United States Constitution, the three of us walked into the Coral Gables City Hall and made our marriage in the US ironclad.

When we got back to the US—after being in Spain for more than three months—I promptly moved out of the apartment and back home with my family. And I legally changed my name to Gene. We both changed our last names to Pérez-Acosta. I kept Mama's name, López, as a middle initial. And we got pregnant again. We rang in 2010 with the birth of a baby girl.

Today is my forty-first birthday and there are so many things to celebrate. Susana is a sophomore in high school and, apart from being the school's top sprinter on the track team, she's thinking of studying structural engineering in college. I wonder where she got that idea.

To celebrate my birthday, I'm having a quiet dinner here in a little while with Martha, Isa, Susana, and Alejandra: my family. I just got out of the shower, and as I wipe the fog off the mirror, my reflection slowly comes into focus. Looking back at myself, I realize just how much I resemble Lui, who looks exactly like Papá—although he has more wrinkles now, and I have Mamá's broody eyes. But everything else is a beautiful combination of my parents' heritage: a blend of roots from the south and the north of Spain, with the people who came before us, and the America of which so many dream.

Thinking of Lui, I realize the little shit hasn't called me to wish me a happy birthday.

"Mamá, joder, ya has terminado?" my fifteen-year-old bellows from downstairs as I run a towel over my hair. Susana speaks to me in Spanish, a heartwarming if not crass effort because her Spanish is so, well Spanish. We Spaniards tend to be foul-mouthed in our casual conversations as it is. She's no exception. Susana keeps in touch with her cousins in Spain, too. But sometimes the language they use on their weekly FaceTime calls makes me cringe.

"Casi," I simply reply, not sure she hears me and not really caring. I'm not in a rush. But I turn my wrist toward my face to check my Swatch. It's only four in the afternoon. I have plenty of time before Isa and Martha get back from their shopping excursion. Knowing them, they'll be back by six or later. Besides, we catered dinner from the Spanish place my parents introduced to Isa's parents a million years ago, so it doesn't matter that I'm not ready yet.

My involvement with Equality Miami and in the community has brought me out of my shell in many ways. In my new role as board chair, I'm making cold calls to people I've never met before, mingling with county leaders, and helping Jay lobby legislators for sound bills that protect our whole community, and it's shored up my confidence.

Isa took her heart valve research to a private hospital and has been making improvements to the procedure. Now, patients have more options, not to mention better odds at surviving than they did with mechanical heart valves that calcify over time.

I dab on a little Agua de Colonia de Agustin Reyes and make my way downstairs. The house seems quiet on my way down. With all the fuss Susana was making earlier, I thought she'd be the first to complain that I still hadn't come down. But the instant I reach the point on the stairs where I can see a portion of the couch in the formal living room, I'm greeted with my dumb brother's crooked grin. Gasping and clutching my heart over my T-shirt, I make it down the last steps to see that Lui, Jasmine, and my nieces—all with big, goofy smiles plastered on their faces—are sitting on our couch. Flor, Paco, and their boys are also in the living room. Over by the front door, the two plotters-in-chief, Isa and Martha, stand with unabashed looks of satisfaction on their faces. They got me, and I'm stunned.

I think it's the effect of the shock that is now filling my eyes with added moisture. Tears pour out and hotfoot down my face. My brother is the first to jump forward, swoop me up, and envelop me in his wiry arms. He smells of Grey Flannel, just as Papá did. I circle my arms around his waist, noticing how muscular his abs still are at forty-six years of age. I hold on to him hard and do a little bit of ugly crying on his shoulder. When I try to pull away from him, compose myself, and say something coherent, the words jam in my throat.

"I...I..." Stammering, I swallow down the emotion. "I can't believe you're all here," I manage with a squeak in my voice.

Isa walks toward me, arms outstretched. I walk into them and feel her warm body in my arms. But it's not until I nuzzle her neck that I really start to blubber. It's been years since my family has been together like this. I don't even know who else is here yet. Everywhere I look, someone new pops into my sight.

Tita Carmen appears in the family room, and the surprise trickles down to my toes. The last time I saw her and Tito Rigo was a couple of years ago when we celebrated our fifth wedding anniversary with a trip through Andalucía. When I see Rigo's olive skin and shiny dark hair, now scattered with grays and looking so much like Mamá, I get a pang of nostalgia for my parents.

"Felicidades, amor," Tita Carmen says with glee. I've missed her so much. But managing Villa Guadalcacín has kept them in Jerez without much time for a proper vacation. She coils her arms around me, and I think I'm going to faint. Rigo joins in the hug a few moments later. The pounding of my jubilated heart against my chest is honestly going to kill me.

Everyone speaks in Spanish the rest of the night, and I feel as if I've come home again. My house hasn't been this bursting with people since my parents were alive, and it feels amazing. Leave it to Isa and Martha to surprise me in my own home with my entire family. It's the best birthday I've had in years.

Just as I try to process the evening's excitement and think it's all winding down, Isa, Susana, Alejandra, and Martha stand as if on someone's cue. Isa, holding a gift box in her hands that I hadn't noticed before, saunters to the front of the room and stands by the staircase with Martha, and Susana holds Alejandra's little hand.

"Honey," Isa says. "Can you get up for a second? It's time for your gift."

"My gift? But isn't this my gift?" I gesture around the room.

"No mi vida," Martha snorts. "This is not the gift."

I stand and make my way, practically leap-frogging my nieces and cousins to get to them. "Okay, now," I say with a suspicious smile. "What's all this?"

"I'm not going to say anything. I'll let this speak for itself," Isa says with the box outstretched in her arms for me to open. It's not wrapped with paper, so I carefully grasp the top and jiggle it loose from its bottom piece. As it comes free, I lift the tissue paper to discover a letter-size piece of official-looking paper waiting inside. At first glance, I notice it's a certificate. It's framed by a thick, blue ornate border. The top reads, "State of Florida." Under that, it says, "County of Miami-Dade" and the third line reads, "Certificate of Live Birth."

The typical items are displayed on this document, like Susana's full name, the date, and her place of birth with the certificate number. But it's what's under that information that makes my eyes sting again with blistering tears.

Parent Name: Isabel Susana Pérez-Acosta
Parent Name: Gene L. Pérez-Acosta

I glance up from the box and into Isa's tear-filled eyes and mischievous grin. Her chin dimples are pools of her own making.

"But how?" I ask. Marriage equality has just been passed, and there are court cases still pending—mine included for both Susana and Alejandra—to add the names of both parents to official birth certificates of children born to gay and lesbian couples.

"While you were working to adopt your daughters, I was working behind the scenes with Jay and Sergio to expedite their birth certificates," Isa says, pointing at Jay and Sergio.

Sergio gets up from his place on the living room couch and says, "Susana's came first, of course, because we applied for it years ago, but soon you'll have Alex's delivered with the correct information of both her birth parents."

The skin that wraps around the bones, veins, and ligaments of my neck tightens so hard it's going to burst. I'm stupefied, flabbergasted, and a sniveling mess. How did I get here? How did this woman—who in the past struggled to come to terms with loving a woman—come to navigate the legal system to bring me this gift? This gift that I've been fighting to obtain for nearly sixteen years. Without hesitation, restraint, or uneasiness, I snatch the box from Isa's grasp to wrap my arms around her torso. And in front of my noisy, nosy Spanish family, I plant a big, wet kiss on her lips.

"Thank you, thank you, thank you," is all my throat allows before it closes, and I begin heaving sobs of joyful tears.

We stand in the living room in each other's arms and no one makes a sound, but almost as if orchestrated by a conductor, I feel Martha, Susana, and Alejandra surround us in a familiar embrace.

"It's what you've wanted the most," Isa quietly whispers in my ear. And that's just the thing. Somehow, she has always managed to give me exactly what I most want.

Bella Books, Inc.

Women. Books. Even Better Together.

P.O. Box 10543
Tallahassee, FL 32302
Phone: (800) 729-4992
www.BellaBooks.com

More Titles from Bella Books

Hunter's Revenge – Gerri Hill
978-1-64247-447-3 | 276 pgs | paperback: $18.95 | eBook: $9.99
Tori Hunter is back! Don't miss this final chapter in the acclaimed Tori Hunter series.

Integrity – E. J. Noyes
978-1-64247-465-7 | 28 pgs | paperback: $19.95 | eBook: $9.99
It was supposed to be an ordinary workday...

The Order – TJ O'Shea
978-1-64247-378-0 | 396 pgs | paperback: $19.95 | eBook: $9.99
For two women the battle between new love and old loyalty may prove more dangerous than the war they're trying to survive.

Under the Stars with You – Jaime Clevenger
978-1-64247-439-8 | 302 pgs | paperback: $19.95 | eBook: $9.99
Sometimes believing in love is the first step. And sometimes it's all about trusting the stars.

The Missing Piece – Kat Jackson
978-1-64247-445-9 | 250 pgs | paperback: $18.95 | eBook: $9.99
Renee's world collides with possibility and the past, setting off a tidal wave of changes she could have never predicted.

An Acquired Taste – Cheri Ritz
978-1-64247-462-6 | 206 pgs | paperback: $17.95 | eBook: $9.99
Can Elle and Ashley stand the heat in the *Celebrity Cook Off* kitchen?